M000315051

MAMMOTH

BOBBY AKART

THANK YOU

Thank you for reading **Mammoth,** a novel by
author Bobby Akart.
Join Bobby Akart's mailing list to learn about
upcoming releases, deals, and appearances. Follow
this link to:
BobbyAkart.com

PRAISE FOR BOBBY AKART AND THE CALIFORNIA DREAMIN' NOVELS

"If Bobby Akart ever decided to write screenplays for the movies, he'd be happy and rich as Croesus. His novels read like a Roland Emmerich disaster movie, which is to say, of the highest quality!" ~ Amazon review for ARkStorm

"I love the way you are drawn into the lives of the characters in Bobby's books. It's like you're there with them and cheering them on to not give up." ~ Amazon review for ARkStorm

"Only Bobby Akart can put together a thriller like no other and can capture the reader with his well thought out scenarios." ~ Amazon review of Fractured

MAMMOTH

by
Bobby Akart

OTHER WORKS BY AMAZON CHARTS TOP 25 AUTHOR BOBBY AKART

Made In China (a Gunner Fox, standalone thriller)

The California Dreamin' disaster thrillers
ARkStorm (a standalone, disaster thriller)
Fractured (a standalone, disaster thriller)
Mammoth (a standalone, disaster thriller)

The Perfect Storm Series
Perfect Storm 1
Perfect Storm 2
Perfect Storm 3
Perfect Storm 4

Black Gold (a standalone, terrorism thriller)

The Asteroid Series (A Gunner Fox trilogy)
Discovery
Diversion
Destruction

The Doomsday Series
Apocalypse
Haven
Anarchy
Minutemen
Civil War

The Yellowstone Series
Hellfire
Inferno
Fallout
Survival

The Lone Star Series
Axis of Evil
Beyond Borders
Lines in the Sand
Texas Strong
Fifth Column
Suicide Six

The Pandemic Series
Beginnings
The Innocents
Level 6
Quietus

The Blackout Series
36 Hours
Zero Hour
Turning Point
Shiloh Ranch
Hornet's Nest
Devil's Homecoming

The Boston Brahmin Series
The Loyal Nine
Cyber Attack
Martial Law
False Flag
The Mechanics
Choose Freedom

Patriot's Farewell (standalone novel)

Black Friday (standalone novel)

Seeds of Liberty (Companion Guide)

The Prepping for Tomorrow Series (non-fiction)
Cyber Warfare
EMP: Electromagnetic Pulse
Economic Collapse

Copyright Information

DEDICATIONS

To the love of my life, Dani, and our little princesses in training, Bullie & Boom. Every day, you unselfishly smother me with your love, support, and merriment. I may be the machine that produces these words. You are the glue that holds me together and the fuel that winds me up each day so I can tell these stories. I will love you forever.

This novel is also dedicated to the brave members of the Ski Mammoth Safety team that includes ski patrol, avalanche search and rescue squads, and of course the Paws on Patrol, the four-legged pups who are trained to search for people in lost in an avalanche. To learn more about Duke, Trico, Luna, Ritter and Oski, visit MammothMountain.com.

Finally, on a solemn note, I want to dedicate this novel to the memory of the three experienced Mammoth Mountain Ski Patrollers who perished on April 6, 2006, while securing a fumarole. The patrollers were fencing off the fumarole when the snow around the vent suddenly collapsed. Two of the patrollers fell into the six-foot wide, twenty-one-foot-deep hole. Two others attempted to descend into the heated vent to rescue their brothers. Three of them died due to asphyxiation from the volcanic gasses. They are:

Walter Rosenthal, a working scientist with a master's degree who was a valued comrade of the ski patrollers.

James Juarez, a popular, fun-loving member of the Ski Patrol who sacrificed his life for the protection of others.

Scotty McAndrews, a Penn State graduate who

devoted his efforts to avalanche control. He'd been voted Rookie of the Year by his peers just two days before he died attempting to make safe the mountains he loved so dearly.

God rest your souls, gentlemen.

EPIGRAPH

HAD the fierce ashes of some fiery peak
Been hurl'd so high they ranged about the globe?
For day by day, thro' many a blood-red eve,
In that four-hundredth summer after Christ,
The wrathful sunset glared.
~ Alfred Tennyson in St. Telemachus

Volcanic eruptions are astral messages sent directly
down to the Earth and of an importance that would
be ignored only at man's peril. ~ Simon Winchester,
British-American Journalist

Civilization exists by geologic consent, subject to change without notice.
~ Will Durant, American Historian

Volcanoes are one way Earth gives birth to itself.
~ Dr. Robert Gross, Volcanologist

Extinction is the rule. Survival is the exception.
~ Carl Sagan, American Scientist

Mammoth Mountain Ski Resort
Mammoth Lakes, California, USA

That late March, spring break was in full swing across America. Some college students descended upon Fort Lauderdale, or Fort Liquordale for those who remained imbibed during the weeklong crazy train. Others hit the resort cities in Mexico—Cancun, Cozumel, and the Baja Peninsula—to find their fun in the sun. Then there was the *Think Snow* bunch. The daredevils who believed everyone deserved a snow day. A spring break party where the only bikini-clad coeds were found in hot tubs, slamming shots. A weeklong respite from the rigors of college, dedicated to high altitudes and getting high for some.

The tiny resort town of Mammoth Lakes, California, with a population of just over seven thousand, had a love relationship with this time of year. In past winter seasons, over a million visitors would make their way from Los Angeles and San Francisco to hit the slopes. Then came the ARkStorm, the series of atmospheric rivers that descended upon the Pacific Coast of California, generating a once-in-a-lifetime atmospheric event that conjured up comparisons to the story of Noah's Ark in the Bible. Although the reference to an ark in the scientific sense was far different. *ARk* denoted atmospheric river, a thousand-year flood event. *Storm*, while easily envisioned, was certainly understated for those who lived through it.

Los Angeles had been destroyed when the Pacific Ocean swept across the city and joined the incredible torrent of rain that rushed through California's Central Valley to greet it. After the deluge of rain had finally subsided that year, Californians had experienced the greatest natural disaster in modern history. The faces of mountains collapsed. Large cities were either swept away by the floodwaters or submerged, subjected to a watery grave.

The rain, combined with massive amounts of snowfall equivalent to the volume of the Mississippi River times twenty-two, had created a new body of water. Known as Lake California, it had stretched from north of Sacramento to near LA. Years later, the state had begun the healing process from what had become known as the *Other Big One*.

It was the weight of the water that led to what the world's scientists commonly referred to as the *Big One*—a series of earthquakes related to the San Andreas fault. Only, it was more than the San Andreas. Other major faults, including the San Jacinto, Garlock, and the Eastern California Shear Zone (ECSZ), experienced major quakes. The result was nothing short of preternatural.

Last summer, as the quakes hit the state in rapid succession, the planet opened up under California. Both hungry and thirsty, the beast within gobbled up everything within its reach and then drank to quench its thirst. Nearly all of Lake California had been drained beneath the Earth's surface or evaporated by the superheated gases emitted from the belly of the beast.

The series of events changed the attitude of many Californians, especially young people. *Carpe diem*, or seize the day, became the rally cry. *Life's too short, make the most of it* was a motto adopted by many. They'd survived the history-making catastrophic events and were determined to live every day as if it was their last.

A group of four college kids from the University of Nevada Reno had grown up together in the bedroom community of Saddlehorn, where they'd been friends since high school. Their lives revolved around hiking and camping in the summer months while they waited for the ski resorts to open around Lake Tahoe in the winter.

Soon, winter sports became their life. They became expert snowboarders and skiers, mastering the slopes at the Lake Tahoe ski resorts. After entering college together, the foursome was inseparable, especially during the winter. They expanded their ski adventures and made their way to Mammoth Mountain, a hundred miles south of Reno.

The three guys and a girl loved the vibe of Mammoth Lakes. It wasn't full of wannabe skiers who'd just lost all their money at the Tahoe casinos.

The skiers and snowboarders at Mammoth Mountain were all about the outdoors and the natural beauty of their surroundings.

Their nicknames were epic considering their love of winter sports. The leader of the foursome, Andy Bulwark, had been teased as a kid because of his last name. As a teen, he began to embrace it and preferred to be referred to as Bullwinkle, especially while skiing. Well, that fit nicely with his friend Bo Richards, whose girlfriend's name was Natasha, the daughter of Russian immigrants who were belittled because of their nationality. The three of them had grown up on the same street together in Saddlehorn. Bullwinkle, along with his besties, Natasha and Bo, now referred to by the friends as Boris, were inseparable.

There was still a void in the group. The cartoon characters needed a fourth. A flying squirrel, so to speak, named Rocky. Along came Paulie Hammond. Paulie wasn't a squirrel, nor could he fly. He could, however, fight. He was undersized, but his fists were fast as lightning. When he was pushed around as the new kid in school, he responded with his fists. Bullies began to fear him, and he promptly earned the nickname Rocky.

So the group of four, Bullwinkle, Rocky, Boris, and Natasha, studied hard, partied a little harder, and skied the hardest slopes they could find. Their spring break vacation was coming to an end. They'd checked out of the hostel they'd saved their money for throughout the year. Located on the outskirts of Mammoth Lakes, they were able to walk to the downtown area and ride a gondola to the slopes. They planned one last day of skiing before they'd make the trip through the Sierra Nevada Mountains to Reno.

The four friends had just made their way to the main lodge after a raucous ride down Andy's Double Gold, a black-diamond designated slope on the east side of Mammoth Mountain. Ski slopes were assigned easily identifiable colors and trail markers based on their difficulty. A green circle was the easiest, followed by a blue square for intermediate-level skiers. Then there were the black diamonds, also known as blacks, but never diamonds. They were the most challenging runs for only the most advanced skiers. The slopes were often steep, ungroomed, and full of obstacles like trees and rocks. Mammoth Mountain had numerous blacks, some of which were high-alpine bowls, terrain above the treeline that was wide at the top and narrowed toward the bottom of the run.

Mammoth also had its share of double blacks, the steepest, most challenging terrain on any mountain. These extreme skiing opportunities included vertical drops off cliffs as well as narrow trails or *chutes* between rocks and trees. To be sure, every expert skier was aware that double blacks could be unpredictable, especially during uncertain weather conditions.

Bullwinkle was feeling exhilarated after the ride down Andy's Double Gold. He and Rocky raced one another, flying over moguls and deftly navigating their way down the nine-hundred-foot-long slope that descended forty-five feet from top to bottom. As he reached the base of the mountain, he raised his poles high over his head in his best imitation of *I just won the Super-G gold medal at the Olympics for my superiority in the super giant slalom event.*

After the others caught up to him, he was grinning from ear to ear. "One more run!" he shouted. His friends pulled to a stop next to him, digging the sharp edges of their skis in the snow, intentionally throwing powder and ice onto his legs. It was a tradition they shared. After flipping them the bird, he adopted a British accent. "The mountain is calling, and I simply must go for one more run!"

"Yeah!" agreed Rocky enthusiastically.

"They're gonna be closing the lifts soon," countered Boris. He was tired from a long night of drinking. He was never able to hold his liquor like his buddies. He and Natasha preferred smoking marijuana. Fewer calories, she always reminded him.

"Come on, man, one last run," insisted Bullwinkle. "The snow must go on. Get it."

"Har, har, har," said Boris. "What are you thinking? Another trip down Andy's?" He pointed toward the slope they'd just tackled.

"No, man. Let's do the Dragon's Back," replied Bullwinkle.

Even Rocky was quiet as his friend's suggestion sank in. The Dragon's Back at Mammoth Mountain was a rugged ridgeline of volcanic rock jutting out of Mammoth's southernmost flank. It formed the steep, southern boundary of the ski resort. Very few skiers had the intestinal fortitude to tackle its double blacks.

When nobody spoke, Natasha, after some reflection, asked, "Can we even get over there before the lifts close?"

"If we hustle," replied Bullwinkle. "We'll take

the lower and upper gondolas to the summit. Find a place to cop a squat and enjoy the view. It'll be romantic for you two lovebirds."

Rocky added, "The timing is perfect. We'll catch the sunset from the peak. Burn one and then hit it!"

"I don't know." Boris was still apprehensive.

Natasha shrugged and cozied up to her longtime boyfriend. "Come on. Do it for me, Bo," she cooed.

How could he resist? "What can I say?" he asked with a laugh. "My girl loves black diamonds!"

Natasha gave him a playful shrug while Bull-winkle and Rocky teased her about being high maintenance.

The four friends made their way to the enclosed gondolas that would take them from the main lodge to a midpoint of Mammoth Mountain. From there, they boarded the upper panorama gondola until they reached the top station building at the summit, eleven thousand fifty-three feet above sea level.

They glanced toward the Eleven53, an interpretive center at the summit that allowed visitors to learn about the geography surrounding Mammoth Lakes and to enjoy a restaurant with an incredible three-hundred-sixty-degree views. It was tempting to call it a day, settle into the warm environs of Eleven53 and enjoy a few beers. However, this was their last run, and the sun was beginning to set. Soon, Mammoth ski patrols would be blocking access to the slopes, forcing patrons to ride the gondola back to the bottom.

"This way," said Bullwinkle, who'd skied the difficult terrain at Dragon's Back during a Christmas vacation with his family. They casually made their way down a gentle slope until they reached an orange-mesh warning fence perched atop a cliff facing the west. The sun was slowly sinking beyond the vast Central Valley that had once been an enormous lake. Now Earth's surface was a muddy mess trying to heal itself.

They lingered for twenty minutes, reminiscing about their trip and plotting their next one. As they smoked one marijuana cigarette after another, they lamented returning to school. They were already talking about returning to Mammoth in late May after finals if the snow was still around.

"If we're gonna do this, we'd better get rolling," said Boris.

"Damn straight," added Bullwinkle, who stood and locked himself into his snow skis' bindings. When everybody was ready, he jokingly gave them their marching orders. "You guys know the drill. Turn right. Turn left. Repeat."

"And never let a good mogul go to waste, right?" interrupted Natasha.

"That's my girl!" shouted Boris.

"Rise and glide, people," yelled Rocky as he shoved off, determined to get a head start on Bullwinkle down the mountain.

Natasha brought up the rear, like always. Although she was an accomplished skier, she wasn't quite as crazy as her friends. She loved hanging out with the guys. Less drama than the girls in her life. As they hooted and hollered, Natasha tried to remain focused on her technique.

The biggest challenge of black runs, especially double diamonds, was in regulating her speed to maintain control. At this level of difficulty, losing control could mean death or a lot of broken bones. Natasha trusted her basic instincts when it came to her capabilities on trails as difficult as those found within the Dragon's Back. That afternoon, it felt right. She, like the guys, had no fear.

As they descended, the foursome made polished, short turns on the sometimes icy, steep slopes. The southwestern side of Mammoth Mountain enjoyed sun throughout the day. Despite the bone-chilling temperatures at the summit, the sun was capable of melting the snow during daylight hours. As it dropped over the horizon, the shadows grew long, and the temperatures quickly plummeted, causing the melted snow to ice over in parts.

Natasha was exhilarated as she followed the paths of the guys. She used the sharp edges of her skis to maintain optimal balance. Her knees acted like shock absorbers as they hit the moguls dotting the landscape. She consciously kept her skis wider apart than on a less challenging slope to maintain stability as they picked up speed through the narrow, rocky chutes.

As they approached Wazoo, the rocky portion of the run began to end, and the spread-out trees began. This gave Natasha a chance to catch her breath and allow herself a deep exhale to relieve some tension. The last part of the run was just ahead—the Dragon's Tail.

There were a series of steep moguls covering rocky outcroppings before they entered the last zone of Dragon's Back. Bullwinkle hit the largest mogul first, perfectly executing a spin. Not to be outdone, Rocky lowered his body into a crouch to gain speed. At the top of the mogul, he performed his signature Rocky the Squirrel move, spreading his arms and legs far away from his body as if he were jumping from the top of the mogul to the top of a tree. Boris was next, hoping to impress his lover with a head-over-skis flip.

Natasha wasn't interested in any daredevil moves as she hit the mogul. There was nobody behind her to impress. She was content with hitting the mogul, getting airborne, and then landing on packed snow.

As she cleared the hill, Natasha had her *oh shit* moment, that defining point when her sense of good judgment finally acknowledged her idiocy. That moment when she knew it was too late to correct the error she'd made.

When she saw the snow cave that had appeared below her emitting steam, she tried to twist and turn her body to avoid landing in it. In those seconds, she could hear the screams of her friends, who'd preceded her into the abyss. She twisted her torso and flailed her arms to gain height or distance. Her contortions served to save her life, for the moment.

Natasha landed hard at the edge of the snow cave. The heated gases struck her in the face, immediately scalding her skin. She struggled to hold onto the rapidly melting snow, to no avail. As the smell of boiling flesh reached her nostrils, she slipped downward into the mouth of the beast that had swallowed her friends. The hot gases from the newly formed fumarole seared through her clothing, melting her skin, brutally separating flesh from bone. Before her body disappeared, she was dead.

Mammoth had awakened, but none of them lived to tell anyone.

And so it begins ...

CHAPTER ONE

USGS Cabin
Bald Mountain
Mono County, CA

Taylor Reed finished up an email and sipped the last of her morning coffee. As she set the cup in the sink, she turned and leaned against the countertop. A lot had changed in her life since that summer day last year when she had been sent to Eureka, California, by her boss at the United States Geological Survey. She'd almost been sucked into the earth by a whirlpool. She'd nearly been buried alive by a collapsing hospital. And now she was engaged to the man who'd unintentionally led her into these potential calamities.

As a volcanologist with the USGS, Taylor was assigned to monitor the volcanic systems beneath the Long Valley Caldera and the surrounding Sierra Nevada Mountains. Her field office, located in nearby Bridgeport, Mono County, was part of the California Volcano Observatory known as CalVO.

She'd met Mac Atwood one afternoon in Eureka, located on the Pacific coast in Northern California. Mac had just emerged from an exploratory mission off the coast where an unexpected rift had opened up in the ocean floor. His discovery concerned him, as it appeared there were heated gases seeping through a previously unmapped seamount—an indicator of volcanic activity. While this discovery was extraordinary in some respects, it was also disconcerting, as it was directly over the San Andreas Fault.

Within a week, five massive earthquakes had taken place along major fault lines in the state. Lake California had drained. The geological landscape of the state had changed drastically. And through it all, Taylor and Mac had fallen in love.

During their ill-fated submersible dive to determine if the earth had fractured beneath the lake, a major earthquake struck at Hollister, perilously close to their position. The ground opened up, creating an eddy capable of tossing their submersible around like a floating duckie attempting to avoid the emptying drain of a bathtub. During the chaos, Mac proposed. Taylor accepted, sort of, and with a lot of luck and divine intervention, they survived the grip the swirling water had on them. Only for their lives to be threatened by another earthquake near Napa.

Through it all, the two fought the demons below. The earthquakes were relentless. Then the rifts that formed at Lake California's bottom resulted in the water being drained or turned into vapor by the superheated gas spewing from deep in the earth.

When it was over, Mac had lost everything, again. First, his home had washed away when the ARkStorm had hit years prior. Then, last summer, as the earthquake struck the fault lines near the Vaca Mountains, his Jeep had been sucked into the water while his boat and floating house had succumbed to the inland tsunami generated by the quakes.

Yet Mac remained positive, buoyed by his love for Taylor. Now the two had lived together since that fateful week in July. He'd successfully lobbied the USGS to establish a monitoring field office to work in conjunction with CalVO. He convinced his boss there was a possible connection between the change in the geologic formation under the state following the ARkStorm and the massive earthquakes happening in rapid succession. With Taylor's help, they both convinced their superiors that these earthquakes could potentially impact the largest volcanic system in the state—the Long Valley Caldera.

Where there's smoke, there's fire, as they say.

Taylor pulled on her orange and blue Denver Broncos sweatshirt, a staple in her wardrobe following her days of growing up in Aurora, located in the Denver metropolitan area. It was an unusually warm, thirty-three-degree day in the Sierra Nevada. She soaked in the sun and paused to watch Mac for a moment.

A heavy snowfall had struck the region a week ago. The moist snow had accumulated on the lean-to attached to their garage that housed two snowmobiles and other outdoor equipment. Because the cabin they lived in belonged to the USGS and was located on federal land, they couldn't own it. However, they were able to treat it like their own, with any expenditures funded by the USGS. After the collapse, Taylor obtained the obligatory three bids, chose the lowest, which was high due to hyper-inflated construction costs during the rebuilding of earthquake-stricken areas, and within days, they received a check. The couple cashed it and placed it in their wedding fund. Mac rolled up his sleeves and decided to fix the lean-to himself.

Although Mac had been fully insured for his losses resulting from the earthquakes and tsunami, he'd only received a settlement from his auto insurance company. The insurance on his boat and floating house was through a carrier that had gone bankrupt. California's pledge to cover the losses for those who lost their property was likely to be paid years from now, at pennies on the dollar. As a result, financially strapped Mac was forced to start his life anew with Taylor. This was his way of contributing to their upcoming nuptials, other than being the man of honor.

Her feet crunched on the iced-over snow as she made her way to the garage. She glanced over the ridge to take in the beauty of the twenty-mile-long valley covered with snow. It was hard to believe their cabin, perched high atop Bald Mountain, was barely half a mile from the Long Valley Caldera, a potentially planet-altering supervolcano formed 760,000 years ago, a blink of the eye, geologically speaking. It was the monitoring of the caldera and the volcanic mountain range to the west that kept Taylor and Mac busy.

And, sometimes, awake at night.

CHAPTER TWO

USGS Cabin
Bald Mountain
Mono County, CA

"Hey, honey!" Mac greeted Taylor cheerily as she approached. He set aside the snow shovel and peeled off his Ski Mammoth sweatshirt. It was one of the first articles of clothing he'd purchased when he and Taylor arrived in Mammoth Lakes together. Mac had never skied before. He still hadn't. Since their arrival, there had been no rest for the weary.

His bright red tee shirt, purchased for him by Taylor, was blinding against the white background created by the snowdrifts. The front of the tee depicted a volcano erupting and the clever caption *Volcanoes Kick Ash*. It had been purchased for him by Taylor as a replacement for his beloved tee shirt he'd lost during the last earthquake that nearly took his life. It had depicted two cartoonish tectonic plates hitting each other and read *Sorry, My Fault*.

It was not unusual for Mac to pick a tee or sweatshirt to reflect his mood. In the office, he had to wear the obligatory USGS-logoed apparel. In the field, he was given more latitude although he was urged to wear something that identified him as a geophysicist with the USGS. You know, he was told, in case of an accident. *Gee, thanks*, Mac had thought to himself. *I appreciate your concern.*

Between the ARkStorm and the earthquake sequence that had fractured the state, Mac had adopted an even more laid-back approach to his job. Certainly, he was the consummate professional. In fact, he was one of the best geophysicists the USGS employed. It was his outside-the-box thinking as the earthquake sequence had unfolded that caught the attention of the upper-level administrators in Reston, Virginia, the USGS headquarters, as well as within the U.S. Department of the Interior. Nonetheless, he made the decision to live life his way, and that didn't include risking said life for the

USGS. At least, that was what he told himself, anyway.

"How's it goin', stud?" asked Taylor as she arrived by his side and gave him a kiss on the cheek. She smacked the only remaining post holding up the collapsed roof.

A huge smile appeared on Mac's face. Taylor had that effect on him. He chuckled. "Yeah, stud. Very funny. Trust me, I'd love to close this thing in and make our garage bigger. There's barely enough room for our vehicles."

Taylor looked through a gaping hole in the outer wall of the garage. "Not my car's fault, I might add."

Her government-issue Chevy Bolt EV Crossover was dwarfed in comparison to the vintage Chevrolet Blazer Mac had purchased with his car insurance settlement. The renovated '76 model had been lifted to accommodate the oversized mud terrain tires. When Mac arrived at the cabin for the first time and saw the Chevy Bolt, he shook his head in disbelief and burst out laughing.

In fact, his thoughts of the puny little car making its way through the winter storms descending upon the Sierra Nevada mountain range threw him into a laughing fit. Taylor assured him it got around just fine, but he wasn't having any of it. He immediately went online and found the vintage Blazer in nearby Tonopah, Nevada.

"Don't get me started," said Mac with a chuckle. He proceeded to bring Taylor up to speed on his project. A notoriously early riser, Mac used to start his day swimming across the glass-like waters of Lake California. His internal alarm clock still functioned, but there was no lake to swim. The closest body of water, Mono Lake, was to the north. However, it was a saline soda lake, owing its high levels of salts to geological forces over millions of years, including volcanism at the base of the Sierra Nevada Mountains.

"How can I help?" she asked as Mac laid out his game plan.

The two of them worked together, alternating between accomplishing a task to make progress on the new lean-to and flirting. Over the nine months they'd been officially a couple, the newness of the relationship had never worn off. The two had settled in as a married couple despite not having exchanged vows. Later that morning, Mac brought up their plans.

"Okay, honey," Mac began. "We've got our date. May 26. You've confirmed your parents can fly in from Germany. My family is on board. We've got a few friends and extended family. What's our head count?"

"Twenty-one if you include you and me."

"Well, I suppose I could bail out to make an even twenty."

Mac's joke fell flat and earned him a barrage of snowballs. Taylor had remarkable accuracy as Mac ran away, seeking cover behind the snowmobiles. She picked up the snow shovel and began marching toward him.

"Do you wanna try that again?" she asked, pretending to be angry. Of course, she wasn't. She loved Mac's sense of humor.

"Twenty-one is perfect."

"I'm glad you agree, Atwood."

She held the snow shovel like a baseball bat as he rounded the protection of the snowmobile. He stopped in his tracks, unsure of whether she'd use the shovel as she intended.

He held his hands up. "I surrender. I'm a lover, not a fighter."

"Not today, you're not. Get to work, mister man!"

Mac earned a kiss on the cheek for his playing along with her. "Did you decide on a venue yet? I know we've kicked around a couple of options."

Taylor shrugged. "If it were up to me, we'd haul a preacher up here and get married overlooking the caldera. Imagine the fireworks we might have."

Mac laughed. "Um, I'd rather not. I've had enough fireworks for one lifetime."

"I'm just kidding. Ironically, I just replied to an email from my mom. She was fussy that I hadn't responded to her, but she forgets that Germany is practically half a day away from us time-zone-wise."

"Did she ask the same question?"

"Yes, of course. I swear, Mac, I'm not procrastinating. I want everything to be perfect."

Mac took her in his arms and held her for a moment. "No pressure, okay?"

"It's two months away. I've gotta decide."

Mac looked into her face. "We've talked about this. This is our wedding, not our families' or friends'. We're going to make memories for a lifetime. You only get married for the last time once."

She hugged him and laid her head against his chest. "You always know what to say."

"Sometimes, maybe. Anyway, which venue gives you the warm fuzzies?"

Taylor sighed. "Without a doubt, it's Mammoth. At the summit. Can you imagine a wedding on the snow looking west? Followed by a reception on the deck of Eleven53 at sunset? Practically on top of the world."

"Highest point in California to get married. And it would be a white wedding. Get it?"

Taylor laughed and hugged her fiancé. "Thank you."

"I can't think of a better spot," Mac replied as he added a quick kiss to seal the deal. "Now, you'd better get with the resort to reserve it. I'm gonna keep working for a few hours."

Taylor shouted, "I love you." She walked briskly toward the cabin.

"I love you back," said Mac. "Hey, when I'm done, whadya think about Bodie's for wings and beers?"

"Stamp it!" came Taylor's reply.

His spirits lifted, Mac whistled while he removed the rest of the lean-to's sagging roof and began rebuilding the supports to hold up the standing seam metal roof panels he'd acquired. As he worked, he glanced to the west as white billowy clouds approached. Yet another wintery storm was brewing and headed their way to add to the already deep snowpack.

He subconsciously glanced down at the dirt he'd cleared to install another post. His trained, scientific mind wandered as it contemplated the weight of the snowpack on the geologic formations below the Earth's surface.

Was it like Lake California? Was it heavy enough to impact the complex seismic system surrounding the Sierra Nevada? A cold gust of wind washed over his body, causing him to shudder. Or was it his thoughts that gave him the chills?

CHAPTER THREE

**Lookout Mountain
Mono County, CA**

There was a time when Finnegan Fergus O'Brien
had the rest of his life planned out. Finn had been a
firefighter with the Los Angeles County Fire Department. He'd assisted in hundreds of search and rescue
operations. He'd risked his life during the many wildfires in the mountains of California. Including, most
notably, Station Fire II, which had threatened to
destroy his own neighborhood in the fall before the
ARkStorm did it anyway.

Then he was informed that his days as a firefighter were over. Forced retirement, the muckety-mucks called it. Time to make room for new blood, lack of experience notwithstanding. Finn, the consummate professional and a proud son of Irish immigrants, took the decision like a man. Yet he didn't.

He couldn't seem to let go, frequently visiting his old pals at the fire hall near where he lived. He enjoyed the comradery and doling out advice to the newbies, while lamenting, at times, the county's insistence that he retire.

Then the ARkStorm hit. Every truck and engine in the fire station had been dispatched to deal with fires and vehicle accidents. Finn volunteered to watch over the station and its equipment until they returned. They never did. The only thing that came his way was a deluge of rain and floodwater, carrying everything from houses to wayward bears.

Afterwards, LA County asked him to return to work. They needed a man of his experience, they'd said. They'd lost so many of their ranks to the catastrophe, or they'd simply left for good, he'd been told. Excited about the prospects of helping others once again, Finn rejoined the fire department. He was an invaluable addition as the leader of search and rescue operations throughout what was left of Los Angeles.

Then, inevitably, things began to settle down as California recovered from the onslaught of water that washed nearly everything into the Pacific Ocean. Trillions of dollars were thrown at Los Angeles County. *"L-A Strong!"* declared the politicians to the cameras. *"Hollywood will rebuild,"* proclaimed the movers and shakers of Tinseltown. And as they did, once again civic leaders turned to younger and presumably brighter firefighters. Finn was put out to pasture, as they say.

He'd had enough of the politics. His home in the Crescenta Valley had been destroyed. He'd been sharing a three-bedroom apartment with other firefighters who lived a fraternity-house lifestyle. He'd already purchased a cabin high above sea level near Mammoth Lakes. So this time, Finn didn't argue. He collected his generous pension and severance package, loaded up his used, military-surplus Jeep, and headed for the mountains.

However, he was not alone. He brought along a friend.

When the fire department had been retooled using youthful replacements for experienced assets, they forced several members of their K-9 units into retirement. Rebel, a Labrador, was as good at sniffing out trouble or locating trapped victims as any dog he'd ever had the pleasure of working with. Her handler had left California when the going got rough, leaving Rebel and others like her to fend for themselves. Some perished in the floodwaters. Others, like Rebel, survived the deluge and did what she did best—rescued people.

Finn had worked with Rebel during search and rescue missions until the duo was asked to move on. He immediately took steps to adopt Rebel, and now they were inseparable. Plus, they were both back in action.

During his first year in Mammoth Lakes, Finn made friends. Naturally, one of his first stops was the Mammoth Lakes Fire Department, where he got to know the small team of firefighters and the top brass. He also ventured up to Bridgeport from time to time, hanging around the Mono County emergency management operations center. Even in retirement, hundreds of miles away from his former home, Finn found a way to be a part of his newly adopted community.

Life was good for Finn and Rebel as he undertook renovations on the fixer-upper cabin. From time to time, the Mono County Sheriff's Office or Mammoth Lakes FD would call upon Rebel's expertise in locating lost hikers. It gave Finn a satisfying sense of purpose.

Then came that fateful telephone call. LA County had struck again.

As the city rebuilt, civic leaders realized their emergency management operations were woefully understaffed. They hired an army of headhunters who systematically reached out to first responders from *dry* counties in the region. A *dry county* was the name given to any county not flooded by Lake California. It didn't take long before the lure of a big paycheck made its way to Mono County. The exodus of the county's first responders happened faster than the local governmental officials could react. Finn suspected that was by design. Los Angeles County had trillions of federal and state dollars at its disposal. It would've been impossible for a modest county government to compete with the offers dangled in front of its employees. So off they went, decimating the ranks of the sheriff's office and the fire departments in Mono County and its municipalities.

Finn was sitting at Bodie's, his favorite hangout, when his cell phone rang. At first, he reared his head back to double-check the number. He'd never received a phone call from Jennifer Katz, the chairwoman of the Board of Supervisors. Yet the display on his phone didn't lie.

By the time the call was completed, Finnegan Fergus O'Brien was back in business as the new Mammoth Lakes fire chief. And Rebel was given a job, too.

CHAPTER FOUR

Station 1
Mammoth Lakes Fire Department
Mammoth Lakes, CA

"Rebel, root beer, please," instructed Finn as he pored over reports prepared for him following a recent structure fire. The past week and the next was the heart of spring break for high schoolers and college kids on the West Coast. Some rented VRBOs, an acronym for vacation rentals by owner. It was not unusual for a dozen college students to pile into a two-bedroom chalet, sleeping anywhere they could curl into a ball after a night of partying. A keg party around an ill-advised bonfire near an A-frame cabin had nearly burned five acres of woods despite the large amount of snow on the ground. The A-frame itself had been reduced to ashes. Fortunately, nobody was seriously injured other than from minor smoke inhalation.

Rebel hoisted herself out of the dog bed lying next to Finn's desk and moseyed to the fire hall's kitchen. She walked past the firefighters on shift, who acknowledged her by saying hello or patting her on the head. Rebel was a member of their unit, and she'd proven on more than one occasion she was worthy of their respect.

As one of the new firefighters prepared lunch for the others, Rebel approached the refrigerator, tugged on the towel tied to the handle, and pulled open the door. She stuck her head inside and retrieved one of the bottles of IBC root beer on the door's bottom shelf with her mouth. Then, dutifully, she performed a seemingly mundane task that somehow evaded the capabilities of the firefighters. She nudged the refrigerator door closed with her snout. A minute later, she delivered the root beer to Finn and reassumed her favorite task—standing by for further instructions.

The phone rang, and Finn studied the display before he answered it. "Seriously? Stop calling me!"

he groaned before picking up his cell phone. It was the mayor.

"This is Finn," he answered brusquely. The newly installed mayor, a former attorney from San Francisco, had gotten on Finn's last nerve since he was elected. He wasn't a local other than the fact he had a vacation home on Mammoth Mountain overlooking the ski slopes. Finn suspected the retired attorney turned mayor simply wanted to notch another feather in his cap or add an additional line item to his epitaph. Regardless, the man clearly didn't have enough to do, as he made it a point to contact daily everyone remotely under his purview. *Tyrant*, Finn had mumbled about Mayor Bill DiGregory more than once.

"Chief O'Brien," the mayor began, drawing an enormous eye roll from Finn. Early on, he and the mayor had been cordial. When the Mammoth Lakes fire commissioner suddenly retired, the mayor had called upon Finn to perform both roles on a temporary basis. After eight months, Finn felt used. He became convinced the mayor was taking advantage of his generosity, so he quit the temporary position in order to focus on his job as fire chief.

This didn't sit well with the mayor, who was used to bullying his way around town hall. The self-importance of this man was unparalleled. He insisted upon formality when speaking with Finn and other department heads situated within Mammoth Lakes. Once, in a heated conversation, Finn reminded the good mayor that he technically worked for the Mammoth Lakes Board of Commissioners, not the city. DiGregory moved heaven and earth to attempt to censure Finn for his insubordination. When Finn threatened to quit altogether, that was the end of that.

"Hello, Mayor," interrupted Finn, hoping to throw DiGregory off his train of thought. He didn't.

"Chief, I'd like to get together with you this afternoon to discuss this most recent fire. I have some ideas of how we can educate the community and our guests about the dangers of open fires, especially the use of firepits near our beloved forests."

Gag me. Once again, he wants to tell me how to do my job.

Finn lied, something that he did often when dealing with the mayor. "Today's not a good day, Mayor. I'm looking at the calendar, and my afternoon is packed." He didn't have a calendar. In his mind, he was still retired, especially in light of the fact he was working for nearly nothing.

"Tomorrow, then?" asked the mayor.

Finn lied again. He planned on spending some time with his friends who were coming to visit. He checked his watch again. Based on their last text, they planned on meeting him at Bodie's in a couple of hours. He'd been looking forward to them visiting since, well, the last time they'd been in town.

"Absolutely, Mayor. I'll call you in the morning, and we'll compare our schedules." Finn noticed the two lieutenants on shift standing in his doorway. "Oh, looks like I'm late for my weekly meeting with my lieutenants. We're talking, um, budget issues and personnel changes and visitor safety. Talk to you tomorrow!"

Finn disconnected the call, opened a desk drawer, and shoved his phone inside. He rested his chin on the top of his hands and looked at the new arrivals.

"The mayor," he muttered.

"We gathered," said the lieutenant assigned to the town's sole aerial, or ladder, truck. Mammoth Lakes only had a few structures that were four stories tall. All were located in the Village at Mammoth, a quaint European setting that was one of the reasons Finn fell in love with the area. It was more Swiss Alps than it was Dublin, Ireland, where his family was from. However, it gave him a taste of the old country.

"What's up, guys?" asked Finn.

"We need to borrow Rebel," began one of the men. "The sheriff's department has asked for our help in locating four missing college students from Reno. They were due back home last night, and their parents reported them missing."

"Already? They're college kids. They probably stopped in Tahoe to party some more."

One of the lieutenants shrugged and grimaced. "Not so sure, Chief. Their vehicle was located at the Canyon Lodge parking lot. It was packed as it they were leaving."

The other lieutenant added, "Everything except their ski gear. Well, maybe snowboards. Not sure."

Finn rolled his neck around his shoulders as he thought it through. He rarely allowed Rebel to undertake a search and rescue without his being present. He asked a few obvious questions to allow him time to make a decision.

"They've checked cell phones, I assume?"

"Yeah," replied one.

"Something's odd, though," said the other.

"How so?" Finn sat a little taller in his chair and

leaned onto his desk. Rebel seemed to notice his renewed interest, so her ears perked up.

"Okay, granted these are college kids. We know what that's like. However, the parents are reporting that they're unable to locate their phones through the Apple tracking capabilities."

"Why does that surprise anybody? I tried to hide from my parents when I was their age, too."

"Yeah," began one of the men. "Except one parent claimed they'd checked on them earlier in the day. They were skiing near Main Lodge. When they didn't show up last night, the parent tried again and found nothing. This morning, after another try, the kid's mom reached out to the other parents. None of their phones were discoverable through the app."

Finn didn't want to belabor the point. His job was fire rescue, not missing persons. He asked, "What does the sheriff's office want from us?"

"They have authorization to break into the car and search for clues as to their whereabouts. We'd like to use Rebel to sniff their clothes and locate them."

"She's not a bloodhound, guys. Besides, it's logical to assume if something bad happened to them, it would've been on the slopes. Has Mammoth

Ski Patrol searched their cameras? They have a gazil-
lion of them."

"Yes, Chief. According to them, the group was
last seen exiting the gondola at the summit. If they
skied the Dragon's Back, there are no cameras to pick
them up until near the bottom of the mountain."

Finn sighed. "Naturally, ski patrol searched the
area this morning?"

"Yes, sir. There was about eight inches of snowfall last night at the upper elevations. The fresh
powder covered any tracks that might have led to the
cliffs."

Finn continued to go through the possibilities.
"Was there enough buildup to cause an avalanche?
Any slopes closed?"

The lieutenants hadn't thought of that. Both of
them were new to the area and could only report
what they had experienced or heard from others.

Years prior, an inbounds avalanche had been
triggered by a skier on a closed portion of the Dragon's Back double blacks. The avalanche was only a
foot deep, but it was fifty feet wide. As it continued
downward, it built upon itself and temporarily
buried several skiers who stood to watch the
spectacle.

Finn continued, "I can tell you aren't sure.

Check back with the ski patrol to determine if there's evidence of an avalanche along the Dragon's Back. Then ask them to identify any ridges they might have skied off by accident. Reach out to Bridgeport and borrow their chopper. Search the ridges along the western slope for their bodies. If they skied off the cliff, this has become a recovery rather than a possible rescue."

"Okay, Chief. We're on it." The men left, and Finn sat back in his chair. Rebel sat up and stared at him. Somehow, she sensed he needed to vent.

"Old gal, I can't have them sending you around that mountain looking for ghosts. They've barely been missing twenty-four hours."

Rebel stared back at him, a slight smile on her face, coupled with her normal panting. It was warm in the fire hall that day, and Rebel wasn't a fan of the heat. She, like Finn, benefited from getting out of LA.

Finn talked out loud, coming up with a million reasons as to why deploying Rebel on an operation without his supervision was not only a bad idea, but unnecessary. That said, he felt guilty for putting his personal feelings ahead of others'.

During the ARkStorm, he'd risked his life to save those of a young woman and her two nieces. Their battle for survival allowed her to reunite with her husband. He could've stayed in the relative safety of the fire hall that day. Instead, he risked his life to protect them. It changed their lives, and his.

He promised himself that if a clue emerged in the case of the missing college kids, he'd drop everything to help. And he'd bring Rebel along without hesitation.

He checked his watch and smiled. He straightened his desk, set his office phone to voicemail since his budget didn't allow for a secretary, and snuck out the door with Rebel in tow.

Next stop: Bodie's.

CHAPTER FIVE

Bodie's Roadhouse
Lee Vining, CA

For someone who never visited California or studied it on a map, it was hard to fathom its size and different geographic regions. Large cities like LA, San Francisco, and San Diego got all the attention for a variety of reasons. Smaller communities like Mammoth Lakes got notoriety because of their resorts and outdoor activities. It was also a state rich in history, most of which began with the Gold Rush following the discovery of the precious metal at Sutter's Mill in El Dorado County, not that far from Mono County.

In Mono County, another famous gold-mining town sprang up in the mid-eighteen hundreds when thousands of prospectors descended upon the state. Bodie became a boomtown when a profitable line of gold was discovered in the hills along the Nevada state line. Ten thousand prospectors filled the town. Sutter's Mill, then the famous Comstock Lode, drew even more prospectors from the Eastern United States.

However, like the other boomtowns, Bodie fell into decline after the turn of the century. Mining profits disappeared. Businesses fell into bankruptcy. And by World War II, Bodie officially became a ghost town.

Since then, Bodie had been designated a National Historic Landmark, and the California legislature created a state park around the one hundred seventy buildings in the town. Volunteers meticulously undertook a preservation project to protect the structures from disrepair. Today, it remains open to visitors.

Jimmy Bodey, a distant relative of W. S. Bodey, the prospector from Poughkeepsie, New York, who discovered the gold in Mono County, undertook an ambitious effort of his own. Mammoth Lakes and its businesses had fallen on hard times in the years after the ARkStorm. The vast majority of visitors to the resort town came from LA, which had been destroyed, and San Francisco, which was no longer easily accessible by highway.

The restaurant on Mono Lake had closed as a result, and Jimmy Bodey, who'd kept up with the area via the historic ghost town's Facebook page, learned of the opportunity to buy it.

First, he had to swallow his pride. He wanted to name it after himself but opted instead to name it after the town his ancestor had founded. A painter had mistakenly created an official town sign but misspelled his ancestor's last name as Bodie. Jimmy Bodey didn't care because he had a vision for the restaurant that would naturally tie in to the nearby historic ghost town.

After acquiring the building and equipment, he immediately remodeled the interior to give it a road-house feel. The interior was made more rustic. Barn buildings were constructed on both sides to resemble stables for weary travelers' horses. They were outfitted with picnic tables, string lights, and individual bars. Jimmy's thought was to separate the rowdy bar crowds interested in drinking and dancing from his patrons looking for a meal.

Once completed, it had the look of a roadhouse

straight out of the Wild, Wild West. Then he had to match the menu and name of his new restaurant concept to the appearance.

Jimmy called it Bodie's Roadhouse and created a menu that tied his restaurant to the legend of Bodie's Ghost Town. At the bar, he served beers named after the famous California Gold Rush towns of yesteryear. Sutter Creek pale ale, Nevada City stout, Eureka Blonde, and Gold Creek lager were just a few of the beers provided by local microbreweries. Of course, he proudly served the offerings from Devil's Creek Distillery in Mammoth Lakes.

When Jimmy opened Bodie's, he blew the doors off with the locals. Located halfway between Bridgeport and Mammoth Lakes, overlooking Mono Lake, the location offered views, lively entertainment, and libations of all sorts. Meals were served on retro-style trays not unlike those that might be a part of a cattle drive's chuck wagon. Meatloaf, roasted turkey, and Salisbury steak were all paired up with mashed potatoes and gravy, sweet corn stuffing, and apple pie.

While people raved about the building and its décor, the magnificent view of the lake, and the incredible menu, it was clear that the star of this show was the man who was found behind the bar most days—Jimmy.

CHAPTER SIX

Bodie's Roadhouse
Lee Vining, CA

Taylor and Mac eased onto the saddle barstools at Bodie's, where they were immediately greeted by the proprietor.

"Howdy, pardners!" exclaimed Jimmy, who hadn't been able to shake his thick New York accent during his few years in California.

Mac laughed. "Gimme a break, Jimmy. Save the cowboy schtick for the tourists."

"You still qualify as a tourist, Mac. Have you even been here a year yet?"

Mac rolled his eyes and pointed at the Eureka

Blonde beer tap to his right. Eureka Blonde had been adopted as the official beer of the couple, as the Pacific coastal town was where they'd met. He held up two fingers in the form of a peace sign, a not-so-subtle reminder to the bartender that he didn't want to fight that day.

Jimmy immediately turned his attention to Taylor. He reached for her hand and gave it a gentle squeeze. The seventy-year-old provided her a toothy grin. "Hello, darlin'. When are you gonna dump this mope and marry me instead? I'll give you half of all this. Hell, you can have it all if you promise to take care of me until I'm old and gray."

Mac interrupted his playful play for his fiancée. "You're already old and gray."

"Zip it, city boy, or there's no drinking for you today."

"I'm not a—" Mac began to protest, but a stomp on the foot from his betrothed encouraged him to zip it.

"Now, Jimmy," Taylor played along, "you already have a wife."

"No, I don't."

Taylor sat a little taller in her saddle and waved her arms around. "Yes, you do. You're married to Bodie's."

Jimmy scowled. She had a point. He'd transitioned from New Yorker to western bartender. "I'd give it all up for you, darlin'."

Taylor smiled and blew him a kiss. "Let me have a few beers, and I'll think about it." She nodded toward the beer tap.

A group of college girls came in and took up seats at the far end of the bar. They immediately grabbed both Jimmy's and Mac's attention, the latter of whom glanced a little too long for Taylor's liking.

"Ow!" he squalled as she gave him a real kick to the leg, unlike the love tap she'd provided earlier.

"See anything you like, MacArthur?"

Mac knew he was in trouble. His given name was MacArthur. His parents, who were of Scottish descent, wanted to name him after his father, Arthur. However, they didn't want to burden their son with the outdated name, or the other possible nicknames like Artie, so his mother dug into the Scottish ancestry websites and learned that the name MacArthur meant son of Arthur in Scotland's Gaelic-speaking tribes.

While it was an interesting surname, resulting in an even cooler first name, it meant trouble when Taylor used it. Especially in that tone of voice.

Jimmy delivered two frosted mugs of Eureka

Blonde and hustled off to flirt with the young women. The brief distraction gave Mac a moment to think about an excuse for the inexcusable ogling.

"Nah, I wasn't looking at them. Um, I was just thinking about, um, our wedding."

Taylor rolled her eyes and gave him a playful shove nearly strong enough to dislodge him from the saddle. "That's so lame, Atwood. If you're gonna lust over something you can't have, at least have several plausible excuses stored in your memory banks from your prior hound-dog days."

Mac felt genuinely sorry. He really hadn't intended to stare at the women. In fact, he wasn't sure what bothered him to make his mind wander like that.

"I'm sorry, honey. I didn't mean to hurt—"

Taylor laughed and picked up Jimmy's New York accent. "Fuhgeddaboudit, you mope. I'm just bustin' your balls." She lifted her beer to toast.

Mac hesitantly picked up his beer. He wasn't sure if she was channeling Jimmy's New York ways or sending him a subtle reminder of what might happen if he stepped out of line with another woman.

"I am sorry. Cheers?" he asked.

She planted a kiss on his cheek and smiled. "Always and forever. Cheers!"

They touched their mugs together and took a long swig of the mid-strength ale that had a slightly sweet taste. The Eureka clocked in at eight percent alcohol content, a nice punch for a beer.

Jimmy served them a couple of trays of his signature naked Buffalo wings smothered in sauce made of butter, Tabasco hot sauce, and a dash of cayenne pepper. They were designed to heat up the mouth, requiring his guests to consume more beer. It was a winning combination for the restauranteur.

Taylor grew quiet as she looked through the plate-glass windows on the back side of the bar. Guests at the bar had an unobstructed view of Mono Lake as well as the twin islands of Negit and Paoha, created by the two most recent volcanic eruptions along the Mono-Inyo volcanic chain.

"Fascinating, isn't it?"

"What?" asked Mac.

She sipped her beer and pointed toward the volcanic islands. The mostly basalt islands were devoid of vegetation for the most part. They were simply a reminder of Earth's powerful forces.

"The islands. Most people have no inkling of what made them. To them, they're just crusty little hills in the middle of the lake. I mean, we understand how they are formed.

"Mountain-making takes millions of years and can happen many different ways. Sediment fills underwater trenches and is hardened over many thousands of years into rock. This rock is subjected to even greater pressure when additional rock is piled on. Then the tectonic plates may rise, forcing the rock upwards to form bigger hills.

"It's the really large mountains that have always captivated me. Growing up in Colorado, I spent most of my outdoor time hiking west of Denver. The Rockies are a young, tall, rough range of mountains. They were formed sixty-five million years ago, an unfathomable amount of time for anyone to relate to, yet they're considered young, even at nearly twenty thousand feet.

"Like anything young, the Rockies are unpredictable and fickle. Full of secrets. Their beauty is, you know, kinda seductive. Yet they're very unforgiving. One misstep, and you'll become one of those insignificant particles of sediment that might make up the next mountain range."

Mac resisted the urge to respond by saying *that's really deep, honey*. Instead, he remained quiet, allowing the love of his life to wax poetic. Clearly, she was feeling philosophical.

Taylor continued. She swallowed hard. "Mountain-making may take millions of years, but death only takes an instant. I wish we could find a better way to warn people of catastrophic events like quakes and eruptions. Certainly, one leads to the other. But not always."

Mac interrupted. "We've made great strides. Think about half a century ago. As late as the seventies, we were using antiquated means of measuring the ground shaking. Volcanologists now have the means to measure magma chambers as well as determine what percentage of the chamber is molten."

Taylor shrugged. "And we can calculate the depth. We spend a lot of time studying the calderas around the world. It's not an exact science, but we're getting better."

Jimmy brought them another round of beers and removed the remains of the Buffalo wings that the couple had devoured. He tossed them a wet bar rag to wipe their fingers. Tourists got the small wet wipe packet. Regulars got the bar rag.

Mac set his beer down and took Taylor's hand. "You and I almost died a couple of times, but we didn't. As a result, what we learned in those moments was relayed to our peers. They'll step up their research on fault-jumping, for example. They'll study the seamount that formed so rapidly. Something that the scientific community swore couldn't happen."

"What was once a wild-eyed theory can become scientific fact, right?" asked Taylor with a nod toward a taxidermied creature hanging from the bar above their heads.

CHAPTER SEVEN

U.S. 395
Near Topaz Lake, CA

U.S. 395, also known as the Three Flags Highway, was a thirteen-hundred-mile ribbon of asphalt that stretched from the Canadian border to the Mojave Desert, where it terminated at Interstate 15. The highway had a cult following much like the celebrated U.S. Route 66 when it was first built, as it linked Mexico, the U.S. and Canada before major road changes around LA altered the termination point. Travelers marveled at the spectacular scenery, high mountain passes, huge lakes, as well as dry deserts along the way. The history and architecture of the route had been preserved by numerous National Historic Register designations.

There had been a moment in time that Sammy Hendrick and her husband, Tyler, swore they'd never return to California. In actuality, during the onset of the ARkStorm, there was more than one moment when they thought they'd met their maker. The two transplants from Florida had made a life for themselves in the Pasadena area overlooking a beautiful golf course while being located just a couple of miles from the Rose Bowl.

Sammy had been a corporate attorney specializing in mergers and acquisitions. Tyler had been the head trainer for the University of Southern California football team, which at the time had been preparing for the big Rose Bowl game against his alma mater, Penn State.

They lost everything that day. Well, at least the material belongings that people tend to put so much stock in. By the grace of God, and the help of a crusty retired firefighter, Finn, the couple survived, as did their dogs, Carly and Fenway.

Forced to start over, they returned home to Pennsylvania. Tyler received a job offer from Penn State, and Sammy joined a law firm in the state's capital of

Harrisburg. However, they didn't turn their backs on California completely.

After Finn purchased his cabin at Mammoth Lakes, well above the potential floodwaters from another ARkStorm, the couple made an annual trek back to California with the proviso they'd only come during the summer months. They had been scheduled to visit Finn last July, but that trip had been derailed when the earthquake sequence tore open the state and emptied Lake California.

Not to be deterred, they put off their gathering until this week, knowing that the greatest threat they'd face would be unruly college kids. While at USC and Penn State, Tyler had grown accustomed to that environment. Now that he'd taken a position as the Assistant Strength and Conditioning Coach with the Pittsburgh Steelers, he was working with more mature players. Plus, following their Super Bowl victory in February over the Dallas Cowboys, the entire coaching staff had earned the month of March off.

They loved visiting Finn at Mammoth Lakes. Sammy loved skiing, and Tyler was an accomplished snowboarder. The slopes of Mammoth Mountain perfectly suited them. As did the Village at Mammoth Lakes and the surroundings. Oftentimes,

Finn would have to be on duty or get called to handle a crisis. They enjoyed the night life the Village had to offer, and during the daytime, they sought out the most picturesque hiking trails to explore.

Their drive along U.S. 395 jump-started the annual, much-anticipated trip for them. In the summer months, they'd rent a sedan or small SUV just large enough to stow their gear during the two-and-a-half-hour drive from the airport. This time, they'd reserved an SUV, but because their flight had been delayed into Reno, the car rental agency had given the four-wheel-drive vehicles to other people with reservations. By way of apology, they had been upgraded to a red Infiniti Q50. Tyler was enjoying the sporty feel of the luxury sedan.

Sammy was taking in the mild temperatures, which meant, for her, anything above freezing as long as the sun was out. She'd insisted on opening the sunroof and cracking the rear windows. Tyler put on his jacket and gloves to keep his fingers from freezing to the woodgrain steering wheel.

They'd just passed the Welcome to California sign where the highway passed Lake Topaz. As she did every trip, Sammy leaned out the passenger window to take a picture. She studied her phone to make sure it wasn't blurry. One time, in her attempt to capture the moment, the wind's velocity had caused her camera to shudder, resulting in a blurred image. Much to Tyler's chagrin, she'd made him do a U-turn and return to the state line crossing so she could have a do-over.

"Okay, I know we made this solemn vow to never consider moving back to California," Sammy began as she turned in her seat to face Tyler. She wanted to study his face to gauge his reaction to what she was about to propose. "But every time we go to Mammoth Lakes, we talk about how much we love it there. Maybe we should consider—"

Tyler cut her off. "We're not moving back to California. No way. Besides, our jobs and dogs and the house we just built are back in Pennsylvania."

"Wait. Wait. Hear me out. We're doin' really well financially. I mean, I could see us owning a second home. Something small. A cabin or A-frame, maybe."

Tyler glanced out his window to admire the snowcapped mountains. Soon, they'd be climbing into the higher elevations, where snow would cover the landscape except for the highway, he hoped.

"I don't know, Sam. I love it here, too. But there's a lot to consider. Carly and Fenway are much older, and I don't think they could fly with us. Those two would be like terrorists on the flight. The drive is twenty-five hundred miles. We'd need to buy a Winnebago or something like that."

Sammy slumped in her seat and appeared defeated. They had always been savers, working diligently to pay off their bills. She wanted to live a little, as if surviving the collapse of a mountain ridge and a biblical flood during the ARkStorm wasn't enough.

"Okay," she said with a pout. "You're right."

"I've thought about it, too."

"You have?" Sammy perked up again.

"Yeah. I can't disagree with you. The logistics of owning a second home this far away doesn't really work. But then, when did we let that stand in the way? So I want us to enjoy ourselves this week while, at the same time, we kinda kick the idea around a little bit."

Sammy leaned across the console and planted a long kiss on Tyler's cheek. She whispered in his ear, "We can close the windows now."

Tyler burst out laughing. It was not what he expected to hear, but as the temperatures dropped, he'd take it. He glanced at the GPS display on the Q50's dashboard. Bodie's was thirty minutes away.

CHAPTER EIGHT

Bodie's Roadhouse
Lee Vining, CA

Taylor pointed at a taxidermy mount of the jackalope. "You and I are scientists. You even have Dr. in front of your name, but you rarely use it. Nonetheless, it's evidence that your scientific education is at the top rung of the ladder."

"Yeah. What's that got to do with the jackalope?" asked Mac, unsure of where she was headed with this conversation.

"You and I have one thing in common. Well, many things, but as it relates to our careers, we both tend to go against the grain. We buck authority. We question accepted principles of geology and volcanology."

"As we should," interjected Mac. "In the 1400s, the accepted science was that the Earth was flat. Then along came this guy named Magellan and proved it wasn't. He questioned the science, and it turned out he was right."

"Just like during the pandemic," added Taylor. "Many people, scientists included, questioned the underlying premise of COVID and the vaccines used to combat it. They were vilified for daring to question the accepted line of thinking. Trust the science, people shouted at them. Then it turns out the so-called conspiracy theorists were correct in many respects."

"I was supposed to get the jab," said Mac. "I found one of those places that would make up a fake vaccine record, and I gave it to Kemp."

"You lied to Director Kemp? And got away with it?"

"Yep. At least, she let me get away with it, I think. I had just started in Sacramento, so she didn't know me that well. Somehow, I think she was onto me after that ruse. She didn't want to get an unproven vaccine shot into her body either. She's a health nut. Vegan and all that."

"Wow, who knew? You're a man of mystery, sir." She still had a lot to learn about her future husband.

Mac laughed. He pointed up at the jackalope, the odd-looking creature that started this whole conversation. "I think I see your point."

Taylor explained. "Right. During those pandemic years, everyone was locked down or told to social distance or forced to follow all kinds of rules. That encouraged people to enjoy the great outdoors, including activities like hiking and spelunking in the Black Hills Caverns in the Badlands of South Dakota.

"Now, prior to that, a jackalope was considered some kind of urban legend, a myth. Anyone who swore they saw one was considered to be loony or a conspiracy theorist. Then those college kids from Sioux Falls wandered into the caverns and found a large burrow of them. The real damn thing. No myth. No photoshopped images. Actual video footage plus the wounds from their antlers to prove it."

Mac interrupted her with a question. "Later, a team from a zoo captured one, right?"

"Yes. Several are in the Brookfield Zoo in Chicago now. I read about the zoologist, Dr. Kristi Boone. Interesting story." Taylor took a sip of her beer and then continued, "So you see what I mean? People didn't believe that jackalopes existed. Those who challenged the science were eventually shouted down. Yet there they were. In the Badlands."

Mac thought for a moment. "This relates to the caldera, doesn't it?"

Taylor nodded. "In two ways, actually. First, the accepted science says that heavy snowpacks don't affect the volcanic system underneath. I don't necessarily agree with that. It's just a hunch based on my knowledge of this region."

Mac struggled to force his swivel saddle to turn so he could face Taylor. "Let's explore the theory together. Nobody ever thought the sudden formation of Lake California following the ARkStorm would impact the seismic system."

"You did, and they laughed at you," interjected Taylor. "I think everyone underestimated the impact of the ARkStorm. You didn't."

"Well, true, but I could have been more vocal about it. You know, put myself out there."

Taylor shook her head. "I saw their reaction in the auditorium when Director Kemp put you in the hot seat. Did any of those assholes apologize?"

Mac laughed. "Of course not."

"Exactly. I've learned not to give a damn about

what people think about me. I'm gonna question everything and prove my point when I can."

Mac smiled at her as he spoke. He loved her for so many reasons, including her feistiness. "Now, I don't know how we would prove the snowpack theory except through simulations, but I'd enjoy doing it with you. What's the other way it relates to the caldera?"

Taylor finished her beer and waved at Jimmy to bring her another. Mac requested one as well. She stared at Mono Lake as she replied.

"The community of volcanologists are firm in their scientific opinion that the Long Valley Caldera magma chambers are separate and distinct from the Mono-Inyo volcanic system. I believe that Long Valley's migrates and may even have merged with Mono-Inyo's."

"Wouldn't that almost double the size of the caldera's chamber?"

Taylor grimaced and nodded. "Afraid so."

As Mac contemplated her statement, Taylor left her seat to use the restroom. While he waited for her return, Jimmy checked in with Mac.

"You guys good? Too serious for happy hour."

"Yeah," Mac replied with a chuckle. "We're talking about some heady stuff."

"Like destroying the world?" Jimmy asked. He wiped away some remnants on the bar from the wings they'd enjoyed. "I sure hope not. Did you know they wouldn't insure my place against a volcano erupting?"

"Well, Jimmy, if it makes you feel any better, when Long Valley erupts, none of us will be around to collect any insurance checks."

"Did you say *when?*"

Mac nodded. As he replied, Taylor rejoined him. "Yeah. This caldera will erupt again. It's like a ticking time bomb beneath our feet. We don't know when, and that's what we were just talking about. We're always looking for a better way to predict these things."

"I heard when this thing blows, we'll be toast," said Jimmy, looking at Taylor, who settled onto her saddle.

Taylor corrected him. "More like incinerated ash. Sorry."

Jimmy poured himself a shot of rye and downed it. He winced as it soaked in. Then he poured another.

"You guys will let me know, right?"

Mac laughed. "We'll put you on our to-be-warned list."

Jimmy looked at Taylor. "Will you do it? I don't trust this one." Jimmy nodded in Mac's direction.

Taylor bumped fists with Jimmy. "I've got ya. No worries." With a friendly sneer at Mac, Jimmy wandered back in the direction of the college girls.

Mac continued their conversation. "So NOAA is predicting a heavier than normal snowfall this winter because of a strong El Niño. Since the ARkStorm, snowfall has already been greater than average across the Southern Rockies and Sierra Nevada mountain range. It's supposed to be off the charts in the next week."

Taylor shook her head in disbelief. "Isn't that just peachy. Here's the problem." She took a deep breath before she continued, "The weight of the snow and ice atop the Sierra Nevada affects the volcanic system's carbon dioxide emissions. We already have evidence of trees dying because their roots are suffocated by the CO_2 trying to seep out of the Earth.

"We've been studying the tree-kill area around Horseshoe Lake on Mammoth Mountain for the last year or so. The results revealed a twenty percent reduction in the volume of carbon dioxide finding its way out of the volcanic system. All of this has happened as the region has experienced record snowpacks every winter since the ARkStorm."

Mac leaned back on his saddle stool to crack his back. "There could be a fault developing beneath the surface around Mammoth Mountain. I need to take a closer look at the topography and vegetation patterns around Horseshoe Lake. It's possible changes in the distribution of stress across the mountain is opening and closing the fault. Think of how the tiny gaps between old floorboards flex as you walk across them."

Taylor perked up. "Like our house?"

"Yup. Except it doesn't make Mammoth Mountain a, quote, *charmer*." Mac raised his hands and made air quotation marks with his fingers.

Taylor continued, "We could compare the GPS data and depth measurements to the seismic activity around the southern side of Mammoth. I'll bet we'll find that CO_2 emission levels dropped where the weight of snow and ice is greatest."

Mac added, "Which, in turn, means that the Earth's crust flexed, squeezing together the rocks on each side of the Mammoth Mountain fault lines."

Taylor's voice was excited. "Mac, you know what this means. The CO_2 emission levels could be a driving force behind both the seismic activity and the volcanic system's response. Our forecasting could improve if the gases are ushering upward, and the ground is deforming at the same time. The alignment of these conditions could give us a clue as to the near-term likelihood of an eruption."

She and Mac exchanged high fives before reaching for their beers. Just as they clinked their mugs together, a boisterous group entered the restaurant, talking excitedly between themselves. Even their dog was chattering away.

CHAPTER NINE

Bodie's Roadhouse
Lee Vining, CA

Finn arrived at Bodie's just as Sammy and Tyler were exiting their rental car. Because of the growing number of afternoon bar patrons, they were forced to park near the small grouping of buildings where Jimmy resided. To announce his arrival, Finn turned on the flashing lights atop the roof of his response vehicle. He was tempted to turn on the siren, but he was certain Jimmy would forbid him to ever enter his establishment again if his patrons left in a panic.

"Finn!" yelled Sammy enthusiastically. During their ordeal during the ARkStorm, she and Finn had forged a close relationship. In addition to their annual visit, the two of them texted one another often and called no less than monthly. In addition to the allure of California's beauty, Finn was a big factor in drawing her to Mammoth Lakes.

Her long legs carried her across the parking lot to greet him before he was able to exit the vehicle. The two hugged, and Tyler soon joined the reunion. Because of the quake sequence and the catastrophic results that had followed, the three hadn't reunited in nearly twenty months.

"How was your trip?" he asked after they finished their group hug.

"Uneventful," said Tyler. He pointed toward the sedan. "The car rental company threw us a curveball. I hope the road to your place is clear."

Finn took a step toward the car and studied it. "City car," he mumbled under his breath before responding, "It's packed ice and snow, Ty. That'll land in a snowbank somewhere along the way. No problem, though. My Jeep's getting new shocks put on at Figueroa's in town. We can park the rental at the fire hall, and you can drive the Jeep this week."

"Sounds good," said Tyler.

Rebel stood on the armrest of the driver door, waiting to be invited to the party.

"She's afraid we've forgotten her," observed Sammy, who loved spending time with the Labrador while her own pups were staying with her mom in Pennsylvania. She hustled over to let Rebel out. The two crashed into one another and rolled around on the soft snow near Bodie's front porch.

Finn pointed toward the entrance, urging the three of them to go inside after he noticed two more cars pulling in full of the *après-ski* crowd. The French term, literally defined as after skiing, was made popular in the mid-twentieth century to mark the end of the skiing day and the beginning of the social activities. Bodie's managed to siphon off a good portion of the crowd avoiding the pricey beers and food located at the Ski Mammoth resort.

They picked up the pace to beat a group of four to the entrance. Finn was cracking jokes about ditching the mayor that afternoon while Sammy and Rebel playfully ran into one another. The joyous reunion was not dissimilar to their other annual get-togethers.

Finn surveyed the restaurant in search of a table. The four-tops were taken, but a large booth around the corner from the front entry was open. It meant that Rebel would have to sit on the bench seat and behave herself. While Jimmy allowed well-behaved dogs inside, he frowned on his four-legged guests getting on top of the table to grab a bite or a slurp of beer.

Sammy ordered a Perfect Margarita. Ty requested a Gold Creek lager, while Finn requested a shot of Devil's Creek Rye, as it was the closest thing Jimmy carried to his beloved Irish whiskey. Jimmy, and his Scottish blood coursing through his veins, refused to accommodate the Irishman.

Once the drinks were delivered and food was ordered, they raised their glasses to toast. In unison, the three toasted loud and proud.

"There are good ships, and there are wood ships. The ships that sail the sea. But the best ships are friendships, and may that always be!"

Finn knocked back his shot of rye and set down the empty glass. "*Sláinte!*" A word from Irish and Scottish Gaelic pronounced slawn-che. *Health!*

Sammy and Ty replied, "*Sláinte agatsa!*" *To your health as well.*

Finn grinned from ear to ear. He didn't have any friends in Mammoth Lakes close enough to enjoy a good toast with. His firefighter buddies who'd survived the ARkStorm had never come to visit him. He wasn't lonely because he had acquaintances. However, there was a chasm of difference between acquaintances and true friends like Sammy and Tyler.

"Jimmy, you lazy old Scot! Another round, please!"

From behind the bar, Jimmy mumbled something in response, but Finn couldn't discern what it was, not that it mattered. Jimmy had that old-codger relationship with all of his regulars. If the day came when he was polite and not crusty, Finn would call the paramedics to look in on him.

"This place wouldn't be the same without Jimmy," said Tyler.

"No doubt," added Sammy. She turned her attention to Finn. "How have you been?"

"Pretty good. You know, since we met at the New Year's Party that day, California has become a real shitshow. I thought the ARkStorm was something only Hollywood could conjure up. Then here comes the Big One. Well, not really the Big One like they portray in the movies. It was more like a bunch of regular ones. But when they happen within days of one another, they add up to the Big One."

"We followed it all on the news, of course," said Tyler. "It's hard to imagine that all that water just disappeared."

"Swallowed by the Earth or turned to water

vapor," added Finn. "It threw so much moisture into the atmosphere that we had blizzard-like conditions above the tree line for months. Then El Niño showed up to pile it on."

"After we crossed the state line, the snow cover really picked up," Sammy interjected. "Plus, we heard on the radio that another system is moving in."

Finn nodded. "It's gonna bring cold air with it. You guys might be spending more time by the fire at the cabin than on the slopes or hiking."

"We're ready for it," said Tyler. "We really love it here. The week we spend with you flies by."

Sammy blurted it out. "Plus, we kicked around buying a second home in Mammoth Lakes." Her voice was enthusiastic and hopeful.

"Well, we talked about it briefly in the car," said Tyler, throwing cold water on the idea. "There's a lot to consider."

Finn laughed as he caught Jimmy's attention for another round of drinks. "Don't get me involved in the decision. I'll have you guys living in my place while I bunk with the firefighters."

The three of them enjoyed a hearty laugh as Jimmy arrived with his hands full of drinks and beverage napkins. Finn rehashed the events surrounding the earthquakes and the aftermath.

After the dust had settled and the rescue missions had turned to recovery operations, the profiteers had swarmed the state just as they had after the ARkStorm. It seemed regardless of the catastrophe, there was always money to be made by one form of vulture or another.

CHAPTER TEN

Bodie's Roadhouse
Lee Vining, CA

The cheerful reunion between Finn, Sammy and Tyler had grabbed Taylor's attention for a moment. She'd only met Finn for a brief moment, instantly recognizing him as the Mammoth Lakes fire chief. She'd been asked to the Mono County Board of Commissioners years ago to make a presentation on volcano evacuation procedures. After that, she never had an opportunity to interact with Finn again. She'd heard nothing but good things about the man who stepped in to fill a huge void in the Mammoth Lakes community.

Mac swung back around to finish off his beer. Jimmy offered him another one, but Mac waved him off. He'd had four and was beginning to feel buzzed. Taylor had matched him beer for beer, and he was certain she was feeling good as well.

Taylor asked, "Isn't it crazy how we live in a county with a population of thirteen thousand, and we never interact with the guy in charge of search and rescue in Mammoth Lakes?"

"I know. Part of it is because the county is so large. Sure, there's the highway running north to south. However, you and I spend our time in Bridgeport, and rarely do we venture into the Village at Mammoth Lakes."

"We're just not village people, get it?"

Mac laughed. Had he downed one more beer, he might've jumped off his saddle and started forming the letters Y-M-C-A while singing the Village People's signature hit song.

"I get it. You're a funny one, Taylor Reed."

"Funnier than you, mister," she said with a grin as she finished off her beer. She looked onto the lake and noticed the shadows were growing long as the sun began to set over the mountains behind them.

Mac gave her a kiss. "I'll say this, before we were funny today, we were actually pretty damn smart.

Our alcohol-fueled brainstorm session actually pointed us in a direction that could save all of humanity one day."

Taylor shook her head and laughed. "I don't know about the all-of-humanity part, but certainly people within the blast zone of Mammoth Mountain or even the caldera." She fiddled with her empty beer mug as she contemplated another. Then she added, "Have you ever heard that saying, I do my best thinkin' when I'm drinkin'?"

Mac chuckled. "Yeah. It came from a song, I think."

"It's actually true," Taylor continued her thought. "I remember a study from years ago that took twenty men, served them vodka-cranberry cocktails until they were on the cusp of legal intoxication. Then they competed against a sober bunch in a series of word association problems to solve."

"What happened?"

"The drunks gave more correct answers than the sober dudes. So the scientific conclusion is drunk people are better at creative problem solving than the stone-cold sober stiffs."

Taylor played with her empty beer mug and raised her eyebrows, hoping Mac would wave down Jimmy for one more beer.

Mac scowled. "Where did you hear about this study?"

Taylor grimaced. "Well, *Harvard Business Review* or something like that."

"A Harvard study?" Mac was skeptical.

"No, um, I think the study was at Ole Miss or Mississippi State. One of those Southern schools."

Mac laughed and shook his head. He adored his soon-to-be-wife. He slid the beer mugs a little closer to the bar rail so Jimmy could see they were empty, when his phone vibrated in his pocket.

Taylor's text message alert began to chirp, so she reached for her phone, which was stuffed in her jeans' hip pocket.

"CalVO," she muttered.

"My people, too. A mini swarm."

The two jumped out of their saddles and headed for the door.

"Hey, guys!" Jimmy shouted after them.

"Put it on our tab, Jimmy. Gotta go!"

As they hit the exit, they heard another text message notification going off to their right. Finn had his phone turned upside down on the table.

Mac held the door open for Taylor to exit as Finn and Rebel scurried out of the booth. He dropped a set of keys on the table and a wad of twenties.

"Sorry, I've gotta go. I'll see you at the cabin. The Jeep's ready to pick up at Figueroa's."

Mac waited to hold the door for Finn and Rebel.

"You get notification of the earthquakes, too?" he said inquisitively.

Mac thanked him for holding the door and hustled past to where Taylor was standing. "No, structure fire near the Horseshoe Lake ranger's station. Propane tank explosion."

Mac walked into the shaded parking lot. "We have reports of earthquakes near the Walker River, outside of Bridgeport. Probably no connection."

"Yeah," said Finn. "Probably not."

Everyone hustled to their vehicles and sped off onto the Three Flags Highway to respond to their seemingly unconnected disasters. Taylor turned in her seat to watch Finn's vehicle speed off.

"Did he say Horseshoe Lake?"

"Yeah."

She remained quiet for a moment and then mumbled, "Oh."

CHAPTER ELEVEN

CalVO
Bridgeport, CA

Both Taylor and Mac were deep in thought as he rushed up the highway to Bridgeport. Their beer buzz wore off minutes after their phones signaled a new text message. The Long Valley Caldera was the most dangerous volcanic system in California. It had potentially worldwide destructive capabilities because of the volume of eruptive ash and poison entering the atmosphere. Any new quake sequence above the norm was a reason for concern.

Mac's mind wandered back to last summer, the July 4 week when the fireworks came from below the surface of the planet. After Taylor was rescued, and he'd survived the onslaught, he'd approached his boss, Director Sierra Kemp, about boosting the USGS presence at CalVO – Bridgeport.

CalVO had undergone upheavals of its own in recent years. At the time the ARkStorm hit, its headquarters were in Sacramento. Its staff and data center were relatively young although it had grown from strong parentage through what had been known as the Long Valley Observatory, or LVO.

In 1980, seismic unrest in the caldera motivated the USGS to begin more intensive study and monitoring of the region, leading to the creation of the LVO. The staff of three worked with local residents and emergency personnel to monitor and share information of volcanic activity.

Over time, CalVO spread to opening other monitoring centers across the state where active volcanic systems existed. An active volcano was defined as one that produced seismicity, or earthquakes, toxic gas emissions, hot springs, and ground movement, especially deformation.

When dealing with a volcanic system as dangerous as the Long Valley Caldera, abnormal seismic activity immediately drew the attention of CalVO and its scientists. After what he'd experienced last summer during the historic quake sequence, he easily convinced Director Kemp that the Bridgeport CalVO offices were understaffed, especially since there were multiple magma chambers to monitor.

Mac reminded her of the societal impact these massive geological catastrophes have upon the population. The region impacted by the quake sequence, or potential volcanic eruption, must not only have sufficient staff to monitor both the seismology and the volcanic system, but there must be sufficient personnel to establish an effective communication strategy, a liaison, between CalVO and local emergency managers.

Director Kemp didn't argue. On the contrary, she established an enormous budget for Taylor and Mac to expand their operations. Today, the couple, a top volcanologist and geophysicist in their fields, would be put to the test. Their system of plans, protocols and resources would be put to the test. Their handpicked staff, most relatively new to the Bridgeport operations center, would be asked to work around the clock with little rest.

And it all started with a little shaking of the Earth just twenty-eight miles away.

As they entered town, Taylor was the first to

break the tense silence. "Mac, I've been looking at the data streaming through the USGS app. These quakes are becoming more frequent, especially to the north around Walker River and to the south of Mammoth. There's a huge disconnect from what I've seen so far."

"That's what they said last year, remember?" he asked.

Of course she remembered. Taylor had been there when they scoffed at Mac's warnings. She had been there when the grim reaper came knocking at her door, twice.

"I'm with you. Anymore, I take nothing for granted. California is volcano country. The state has eruptions about as frequently as M6 or larger earthquakes occur on the San Andreas. Yet your department gets all the attention."

"Personally, I believe the media, and by media, I mean news and entertainment," Mac began, "the media focus their attention on catastrophic events people can relate to. Like earthquakes. In the U.S., the largest eruption of a volcano in recent memory was Mount Saint Helens forty-some years ago. We weren't born yet."

"True," she interjected. "Not to diminish Mount Saint Helens, but it's a planetary burp compared to what the Long Valley Caldera is capable of."

Mac raced into the parking lot. Unlike the USGS campus at Santa Rosa, parking was abundant. When he was tasked with creating this new facility, office space was a challenge. Mammoth Lakes was out of the question. There was precious little office space, as retail stores and hospitality businesses were more profitable. In Bridgeport, there hadn't been a new commercial office building constructed since before the ARkStorm.

The only option was a high school auditorium mothballed when the new school had been constructed several years ago. When Mac first entered the building, he'd muttered the word *perfect*. He'd converted it to a massive operations center for both the seismic teams and the volcanic observers, both of which worked hand in hand in a crisis. The stage remained, and massive projector screens had been installed to be used by Taylor and Mac to review data and view the area through their many solar-powered observation cameras.

Taylor and Mac quickly exchanged pleasantries with a receptionist who tried to corral one of them into the media room, where a few news reporters had already gathered. They didn't even consider it. Once inside the operations center, Mac grabbed one of his assistants.

"Make sure nobody comes through that door without clearing it with me."

"LEOs, too? The sheriff has already called."

"Everyone. We need time to determine what we're dealing with here."

"Mac, you'll wanna see this!" shouted one of his geophysicists.

Mac nodded to Taylor, who hustled off to meet with her team. He walked briskly toward the front of the old auditorium.

"Put it on the big screen!" he instructed as he took the stairs onto the stage two at a time. Mac stood with his hands on his hips for a moment. He stared at the screens, growing impatient. He turned to look in the direction of the geophysicist, who pointed past Mac at the screens.

There were two quakes. Near simultaneous. He was about to turn to summon Taylor to join him when she suddenly appeared by his side.

"That's at least an M4 at Mammoth Mountain," she said.

Mac turned to his team. "Give me the details on the Mammoth Mountain quake!"

"Magnitude 4.4. Depth is approximately five miles beneath the surface."

Taylor swung around. "Did you say five miles?"

"Yes, ma'am."

She turned to Mac. "Finn said he had a fire near Horseshoe Lake. Our CO_2 readings have been off the charts in that area recently. I even contemplated closing the hiking trails and access to the lake because of it."

Mac pointed to the map again. "I assume this quake is what brought about the alert to us?"

"Yes, sir. It happened several minutes before Mammoth. We're gauging it as an M3.2. Depth is approximately six miles, sir."

"Both are very shallow," said Mac. "This concerns me, Taylor. Shallow earthquakes are more damaging than deep ones. The seismic waves lose energy the farther they're below the Earth's surface."

Taylor's face revealed her concern. "My question is whether this is coincidental. The two quakes are seventy miles apart."

Suddenly, one of the seismologists raised her hand and shouted, "We have another one! And another."

"Where?" asked Mac.

"South County," she replied. "South of Mammoth Mountain."

Mac remained calm. "Bring up a map of the activity around Mammoth for the past two hours."

Taylor and Mac stared at the graphic for a moment until she expressed both of their sentiments.

"Oh, shit."

CHAPTER TWELVE

CalVO
Bridgeport, CA

"That's in real time, Dr. Atwood," the analyst reminded him. Although it was necessary, he reminded everyone observing the screen what the symbols meant. "Of course, disregard the instrument designations for the GPS, gas monitors, tiltmeters, and the seismometers. For purposes of this graphic, the larger the circle, the larger the magnitude. The color scheme is shown in hours. White is the last twelve hours, yellow is four hours, and red represents the last hour."

Dozens of earthquakes had rocked the mountains south of Mammoth over the last twelve hours. Only the strongest had been observed in the last hour.

Taylor turned to a member of her team. "Call the Mammoth Lakes Fire Department. They were responding to a call near Horseshoe Lake. Supposedly a structure fire at the ranger's station. See if there was anything else unusual about the incident."

"Do you think there's more to it?" asked Mac without taking his eyes off the screen.

She shrugged. "I don't know. Just a hunch. Horseshoe Lake has emitted more CO_2 than at any time since I've been here. That doesn't just happen. It's possible something is going on in Mammoth's plumbing. This quake sequence won't help matters."

Without warning, the lights in the building flickered and went out. Power to all the computers remained, as Mac had had the foresight to install a large Generac backup power generator coupled with uninterruptible power supply devices. His aide who was responsible for facility emergency relayed his intention to make the switch over to backup power before Mac asked.

A seismologist announced, "Another quake at

Walker Lane, approximately twenty miles west of here at the base of Walker Mountain."

"What the hell, Mac?" asked Taylor.

"I was afraid of this," he began in reply. "Listen, the quake on both sides of Ridgecrest put us on notice that Walker Lane is still active. The Walker geologic trough eventually intersects at the Garlock Fault. It's not commonly known, but the San Andreas fault only takes up seventy-five percent of the boundary motion between the Pacific Plate and the North American Plate. The other twenty-five percent occurs just to our west along Walker Lane."

"Are you saying that's the reason for seismic activity occurring simultaneously, yet seventy miles apart?"

"Sure," replied Mac. "Think about it. Hollister occurred along San Andreas right before the Mettler quake along Garlock."

"Then came Parkland Junction and then Green Valley," she added.

"Do I need to sing the song again?"

Taylor rolled her eyes and recited it for him.

"The thigh bone's connected to the hip bone.

"The hip bone's connected to the backbone.

"The backbone's connected to the neck bone.

"Shake dem skeleton bones."

Mac quietly clapped and smiled. "Very good. Now, we never addressed it before, but Walker Lane is a part of the same skeleton."

The overhead lights came on as the power of the massive generators shook the side of the building. Mac had learned from experience at the Santa Rosa facility. If you're gonna put observation outposts in the middle of an active seismic zone or down the street from a supervolcano, you'd better make sure the power stays on so you can actually help people.

"You've studied the Walker Lane Tectonic Belt, right?" asked Taylor.

Mac exhaled and shook his head side to side. "Taylor, it's the most discombobulated, hot mess of a seismic system you'll ever encounter. First of all, it's massive. Running up and down the state while also invading much of Western Nevada. Second, it's discontinuous. Technically, the faults are all part of the same seismic zone, although composed of separate segments. This segregation gives us both northwest-striking trans current faults near Bridgeport as well as dip-slip faults closer to Garlock."

"Impossible to predict," Taylor muttered as she studied the live view of the graphic. More small quakes were beginning to dot the landscape. Thus far, none of them were within the Long Valley Caldera.

"No doubt," said Mac. "That said, it was my study of the Walker Lane Tectonic Belt that led me to the theory that seismic events can jump faults. Sadly, my theory was proven last summer."

Taylor pointed at the large screen that filled the center part of the stage. Dots continued to show up at Mammoth Mountain as well as Walker Mountain to their west. "Are you saying these two quake storms are unrelated? Simply a coincidence?"

Mac grimaced. "Yes, that's one possibility. I'm puzzled by the lack of seismic activity in between. You know, why aren't the dots being connected along the entire fault zone?"

"Sweet Jesus!" shouted one of the volcanologists along the front row of the operations center. He stood and ran his fingers through his hair on both sides of his head. "We have an eruption!"

Taylor and Mac ran toward that side of the stage. "Say that again!"

"We have a volcanic eruption." His voice shook as he spoke.

Taylor fired off the questions, logically answering

them as she asked. "Where? At Walker Mountain? Mammoth?"

The man's face became serious. "No. It's at Panum Crater."

Taylor cocked her head to the side. "What? That can't be possible."

CHAPTER THIRTEEN

Horseshoe Lake
South of Mammoth Mountain, CA

Finn rushed down Highway 395, being mindful of the speed limit. Not because law enforcement would stop him. With his lights and siren on full display, he wouldn't be challenged if clocked on radar. Rather, he was careful to be fully aware of road conditions and other vehicles since he'd thrown back three shots of rye before receiving the text.

He avoided the Village and the throngs of tourists enjoying their vacation. He traveled Old Mammoth Road, a direct route into the Horseshoe

Lake area. Dispatch had concerns about two full-size recreational vehicles parked near the ranger's station. Eventually, the flames from the propane tank would burn themselves out. However, the RVs had propane tanks and large gasoline fuel cells of their own. If they became involved in the fire, a chain reaction throughout the parking lot might occur. A hot mess, in Finn's mind. Literally.

To their credit, his squad had had the presence of mind to shut off access to the area farther down the mountain at the entrance to the Twin Falls Overlook. Visitors would be rushing to move their vehicles away from the fire, causing difficulties for his firefighters. Once the flames had been put out, visitors could retrieve their undamaged vehicles.

The first thing Finn noticed when he entered the loop at the lake's basin was the spread of dead trees on the upward slope of the mountain. For more than a decade, the carbon dioxide seeping out of the ground had killed a hundred acres of forest around the perimeter of the lake. He hadn't had an opportunity to drive up to the two-mile-long Horseshoe Lake Loop since the spring of the previous year. He was astonished at how far the deadly gas had spread toward the ski slopes at Mammoth.

His firemen were successfully battling the blaze and were confident the two recreational vehicles at risk could be moved if the owners returned. Finn walked around the RVs to confirm the reports he'd been given. He walked up the steps of one and looked inside. There was a body lying prone on the floor.

"I've got a body! Truck, bring a Halligan!" A Halligan bar was used by firefighters as a way to force open doors and other obstructions. It was designed with a claw, a blade and a pick, enabling it to breach locked doors. He stepped aside as his firefighters worked together to pry open the door.

"Masks!" shouted Finn, not wanting to take any chances for his firefighters as they entered the enclosed space.

"Rescue squad, breach the other RV."

"We have another body, Chief! Both alive but labored breathing."

"Get them outside!" Finn shouted. "Medics, portable air. Now!"

"Dispatch, we need another wagon sent to Horseshoe Lake. Possible multiple victims from carbon dioxide poisoning."

Finn was pacing back and forth, watching as his firefighters breached the second RV. It was empty. The man and woman from the first RV were loaded onto stretchers and hauled across the snow-covered, dusty soil. Finn knew it was filled with carbon dioxide below the surface, but he'd been assured it was not harmful, as the bulk of the poisonous gas had mostly dissipated into the atmosphere.

Suddenly, a woman began screaming for help. She ran out of the woods, flailing her arms over her head.

"My boys! Please help my boys. They've passed out!"

Finn began racing in that direction, followed by two sheriff's deputies who'd arrived to handle crowd control. The vehicle owners had found a way around the roadblock, trekking through the forest or in snow-filled creek beds at the base of the mountain.

"Where?" asked Finn.

"There! Where the trail dips down between the hills." She pointed ahead to the trail that meandered toward Mammoth Mountain. When it had been built, it avoided steep slopes. Instead, it made its way through low-lying areas as it led to higher elevations.

Finn rushed toward the trail, with the deputies close behind. As soon as they entered the lower ground at the base of the mountain, Finn began to feel light-headed, and his lungs felt like they'd been stuffed with cotton.

Ordinarily, carbon dioxide was colorless and odorless. As he dropped to his knees to assess the boys' condition, he detected a sharp, acidic odor. He directed the much younger deputies to scoop the kids up and rush them to higher ground where the air was fresher. He forced his body to follow them as he became unexpectedly lethargic and drowsy. Something in the snow caught his eye. He glanced to his right and saw several small animals, including a long-tailed weasel and a couple of white-tailed jackrabbits. They were all panting heavily before they succumbed to the high levels of poisonous gas.

Finn mustered the energy to get to the upper part of the trail before it descended back into the parking lot. The farther he got away from the shallow part of the forest, the easier his breathing became. He walked briskly down the trail until the ground began to shake ever so slightly. It lasted ten seconds. Finn ignored the shouts and screams coming from the parking lot.

He was feeling woozy. He took a few more steps up a slight incline. He forced himself to take deeper breaths, thinking the recycling of oxygen would replace the poisonous CO_2 that had invaded his lungs.

The earth shook again, a little more violently. Enough to cause him to lose his balance. Screams filled the air as the people attempting to retrieve their vehicles rushed past the roadblock and ran toward their cars. Finn had experienced many earthquakes, including one several years ago that registered as a magnitude 6.2. It had caused minimal damage to Mammoth Lakes, as it was located along the west side of the mountain's summit. This one was not as strong, but the fact it was close in proximity to the mountain caused him concern.

He picked up the pace to assist his unit in getting the injured to the hospital. Then, just as he made it into the clearing, an enormous explosion shook him to his core. He spun around, thinking another propane tank or gasoline storage vessel had been missed by his firefighters. However, the sound was far away, yet close enough to register with everyone at Horseshoe Lake. It was also different. Like a bomb being dropped.

Panic ensued.

"What the hell?" he asked himself as he took several deep breaths to prepare himself for what might be coming. He spun around to get his bearings, naturally looking toward the top of Mammoth Mountain, where skiers were finishing up their day. He fully expected to see lava bombs shooting into the sky and a massive ash cloud spewing into the heavens. He was relieved when he didn't. Then his phone rang. It was dispatch.

"You're not gonna believe this, Chief."

CHAPTER FOURTEEN

Bodie's Roadhouse
Lee Vining, CA

Sammy and Tyler had seen enough of an unfolding natural disaster to last a lifetime. They'd watched the sides of mountains collapse and turn to mud, tearing down homes and lives in the process. They'd witnessed torrential rains and disastrous floodwaters rush through a valley, carrying thousands of people to their deaths. They'd been chased by mudslides and bears. They thought they'd seen it all and assumed those days of disaster were behind them.

It would not be unexpected for the couple to be paranoid at the first inkling of trouble. Their flight-

or-fight response might be triggered, with their instinct leaning toward flight. However, for Sammy and Tyler, it was just the opposite.

When the ground first began to rattle Bodie's Roadhouse that afternoon, many of the patrons, including the restaurant's proprietor, took it all in stride. This was California. Earthquakes happen. Still, the frightened looks on some of the visitors' faces were childlike. In the same way parents tried to hide their abject fear when a child was injured in an effort to calm the little tyke, locals shrugged off the occasional earthquake to soothe the nerves of the visitors.

During those initial twenty-six seconds, the ground shook, bar glasses rattled, and people shrieked and then laughed out of nervous embarrassment. It was the next few seconds that threw Bodie's into mayhem.

Some sitting at the bar saw the lava dome blow off the Panum Crater. The shock of the volcanic eruption left their mouths agape and their voices muted. When the shock wave made its way across the lake, it struck the plate glass of the restaurant, sending hundreds of shards of glass throughout the restaurant. There were barely a few seconds' warning of the impending impact. Only the explosive sound the small volcano made when it blew its top preceded the near simultaneous arrival of the shock wave.

Nervous laughter turned to primal fear in an instant. The only warning was a tremor. One among many that people experienced in the Sierra Nevada Mountains. It was expected.

The eruption at Panum Crater was not.

Sammy and Tyler had just finished dinner and were taking a moment to exchange text messages with friends when all hell broke loose within the restaurant. Having survived a natural disaster, their instincts to duck and cover served them well. They both fell over into their booths and stuck their heads under the table. Glass pelted their clothing and embedded in the vinyl backs of the bench seats. However, none of it struck their skin.

Now, as the volcano erupted, the noise was deafening, as the sound easily carried across the Mono Basin and the lake known for its high alkalinity from the volcanic system beneath. Even the shouts and screams of panicked guests were drowned out by the continuing eruption.

"We've gotta go!" shouted Sammy as the last of the glass pelted her turtleneck sweater. She rose, careful not to sit on or touch any shards of glass.

Tyler did the same but warned her against moving out of the protective confines of their booth. "Not yet! Look!" They had to yell in order to be heard above the roaring volcano.

A human scrum was taking place at the single-door exit from Bodie's. The saying *every man for himself* was on full display, as chivalry had died for the moment. Finally, as the last of the panicked patrons shoved their way into the parking lot, Sammy and Tyler stood to surveil the situation. They were both immediately awestruck by what they saw.

They eased toward the bar, where Jimmy was standing, staring through the gaping opening of the back windows. Cold air was momentarily displaced by a gush of hot wind as the eruption of Panum Crater released superheated gases and magma from the planet. However, it was not the odd temperature changes that mesmerized the three of them. It was the display the volcano was putting on.

Lava bombs and sparks of fiery magma shot into the sky, arcing upward before falling to the Earth's surface. At that late hour, the bright orange and red magma stood in stark contrast to the midnight blue sky of twilight.

With remarkable composure, Sammy had the

presence of mind to open her iPhone's camera app to video record the spectacle. Tyler stood silently by her side, taking in the power of the planet on full display. Only Jimmy's cell phone ringing broke the two of them out of their trance.

The restauranteur walked away for a moment, crunching on broken plate glass while sloshing through destroyed liquor bottles. Had it not been for the odor of the volcano reaching their nostrils, the smell of the multiple types of liquor would've made anyone nauseated.

After he returned, he addressed Tyler. "Aren't you two gonna go screaming into the night like the others?"

Tyler laughed. "Nah, we've seen worse."

"Worse than a volcano erupting across the lake?" asked Jimmy, pointing behind him with a thumb.

Tyler raised his eyebrows and nodded. He glanced at Sammy, who continued to document the eruption. "We were in Pasadena when the ARkStorm hit on New Year's Day. It was brutal, but we survived it."

"How do ya know the Irishman?" asked Jimmy, who recalled that Finn had been sitting with them.

Sammy answered that question. "He saved the

lives of our nieces, and ours, too. We've remained friends even though we moved to Pennsylvania."

Jimmy nodded and laughed, admiring the sense of calm the unflappable couple maintained. The lights began to flicker.

"How about a beer?" he asked Tyler.

"Sure."

Jimmy looked around for an intact beer mug. They'd all landed on the floor and were covered in broken glass. Then the power went out.

"Well, shit," he muttered as he fumbled through his pockets for his phone. Once he found it, he illuminated the flashlight. He found the bottle of rye and an open Jose Cuervo 1800 tequila. He rose out of a crouch and set them on the bar. "Young lady, if I recall, you're a margarita gal."

Sammy laughed and pointed at the 1800. "Tequila is fine. No glass. Just the bottle."

Jimmy grinned. Pointing at Sammy, he said to Tyler, "She's a keeper."

"So she keeps telling me." Sammy rewarded him with a playful shove that almost toppled him over one of the saddle barstools. "I'll take a swig of the rye. It's Finn's favorite."

Jimmy pushed the bottle toward him. After Tyler took a long drink, he passed it back. Jimmy did the same. "Finn would rather drink Irish whiskey. I tell him that I won't carry it because he's Irish and I'm a proud Scot. Truth be told, I keep a bottle of Jameson behind the bar for other customers. I just don't tell him about it."

The three of them enjoyed a laugh and another round of shots straight from the bottle. They debated what to do next. Jimmy felt compelled to stay with the bar to prevent looting. Besides, he had a pretty good view of the fireworks, he said. After Jimmy assured them the highway was well away from the erupting volcano, Sammy and Tyler decided to make their way into Mammoth Lakes to trade their rental for Finn's Jeep.

As they were leaving, Tyler turned to ask, "By the way, there were two people sitting at the bar who seemed to get text messages the same time Finn did. Do you know them?"

"Yeah. They're with the USGS up in Bridgeport. Run the place, I think. Anyway, that's who called. They wanted to watch the show through my live cam. My guess is they have their hands full."

CHAPTER FIFTEEN

CalVO
Bridgeport, CA

"Show me, dammit!" Taylor exclaimed, waving her arm at the screens behind her. She turned to Mac. Her voiced reflected her anxiety over the eruption's location. "How the hell? Where are the seismic precursors? For Pete's sake, we were sitting at the bar staring at the damn thing two hours ago!"

Mac quickly moved to her side and took both of her hands. "Deep breath, honey. Let's see what we're dealing with. Let me get eyes on the crater." Taylor slowed her breathing, so Mac felt comfortable giving direction to one of his aides.

"Call Jimmy at Bodie's. Ask him to turn his live cam toward the south side of Mono Lake."

"On it."

Two of the three screens on the stage changed to address the volcanic eruption. The earthquake swarm continued to be displayed on the far right. In the center was a map of the volcanic system where Panum Crater was located. On the left was a graphic displaying the data CalVO had access to near the erupting volcano.

Taylor walked closer to the screens and studied every aspect of them. Her eyes darted between the earthquake monitoring feed from the USGS and CalVO's own data being transmitted from nearby.

The Mono-Inyo Craters were a volcanic chain that stretched twenty-five miles along U.S. 395 from the northwest shore of Mono Lake to the south side of Mammoth Mountain. The northern end of the chain, known as the Mono Lake Volcanic Field, was made up mainly of steam explosion volcanoes that had either been plugged or overtopped by lava flows. Panum Crater was on the south side of Mono Lake. From the air, it looked like a grayish-white pockmark caused by a near-earth object. Then, over time, as eruptions took place, eruptive sediment began to fill the crater, leaving a mound in the center.

"Will somebody talk to me?" Taylor demanded. "Explosivity? Is it a steam eruption? Evidence of magma? Gases?" Her brain was moving faster than the data could be analyzed.

"I've got video!" shouted Mac's aide.

"Can you mirror it?" asked Mac.

"Hold on."

Seconds later, the center monitor, which had displayed a map of the volcanic field, was replaced with a feed from Bodie's live cam.

"Sir, I have a message from Mr. Bodey."

I can only imagine, Mac thought to himself.

"What is it?"

"Sir, he said you owe him forty-six dollars for earlier. He'd like his money before he dies today."

Mac shook his head and laughed. The fact Jimmy was still in his bar indicated he knew he wasn't in any real danger. Nonetheless, Jimmy would find a way to blame him for the volcanic eruption. Panum Crater was diagonally across the lake from Bodie's. Roughly six miles away. From what Mac could see on the screen, it was a magnificent sight, but hardly deadly. If Jimmy were to perish, undoubtedly he'd find a way to haunt Mac from beyond.

"Look at that, Mac," began a mesmerized Taylor.

Her panic had subsided, at least for the moment. "The pyroclasts of lava are rising out of the crater and falling to the ground in an arc. The ejecta ring is being built upon. Just like it did seven hundred years ago."

"We have deformation at Crater Mountain!" shouted one of the volcanologists from the rear of the auditorium.

The Panum Crater was the youngest vent of the North Mono volcanic field. At an elevation of seven thousand feet, it was dwarfed by Crater Mountain at nearly ten thousand feet. Crater Mountain, located a mile to the south of Panum, was considered the most potentially destructive of the Mono craters.

"Explain, please!" shouted Mac.

"Readings show the rhyolite dome has dropped several hundred feet. It's like the bottom dropped out."

"Eruptive material?" asked Taylor.

"Not based on our readings. Temperatures are normal."

"Why don't I see any tremors associated with the dome?" asked Mac. "Don't we have seismometers up there?"

"Yes, sir, we do. They're not transmitting."

One of Taylor's analysts added, "Ms. Reed, the

same must be true of our infrared absorption instru-
ments. None of the sensors are providing us data on
the volcanic gases being emitted, if any."

Mac took Taylor by the arm and pulled her to
the side so they weren't on full display. After they
were in a dimly lit part of the former auditorium's
stage, he ran his fingers through his hair and paced
the floor.

"I hate being in the dark. So far, we only have
one reported instance of deformation. We have
quakes on both sides of this dome but nothing
underneath."

"Are you thinking what I'm thinking?" asked
Taylor.

Mac nodded. "Let's go see."

CHAPTER SIXTEEN

The West Wing
The White House
Washington, DC

While the West Wing of the White House was being built in the early 1900s, President Theodore Roosevelt's office was temporarily located in the present-day location of the Roosevelt Room. It was so named by President Richard Nixon in honor of both Roosevelts—Theodore for building the West Wing and Franklin for its expansion years later. The windowless room in the center of the West Wing had always been an all-purpose conference room used by the White House staff and, now, for the president's daily briefings. Like its more secure counterpart, the Situation Room, it had been upgraded over the last several years to include a wall of televisions and a large screen for multimedia presentations.

Every day, whether weekend or holiday, the director of National Intelligence and his team prepared the President's Daily Brief, commonly referred to by the acronym PDB. It consisted of reports from the nation's intelligence community as well as his cabinet secretaries.

President Alan Caldwell requested the meeting be divided into international and domestic issues. In his mind, they were two separate and distinct issues. International affairs required an eyes and ears only approach, thereby limiting those in attendance to those with the highest security clearances. His domestic agenda, of tantamount importance to him, was expanded to include many aspects of American life. As a result, it received the bulk of his attention.

As he strolled down the hallway toward the Roosevelt room, the president thumbed through the binder to the highlights section that he insisted on being included in each briefing. If there was a topic of interest that he wanted to see fleshed out, he'd bring it up first. On this day, the reaction of the Chinese to sanctions his administration had imposed on Taiwan appeared to dominate the international part of the briefing.

His secretary and chief of staff awaited him outside the closed door to the Roosevelt Room, where everyone awaited his arrival. The president, who was notoriously tardy, had received his binder filled with the PDB when he awakened that morning. He'd stayed up late into the night following the news coverage of the volcanic eruption near Mammoth Lakes. The scientists brought on for analysis had given him cause for concern that the Panum Crater eruption was only the beginning of something far worse.

After his secretary returned to her post outside the Oval Office, the president whispered to his chief of staff, "I'm in a primary fight, and I have no intention of letting this damned volcano derail me like Hurricane Katrina derailed Bush the second." He was referring to the George W. Bush administration's response to the Category 4 hurricane that had struck New Orleans decades ago.

"It's all about public perception, too, Mr. President," said his chief of staff. "If we control the media narrative, your decisions won't suffer the same negative scrutiny that Bush did in 2005."

"I agree. So, frankly, I have all the briefing I need

on the matter. What I want this morning is political cover for what we do next."

"Then we'll handle it the same way the prior administration handled the pandemic. We'll lay it in the lap of the scientists and experts. You're the president, not a frickin' geologist, or whatever."

The president slapped the former congressman on the back and smiled. "This is why I needed a Washington insider like yourself to run this show. You get it."

"Good morning, all," said the president as he entered the room. Everyone stood from their chairs out of respect and returned the greeting. He glanced around to see who was in attendance and saw a couple of new faces as well as one who had been absent for several weeks. Most importantly, he wanted to make sure the Secretary of the Interior and the Secretary of the Department of Homeland Security were there.

"Good morning, Mr. President," they dutifully replied in near unison.

After everyone settled in, President Caldwell thumbed through the binder to the domestic highlights section. On this day, the volcanic eruption near Mammoth Lakes dominated the first part of the briefing.

The president got started. "Let's talk about the aftermath of this volcano. I see a couple of new faces. I assume you two are from Interior or DHS?"

The Secretary of Homeland Security replied, "They're with me, Mr. President. Jane Law leads the FEMA Office of Response and Recovery. Carla Jennings heads up our National Advisory Council, which advises us on all aspects of emergency management, including overall preparedness for natural disasters."

The president looked around the room for any other new faces. He scowled and then turned his attention to the Secretary of the Interior. He'd been perturbed with his appointee over the last three years since he took office. He'd expected the Interior Secretary to surreptitiously ramrod his climate agenda into law, but she'd failed him. Unfortunately, she was popular with a key constituency to his reelection, so he couldn't replace her. Yet. After his reelection, his hands wouldn't be tied.

He was snarky as he addressed her. "You didn't think it would be a good idea to have someone here from the USGS? Did you expect me to be briefed by CNN?"

"No, Mr. President. Um, I mean, I feel the report we included in the PDB was thorough, and

I'm certain I can answer any questions you might have."

The president grew angry, in part for his disdain for the Interior Secretary and in part because an important decision was weighing on his shoulders—what to do next?

"Fine. Is there going to be another eruption? There are some very bright people making the rounds on the news networks who think a damn supervolcano out there could be next." He was surly because the volcanic eruption had thrown a wild card into his perfectly orchestrated reelection effort.

"Mr. President, nobody knows with certainty," she replied as she thumbed through her copy of the PDB. She was looking for an answer in the report prepared by her staff.

He pointed at the contingent from FEMA, who sat directly across from the Secretary of the Interior. "I'm about to ask these folks if they're prepared to evacuate most of the population of the western United States. Don't you think it's logical to know whether or not that is necessary?"

The flustered cabinet secretary fumbled through the binder and stammered as she tried to buy time. The president grew impatient and continued, lowering his voice to an ominous snarl.

"Here's what's going to happen. Tomorrow, I want two people sitting in front of me and these folks from Homeland Security. I want someone intimately familiar with this extraordinary volcanic system at Mammoth Lakes that the media is talking about. I don't want bureaucrats from Reston or attention-seekers from their California offices in Santa Rosa. I want the people who live and breathe the same air as this monster. We dodged a bullet this time. The next round Mother Earth fires at us might be the size of a nuke. Do I make myself clear?"

All she could do was gulp and nod in response.

CHAPTER SEVENTEEN

USGS Cabin
Bald Mountain
Mono County, CA

The night before, Taylor and Mac had raced to Bodie's to check on the restaurant and found Jimmy to be in good spirits, literally. He made a fortune selling unopened bottles of liquor to people who'd descended upon the shores of Mono Lake to get a look at the erupting volcano. Jimmy had little concern that the California Department of Alcoholic Beverage Control was interested in auditing his battered restaurant. He made a lot of money that evening, which he'd need to carry him through the repair period. The crafty Jimmy even had a plan for that. He would reopen soon, one way or the other.

The couple had been ordered out of CalVO by their subordinates. They were driving the team bonkers as they sought answers to the millions of questions about what was happening under the planet's surface. The data was coming in, and the analysts were processing it as quickly as possible. However, there were a lot of gaps in their reporting due to the deformation occurring around Panum Crater and nearby Crater Mountain.

By the time they arrived at Bodie's, the crowd around the lake's edge was a dozen people deep. There was little doubt that news of the eruption brought people from hundreds of miles away.

Mac suggested returning to the house, where they'd have a bird's-eye view of the eruption. After speaking with Jimmy, they hustled up the snow-covered access road in Mac's truck, glancing toward Mono Lake every time they got the opportunity.

After making coffee, they stood on the front deck, captivated by the view of Mono Lake off in the distance. They talked about the potential ramifications of the day's seismic and volcanic events.

Naturally, their minds went to the worst-case scenario. When they finally dragged themselves to bed, they turned on the television and surfed news channels covering the event. They recognized many of the scientists called upon to render expert opinions. Of course, everything was based on conjecture, as the data was still inconclusive. That didn't stop the pundits and the media from declaring the Long Valley Caldera to be awakening from its slumber. Eventually, they fell asleep to CNN's interview of Bill Nye, the Science Guy, the couple's least favorite *expert*.

The next morning, Mac woke up first, which was not unusual. He didn't have a lake to swim in, but he certainly had a brain wired for early rising. After fixing coffee, a morning habit he'd adopted since moving in with Taylor, he immediately checked on the volcano.

The cold air was refreshing. Mac didn't bother with a jacket. He'd slipped on a pair of jeans and his Ski Mammoth sweatshirt. From a distance, in the early dawn hour, the eruptive material being ejected from the Panum Crater seemed to be lessening in volume. This didn't surprise him, as he doubted Panum was connected to the larger magma chambers beneath Mammoth Mountain and the Long Valley Caldera.

He received a text message from CalVO. They'd

updated their reports to include all the overnight data. It would provide Taylor some insight as to whether this was an isolated volcanic event or the start of something bigger.

The sliding glass door opened, and she stuck her head outside. "Did you get the text?"

"Yeah. I'll come in and print it." He turned to walk toward her, immediately taking in Taylor's beauty even in her disheveled, just-woke-up appearance.

She craned her neck to look around him. She had a robe wrapped around her with no shoes on.

"It's calmed down, right?" she asked.

"I believe so. It doesn't look quite as magnificent during the daytime. I'll be curious to see what the numbers reveal."

Mac kissed her and slid into the living room. He whispered into her ear, "Get dressed, or we'll be late for work."

"Do tell," joked Taylor. "Even in the face of the eruption of a supervolcano down there, you can think about monkey business?"

"You betcha. End-of-the-world sex is the best."

She pulled away. "How would you know? Have you ever experienced the end of the world?"

"No. I read about it on the internet."

She removed her robe and threw it at him, causing him to spill a little of his coffee. He barely recovered in time to see Taylor's bare body rushing into the bedroom.

She playfully shouted back to him, "Stay away from me, you doomsayer! The world isn't going to end until I say so." She disappeared for a moment and then appeared in the hallway, partially dressed. "And I'm not convinced that's gonna happen on our watch."

Mac draped her robe over the couch and made his way to the coffee maker. He fixed her a mug of coffee with cream and sugar. He topped off his own USGS mug before taking a sip.

"So you don't think this is just the beginning?" asked Mac. He studied the USGS logo on the mug and looked around their living area. There was a USGS tee shirt draped over the office chair. His USGS camo ball cap was tossed on the sofa. Taylor's USGS duffel bag lay on the floor by the door. Their home had more USGS-logoed merchandise than adorned their offices. But why not? Mac asked himself. They never stopped working, even at home.

Taylor emerged fully dressed and ready to go. Mac handed her the mug of coffee, smiling as the USGS logo stared at him.

Taylor responded to his question. "Nope, at least not until we have deformation at the caldera. Crater Mountain doesn't count."

Mac wasn't so sure. "Crater Mountain will be a much larger eruption than Panum. It could destabilize the entire region."

He made his way to the computer and began printing duplicates of the reports prepared for them by CalVO. He also noticed an email had arrived from Director Kemp looking for an update from the field. She could wait because he didn't really have an answer to give.

They sipped their coffee and pored over the reports. Ten minutes later, they sat back in their chairs at the dining table and compared notes.

"Let's look at the evidence," began Mac. "We have the Panum eruption adjacent to Mono Lake, and now we have the deformation at Crater Mountain that is at least a few hundred feet per the report. A substantial change in a short period of time is a pretty strong indicator that an eruption is imminent."

"However," said Taylor, holding up her index finger in the air, "we've had no quake activity around Mono Lake except for the tremor leading to the immediate eruption. There's no noticeable steaming or fumarolic activity around Crater

Mountain or the other craters in the North Mono volcanic field. Of course, it figures we lost a lot of our monitoring equipment. In any event, other than the Crater Mountain deformation, there's nothing else."

"Okay, I can make the argument that Panum was isolated and that the collapse of the peak at Crater Mountain was a result of the magma chamber emptying below it. What about the quake sequence on the south side of Mammoth and up at Walker Lane?"

Taylor furrowed her brow and slowly shook her head. "Yesterday, before the eruption, I considered it to be coincidental. The problem is that the geology doesn't match up. From the reports here, it should've been Mammoth that spewed lava last night, not tiny, relatively insignificant Panum Crater."

Mac thought for a moment. "What should we do next?"

"It seems our next logical move is to get eyes on Crater Mountain. Let's take some readings on-site to determine if there is a change in the composition or relative abundances of fumarolic gases."

"Drones?" asked Mac.

"Us," she replied.

Before Mac could protest, Taylor's phone rang.

She looked at the display, which read Mammoth Emergency Management. She put it on speaker.

"Hello?"

"Good morning, Miss Reed." Taylor immediately recognized Finn's Irish accent. "I'm sorry to trouble you so early in the mornin'."

"Not a problem, Chief. How can I help?"

"Well, there are a couple of things. There was an incident at Horseshoe Lake yesterday. Plus, a couple of days ago, we lost four young people last seen skiing the summit. Ski patrol hasn't located them, but they have reported some enlarged areas of hot ground on the southwest side of the mountain."

"Okay, Chief. Thanks for letting us know. We'll check it out."

"Wait, there's one more thing. The local big shots have convened a meeting at town hall for eleven this morning to discuss what steps, if any, need to be taken. You know, in the event something larger is on the horizon. Is there any chance you could join us? It would be nice to have a voice of reason."

Taylor looked at Mac, who shrugged in response. Then he nodded.

"Sure, Chief. I'd be glad to tamp down any concerns or fears."

"Oh, I'm sorry, Miss Reed. I should've been clearer. They're not afraid. They're blind and stupid as to the potential catastrophe that might be on the horizon. These people are all about making money even if it means the Earth will swallow them up before they can cash their checks. They want to adopt an action plan without scaring off the tourists."

Taylor rolled her eyes. She and Mac would be put in a no-win situation.

"Okay, Chief. We'll be there."

Taylor disconnected the call and rested her chin on her hands as she stared at Mac. All she could say was, "Marvelous."

CHAPTER EIGHTEEN

Mammoth Mountain Ski Resort
Mammoth Lakes, CA

While Taylor got ready for the day, she decided to stop by the ski resort before the meeting at town hall. She called Finn back, and he made the arrangements for the ski patrol together with two snowmobiles to meet them at Eagle Lodge to drive them up the mountain. When Taylor mentioned she and Mac were skilled snowmobile drivers, Finn shut the notion down. "Not where you'll be going."

After introductions were made, Mac and Taylor chose ski patrollers to double up with. Riding double on a snowmobile was challenging, especially on the steep slopes where the fumarole was reported.

The head of the patrol explained a few basics before they got started. "We'll be climbing the Dragon's Back, the most challenging slopes and trail at Ski Mammoth. Because of a couple of incidents recently, Dragon's Back is closed to all guests. However, especially during spring break, skiers and snowboarders think it's funny to circumvent our barriers blocking access. As we climb, it may require us to shift course abruptly. Just hold tight to our waists, and it'll be fine."

"If I'm riding behind you, will I be able to get a good grip with that backpack on?" asked Taylor, pointing to his red backpack.

"We'll be sitting one behind the other, just like on a motorcycle," replied the ski patroller. He removed his backpack and set it down next to the snowmobile's running board. There was a similar pack on the other side. He nudged the running board with his boot. "The backpacks have first aid and survival gear for each of us. We'll strap them to the tunnels on both sides so we can get snug. These seats aren't as large as the tandem jet skis people are familiar with."

The other ski patroller added, "We'll strap them

on, but just be aware the straps can come loose and flap at times. Just ignore them. The backpacks won't go anywhere."

The head ski patroller turned to Taylor. "Because you're petite, we're gonna ride princess style. Essentially, to have a safe weight distribution, you'll ride in front of me on the seat. I'll stand to operate the sled on our ascent. On our descent, we'll ride tandem, with you behind me."

"Are you guys good?" asked the other ski patroller. Both men were no-nonsense, an approach Taylor appreciated under the circumstances.

"Yeah, let's do this," said Mac.

Until he met Taylor, his life had revolved around the lake as his preferred recreational outlet. Skiing was a new thing. His athleticism could take him to a solid intermediate level. However, his lack of time to practice kept him on the beginner trails, also known as the bunny slopes. Snowmobiling was his passion. Much like riding his jet ski growing up, he enjoyed exploring the terrain around Mono Lake in the winter. Nevertheless, he was relieved to ride double with the ski patroller on the challenging mountain.

They took off, Taylor and her ski patroller taking the lead up the gradual slope of the Pumpkin Trail. This area represented the southern boundary of Ski

Mammoth. Once they passed the loading area for the Cloud Nine Express chairlift that ran the length of the Dragon's Back ski area, the terrain became extremely steep. The back sides of rock outcroppings were evident. The feeling that they were on top of the world overtook them.

Taylor had been here before on more than one occasion over the years. Fumaroles, like the one she was coming to inspect, popped up from time to time throughout the year. The Ski Mammoth patrols and emergency response teams were aware of the potential for the earth to open up. They'd learned to watch for suddenly melting snow and noxious gases being emitted from the crevices that widened due to seismic activity.

As they climbed higher, an area very familiar to her, as well as every member of the Ski Mammoth ski patrol team, approached. She pointed toward the left, near the base of an outcropping.

Taylor raised her voice so her ski patroller could hear her over the snowmobile's high-pitched engine. "Can we stop by there first? I'd like to show it to Mac."

The ski patroller nodded and backed off the throttle. He momentarily took his left hand off the handlebar. He motioned toward the rocky ledge and eased over to it. Seconds later, they were parked on a flat spot at the top of the Dragon's Back. Nearby, at the top of the ridge overlooking Horseshoe Lake, was a stone monument.

After everyone dismounted, Mac asked, "Is this the right place? I don't see a fumarole."

Taylor stretched out her arm and took Mac's hand. "I need to show you something."

They began walking toward the monument, which consisted of three pillars wrapped in stone veneer. Plaques were affixed to the front of the three pillars as a memorial. Taylor explained.

"In early April 2006, four ski patrollers were alerted to a fumarole that opened up on the side of Mammoth Mountain. The men worked to secure the heated vent by blocking off that portion of the trail by surrounding it with orange safety netting and trail closed signs. As they worked, what they hadn't realized was that a heavy snow the night before had obscured the actual size of the vent. When they got too close to the opening, two fell in, sinking twenty-one feet below the snowpack.

"The other two worked to rescue their fellow ski patrollers. One succumbed to asphyxiation in the process, as did the original two who'd fallen to the bottom of the vent."

Taylor sighed and turned to Mac. "People have no idea what we're standing on. Some, like our escorts, work here to keep visitors safe and to rescue them when necessary. People who come to ski, or even those who live all around us, lose sight of the fact we're in the midst of a massive active volcanic system.

"It doesn't take a cataclysmic eruption to take a person's life here. Earthquake swarms, toxic gases, and fumaroles are just as dangerous. The high concentrations of CO_2 can kill entire forests. You and I know what it can do to human lungs.

"The ski patrollers, like these three who died, and the two who are about to show us the latest fumarole, risk their lives every day to allow skiers and snowboarders to enjoy the beauty and challenges of this mountain. It's up to us to warn them that this volcanic system is no joke. It's very real."

Mac held Taylor as they read every word of the dedications. She wiped away her tears and then nodded to the ski patrollers, indicating they were ready.

It took an hour to inspect the newly created vent and to mark its location with global positioning coordinates. They sent the data to CalVO in Bridgeport to compare it with prior sightings along Dragon's Back.

Mapping fumaroles on the south and west sides of Mammoth Mountain because of the sun exposure was a treacherous, yet necessary undertaking. Despite below-freezing temperatures throughout the day, the snow melting from the heat of the sun caused newly formed vents to become filled in. Then, overnight, when snow frequently falls at that elevation by more than a foot, a snowcap of sorts covered the heated vent.

The vent doesn't simply close up or freeze over. In the battle of supremacy on planet Earth, heat beats ice every time. Otherwise, we'd all be frozen. The fumaroles were simply hidden for a while until they melted the snow again or until an unfortunate skier found them by accident.

After they reached the base of the mountain and said their goodbyes to the ski patrollers, Taylor and Mac made their way to the town meeting. Visiting the monument memorializing the fallen ski patrol heroes had a profound effect on the scientists. They were both reflective as they followed the GPS directions on Taylor's iPhone to the city's town hall.

"We're in a no-win situation with these people," began Mac. "They want us to tell them what they want to hear or, in the case of the politicians, to cover their respective asses."

Taylor shook her head as she stared out the window. Traffic in town hadn't been this congested since New Year's Eve. "Exactly. I can hear it now. The USGS people said everything was copacetic. Nothing to see here, move along. These things only happen every seven hundred thousand years, for the love of Pete."

Mac laughed. "Who is this Pete guy, anyway?"

"Huh?"

"You know. For the love of Pete. For Pete's sake. It seems a lot of people were concerned for Pete's well-being back in the day, whoever he was."

Taylor began laughing. "Why do you think up this shit?"

Mac pointed at her grin. "Because of that. When you're too serious, I need to replace that frown with a smile."

Taylor playfully punched him. "Because you love me?" she asked.

"No. So you don't get frown wrinkles."

The next punch that came his way hurt and almost caused an accident.

He regained his composure as the electronic

female buried deep inside the artificial intelligence of Taylor's iPhone told him what to do.

In one hundred feet, turn right to reach your destination.

"Is this right?" asked Mac as he wheeled his truck into the parking lot of a strip center.

Taylor imitated the iPhone's robotic, female voice. "Do not question me!"

Mac jumped and glanced over at his betrothed. She was holding up her phone next to her face.

"She means business. Both of us do."

"Sheesh," said Mac as he slowed to a stop in the middle of the strip center's parking lot.

He nodded to the right. "I see a Vons grocery store taking up the whole right side of this place."

"My guess is the meeting is over there," said Taylor as she pointed to the left side of the L-shaped shopping center. A hundred people were gathered around the parking lot, speaking excitedly, many animated as their gestures tried to accentuate the opinions they shared.

Mac parked near the entrance to Vons Pharmacy. After he shut off the truck, he took a deep breath and exhaled. "Well, this should be fun."

CHAPTER NINETEEN

Town Hall
Mammoth Lakes, CA

Taylor and Mac walked along the sidewalk toward the stairwell leading to the second level. People were raising their voices, arguing back and forth. Opining with absolutely no idea what they were talking about. They slowed as a crowd seemingly unrelated to the town hall meeting had gathered near the entrance of the Booky Joint, a small independent bookstore.

Despite the cool temperatures that morning, the front doors were propped open. Flanking one side was a life-size cardboard cutout of a smiling author holding his newest novel titled *Behind the Gates.* Above the cardboard likeness was a banner that read *Book Signing Today.*

"Oh, *Behind the Gates,*" she said in a soft, gentle voice. "Sounds mysterious."

Mac shrugged, but he got her point. "Think about it. When you're driving some back country road or even by a neighborhood that's guarded by a gate, don't you wonder who lives behind the gates?"

"Yeah, for sure. Like I said. Mysterious, and it makes me wonder what they're hiding."

They reached the stairwell, where two armed law enforcement officers checked people's identification against a printed list on their clipboards. Some were turned away, and others were allowed inside.

Mac leaned over to Taylor and whispered, "With a little luck, we didn't make the list. We'll go help Jimmy empty his beer cooler before it spoils."

Taylor smirked and shook her head. She wrapped her arm through Mac's and dragged him toward the burly officers.

"Taylor Reed and Mac Atwood. We're with the USGS."

While the officer ran his fingers down the list, someone in the crowd shouted, "Hey, they're the scientists!"

People started pushing and shoving to get a look at the guests of honor.

"Is it over?"

"Is the caldera gonna blow?"

"Yeah! When?"

"Do we need to evacuate today?"

"Do I have time to sell my house?"

"Yeah! Great question!"

The officer seemed to be taking his sweet time about confirming their approval to attend the meeting. Mac tried to weasel out of the guest appearance.

"Hey, if we're not on the list, that's cool. We'll just be on—"

The officer scowled as he compared their driver's licenses to their faces. "You're good to go. Head on up."

"Our lucky day," Mac mumbled as he retrieved their licenses. Then he whispered to Taylor as he glanced back at the crowd, who were pushing and shoving to get a look at them, "You just had to add that part about the USGS, didn't you?"

"Mac, I didn't even think about it. These people are nuts."

Mac nodded. "Some are justifiably scared. Others need to be. There has to be a point in the middle that makes sense."

"But what is it?" she asked as they approached the top of the stairwell.

"I don't know, but I know you're gonna do great coming up with an answer on the fly."

"What? Me?" She grabbed his hand and pulled him over to the balcony railing.

"Oh yes, Miss Reed. This meeting is about volcanoes. That's your department. I'm the earthquake guy. That was soooo last summer."

Taylor rolled her eyes as she waved to Finn. "You're a coward, Atwood."

"I am today," he replied with a smile. He gently pressed his hand behind her backside to urge her forward through the crowded room. She swatted it off. The meeting had not yet been called to order, giving them time to talk to Finn and gauge the temperature of the locals.

"Miss Reed, thank you for coming," greeted Finn as he gestured for her and Mac to step toward the back wall. His friends from Bodie's were standing alone, studying the crowd.

"Please, Chief, I know we haven't interacted much in the time we've both been in Mono County, but at this point, call me Taylor. And, so you know, this is my fiancé and renowned USGS geophysicist, Dr. Mac Atwood."

Mac scowled. He suspected she was using the faux accolades and the word doctor before his name for a reason. He extended his hand to shake Finn's. "Mac. Nobody really calls me Dr. Atwood. Even my team calls me Mac."

"Nice to meet you, Mac."

"Finn, he understates his title. Mac is an earthquake expert. He's known throughout the USGS offices on the West Coast as the seismic detective or even the earth whisperer. If there is anyone who can sense what's happening beneath our feet, it's Dr. Atwood."

If Taylor and Mac could communicate via extrasensory perception, an unproven paranormal phenomenon although many couples seem to exhibit it, Mac's glance at Taylor would say *don't you rope me into this*. Taylor's ESP response would be *consider yourself roped*.

"Is that right, Mac?" asked Finn.

"They give me more credit than I'm due," he mumbled.

Finn waved for Sammy and Tyler to join the group. "I'd also like you to meet some very special people in my life," he began as he gently took them by the hands. "They're my family, really." Finn appeared to be nostalgic, as if he was brought to tears by saying his feelings out loud.

Tyler picked up on the moment and gave Finn an opportunity to regain his composure. "Hi, I'm Tyler, and this is my wife, Sammy. I think we saw you guys at Bodie's the day the volcano blew."

"That's right," said Taylor. "You were sitting in the booth behind us."

Sammy added, "After y'all were called away, Ty and I stayed for dinner. We were there when the volcano exploded. I've got video, too."

"Wow!" exclaimed Mac. He hoped they could share their firsthand account of the Panum Crater eruption. "I'd like to ask you a few questions about what you experienced if it doesn't bother you to talk about it."

"Bother us?" asked Sammy with a chuckle.

"That was nothing," interjected Tyler. "When everyone panicked and ran out the door, we hung around the bar with Jimmy."

"Yeah, free Cuervo 1800 trumps volcanic eruption. Right?"

Taylor started laughing. "I love this girl. You really could give us some insight, if you don't mind. And a look at that video."

They were startled when someone near the front

of the room began to slam a gavel against a wood block, indicating it was time to get the meeting started.

Finn leaned in and whispered to everyone, "We can reconvene at the fire hall after the meeting so you can trade notes. I also have some questions about response protocols that I'm sure won't come up in this meeting."

"Sounds good," said Tyler.

The meeting began with the mayor speaking to those in attendance. "I'm sure all of you know me by now, but if you don't, I'm Mayor Bill DiGregory."

Finn leaned over to whisper to Taylor and Mac, "He's a real piece of work. A windbag and a narcissist. Selfish, too."

"I gather you didn't vote for him," Mac whispered back with a wink.

"Hell no, I didn't."

The mayor continued his opening remarks. "I called this emergency meeting in light of the recent activity nearby, namely at Mono Lake. Everyone in this room is part of our fair town's government operations, or they are civic leaders and businesspeople. I wanted you to have an opportunity to voice your concerns in an open forum, and also, after that, we'll listen to the opinions of two individuals from the USGS offices up in Bridgeport."

Because the mayor stood on his toes a bit to see the back of the room, nearly everyone seated turned to gaze upon Taylor and Mac as if they were something out of the ordinary.

The mayor began by calling upon a predetermined list of civic leaders to voice their opinions. One by one, they stood and called for temperance. Now was not the time to panic, a phrase Taylor heard more than once.

She whispered to Mac, "Are you sensing a pattern here?"

"No doubt about it. The mayor wants to assuage people's fears so the show, meaning business, can go on. His cronies are singing the same tune, even using the same buzzwords. By the time he's done giving them their say, it will appear they're the consensus, and nobody else will dare go against the will of the mob."

Taylor jutted her chin out. "Well, wait'll they get a load of me."

"Chief O'Brien, I believe you have arranged for our honored guests to join us?" asked the mayor.

"I've got this," said Taylor to Mac. She turned to Finn. "Just me if that's okay."

Mac had seen the determined look in her eyes before. *This should be fun*, he said to himself as he folded his arms and leaned next to Tyler by the wall.

Finn nodded and led Taylor up the center aisle of the folding chairs. All eyes followed her as she approached the folding tables arranged in a semi-circle at the front of the room. The local administration officials filled the folding chairs, with the mayor sitting next to the podium in a cushioned office chair on rollers. *The king must have an extraordinary throne*, Taylor thought to herself.

Finn stood off to the side as Taylor moved behind the podium. She thanked the mayor for inviting her to the meeting. Then she took a deep breath and began by making a simple statement that set the tone for the rest of the meeting.

"Nobody believes in volcanoes until they're surrounded by molten lava and the lava bombs are coming toward their heads."

CHAPTER TWENTY

Town Hall
Mammoth Lakes, CA

Taylor didn't hold back. Despite the fact she wasn't convinced that the recent seismic activity or the eruption of the Panum Crater had anything to do with the Long Valley Caldera, it was very possible. These so-called civic leaders were trying to sway public opinion in favor of doing nothing so they didn't frighten off their visitors, resulting in their economic engines shutting down.

"So what do I mean by that?" she asked rhetorically. "I've heard your comments. Some of you have referred to the eruption at Panum Crater using fireworks analogies. Something akin to a large sparkler or even a Roman candle. To be sure, the Panum eruption was benign, fortunately.

"It could also precede a much larger eruption at her sister volcano—Crater Mountain. However, the possibilities don't end there. These separate and distinct volcanic systems beneath the Mono-Inyo craters, Mammoth Mountain and the Long Valley Caldera may or may not be interconnected. Their magma chambers are believed to be separate, but nobody knows for sure because it's impossible to be precise when they are in close proximity to each other.

"Last summer, we learned that fault lines, previously believed to stop and start many miles away from one another, still have a connection. On two occasions last summer, earthquakes along the Garlock and San Jacinto fault lines jumped to trigger quakes on San Andreas. Earthquakes in the Mojave Desert, to the southwest of Ridgecrest, also encouraged quake storms to the south of Mammoth Mountain, which is many miles away in the Sierra Nevada seismic zones.

"One quake can trigger another quake, which can trigger another. And you know what happens when the Earth shakes violently around here?

Volcanic systems get pissed off!" Taylor paused to catch her breath and compose herself. She'd made her point. Now she needed to convince the attendees to maintain a heightened state of awareness.

"Please understand, it does me no good to scare the bejesus out of our residents and visitors by talking about supervolcano eruptions. When I'm wrong, I would be transferred to the volcanic observatory near the Arctic Circle. It's a place that makes Russia's Siberia seem like San Diego.

"That said, we have certain indicators that are raising red flags. Warnings that apply to the Mono-Inyo craters and to Mammoth Mountain. Besides the recent quake swarms and the eruption at Panum Crater, we have other precursors like dead animals, sulfur emissions, fumaroles and hot vents spewing carbon dioxide, and now deformation at Crater Mountain.

"So I suspect you want me to pull out my crystal ball and give you a prediction. I can't do that. All I can do is share the science with you."

"What's the worst case?" asked the mayor, who Taylor sensed wanted to interrupt her in order to change the narrative.

"Of course, an eruption of the Long Valley Caldera. Now, let me say this. Some of the largest volcanoes in the world never explode. They effuse basalt, which flows easily to gradually release the energy necessary for an eruption. Others are surrounded by volcanic systems that take the pressure off the caldera by erupting enough volcanic material to release the pressure valve, so to speak. Arguably, the eruption at Panum Crater might be part of that process. The deformation indicates Crater Mountain might be the next valve to relieve pressure."

"Do we have to evacuate Mammoth Lakes for that?" asked the mayor.

"I haven't run the possibilities through our simulation programs, but at this time my answer is no. We need to study Crater Mountain in depth to make that determination."

"What about Ski Mammoth?" asked a woman in the middle of the room who hadn't been asked to speak. "Will you have to close down the resort?"

"Mammoth Mountain is more likely to erupt than the caldera. At this time, it's less likely to erupt than Crater Mountain. That said, over the last forty years, CalVO has noted significant numbers of earthquake swarms, changes in the thermal springs, ground deformation, and significant gas emissions that have killed vast swaths of the vegetation around the southern and western sides of Mammoth."

One of the men the mayor had called on earlier to speak now addressed Taylor directly. He turned to the others in the room as he spoke. He was condescending and brusque.

"I don't know about you, young lady, but I was here in '82 when these people caused a panic in this town. We were crushed financially because the USGS ran everybody off. My family's business went broke, forcing us to start over. I don't plan on going through that again at my age."

Another man stood, again one of the mayor's cohorts. "He's right. I was here that May as well. The *LA Times* wrote about the tremors and earthquakes and how it meant there might be an eruption at Mammoth or, well, between there and the caldera. They wrote about the brewing lava eruptions. There were all kinds of quotes from the so-called experts at the USGS. They raised the threat level from notice to watch.

"Well, we watched all right. We watched as nothing happened. We watched as all the tourists skipped town. The USGS blindsided us back then, and I, for one, will not be duped again."

Exasperated, Taylor wanted to walk away

without saying another word. She was familiar with the 1982 incident. In fact, her boss had made her study the circumstances in detail so she'd be aware of the locals' attitude toward CalVO when it was established. The 1982 false alarm, as it had been called, was the primary reason the USGS had located their offices sixty miles away in Bridgeport. The USGS scientists had been threatened with nasty messages on their cars. They were ridiculed by the locals, who referred to them as the United States Guessing Survey.

Instead of giving up, Taylor said her piece and laid blame squarely on the shoulders of the responsible party. "I don't blame you for being upset about those events, which, let me remind everyone, were way over forty years ago. However, it was the news media that took the USGS official statements out of context. What has been forgotten is that because of the Mount Saint Helens eruption, the deadliest in modern U.S. history, the nation was on edge. Even though the USGS only issued its lowest-level volcano warning alert, it was the *Times* article and subsequent sensationalist news outlets that blew it out of proportion."

The room erupted in conversation as people talked among themselves. Tempers seemed to flare as neighbors, friends, and fellow business owners argued over what was the right thing to do. The mayor finally stepped up to restore order. He pounded the gavel repeatedly and stood next to Taylor.

"Ladies and gentlemen, this young lady is a guest of ours and is here to help. This is not the time to rehash the events of 1982. I wasn't here during the so-called *summer of discontent,* but I'm keenly aware of what happened."

He paused to smile at Taylor. "Miss Reed, is the USGS prepared to issue any kinds of warnings or change the threat levels based upon what has happened?"

"Mr. Mayor, that is not up to me although as the scientist-in-charge of CalVO, I will be asked for my recommendation."

"And what will that be?" he asked.

This was Taylor's chance to provide a plausible assessment while explaining in the simplest terms to those in attendance what was likely to happen.

"With regard to the volcano alert levels, its customary for the USGS and the Department of Homeland Security to make a common-sense assessment of the threat based upon the activity exhibited.

"Prior to the eruption at Panum Crater, we were

at a normal alert level. The sudden appearance of fumaroles and the random seismic activity in Mono County is deemed typical for the noneruptive volcanoes.

"Now that we've had earthquake swarms on the south side of Mammoth, up near Bridgeport, coupled with the volcanic eruption at Mono Lake, it would not be unreasonable to expect that alert level to increase to an advisory. Any time a volcanic system is exhibiting signs of elevated unrest, which the Panum Crater eruption clearly does, the advisory alert level is warranted."

Once again, the attendees spoke amongst themselves although the crescendo of voices resulted in a minor roar in the enclosed space. The mayor once again pounded the gavel to calm everyone down. All this did was give one of the mouthy men an opportunity to put Taylor on the spot.

"Is that what you're gonna tell the media? Exactly the way you explained it."

"The USGS spokesman, who will be very much aware of your feelings when I report our conversation to him, will likely explain it like I did."

Taylor sighed. Luckily for her, that type of interaction on the national stage was way above her pay grade, or so she thought.

CHAPTER TWENTY-ONE

Station 1
Mammoth Lakes Fire Department
Mammoth Lakes, CA

Taylor and Mac followed Finn's truck back to the fire station. The sunny day prompted the firefighters to open up the large bay doors to allow fresh air to wash through the garages holding their emergency response vehicles. The MLFD's engine company had responded to a call, leaving an open view of their vintage Dodge V-series fire truck built in the 1940s.

Sammy and Tyler were immediately drawn to it. "Check this thing out!" Tyler exclaimed as he rubbed his hand across the Art Deco-styled metal front end. It was designed to be a multipurpose, four-wheel-drive vehicle used in the military and by first responders. Eventually, it was made available in a civilian model.

"That looks like what we have back in McVey-town," said Sammy with a laugh. Then she added, "We don't have anything that resembles a real fire truck." Finn teased her about her statement and then confirmed she was serious. A town of a hundred people didn't warrant its own fire department.

Finn took them inside and introduced them to some of the members of second shift who were in the recreation room, which included a full kitchen and dining area. After the activity the day before at Horseshoe Lake, the smoke eaters were enjoying the calm.

"Let's go in here where we can talk," he began as he led them down a hallway toward his office. He gestured for them to enter a large conference room with chairs and tables set up, all facing toward a long wall covered with bulletin boards, maps and a white-board in the center. "Each shift begins here. We have forty-eight full-time firefighters and rescue personnel on our team, roughly divided into thirds for each shift." He closed the door behind them before he continued.

"We also have another dozen or so volunteers. Each year we conduct a fire academy for anyone who'd like to help their community on a part-time basis. Now, we don't send our volunteers into a structure fire or anything like that. However, when we're responding with all units to a challenging call, they can help us with crowd control, delivering gear, and assisting the paramedics."

"It seems like you've transitioned well from your days in LA," said Taylor.

"You know about that?"

"Yeah, you know, small county. Population-wise, anyway. I can tell you that the sheriff speaks highly of you."

Finn nodded and smiled. "Good guy. No nonsense. People would be stupid to commit a crime in this county. I'll just say that."

He walked to a file cabinet and pulled out a three-ring binder. The cover sheet inserted into the front read Town of Mammoth Lakes, Emergency Operations Plan, adopted August 16, 2017.

Mac thumbed through the contents to the end. "Well, it's extensive. Well over a hundred pages. But it hasn't been updated since 2017. California's been through a lot since then."

Finn grimaced. "Yes, it has. If you take a closer

look, you'll see that there are a lot of unnumbered pages and handwritten notes throughout. That's my working copy, which has not been approved by the powers that be. It seems the town is focused so much on tourism dollars, and rightfully so because it pays the bills. However, with the growth following the ARkStorm, we face greater challenges than we did nearly ten years ago. I brought my copy of the Los Angeles County emergency operations plan with me after retirement. I worked some useful provisions into this one." He tapped his finger on the front cover as he took it from Mac and handed it to Taylor.

"Since it's a work in progress, maybe I can help," said Taylor. "After the earthquakes of last summer, I thought it would be appropriate to revisit the USGS Response Plan for Volcano Hazards around the caldera and Mono Craters. Hot off the presses." She handed him the sixty-page document, which was held together with a large binder clip.

As Finn thumbed through it, Taylor made some suggestions that would save him some time and eye strain. "A lot of this is typical government documentation. The USGS, like other agencies, seems to get wordy. Everything in the Appendix dealing with the history of volcanism in the Long Valley region can be found by research on the internet. This response plan takes the hours of research out of it. Also, half of it tells you the hierarchy of the government response team. That might be useful when the shit hits the fan and you're unsure who you are dealing with." As Finn thumbed through the pages, she stopped him at page thirteen.

"Okay, this is useful, and you might want to copy it into your own plan. Also, the last few pages that compare the types of eruptions will prevent you, and your mayor, from panicking. For example, the eruption at Panum Crater was a lava fountain, typical of basaltic eruptions. Certainly, ash and coarser material, together with minimal lava flows, would be present. However, their range would be small, mostly confined to the crater and only up to six miles away."

"What about Mammoth?" asked Finn.

"A rhyolitic magma eruption at Mammoth would look very much like Mount Saint Helens," replied Taylor. "Probably larger, if my theory is correct."

"What's that mean?" asked Finn.

"Large eruptions are generated when there is a combination of material and stored energy to create them. Mammoth Mountain and the Mammoth Knolls, north of town, were formed this way. The more energetic the eruption, the larger the volumes of coarse pumice and destructive pyroclastic flows will be."

"What does that mean in terms of damage?" asked Sammy, who'd been listening intently.

"It all depends on how Mammoth erupts. Volcanoes look for the easiest path to vent. Usually, it's at the top. But not always. Flank eruptions can occur if the pressure seeks the path of least resistance.

"However, if Mammoth were to erupt by blowing off the summit, near total destruction within a twelve-mile radius. The ash could spread across Nevada, based upon the science."

"Is that the same as the caldera erupting?" asked Tyler.

"No, if the accepted scientific study is taken into account. Based on current accepted principles, the magma chambers of Mammoth Mountain and the caldera are separate. An eruption at Mammoth would not necessarily result in an eruption at the caldera."

"What if it did?" asked Tyler.

Taylor sighed. "Let's just say you wouldn't want to be here."

Suddenly, both Taylor and Mac received a text message. The notification sent a jolt of adrenaline through Taylor's body. Her thoughts immediately went to the possibility of another eruption at the Mono-Inyo craters.

"Washington?" mumbled Mac.

"They can't be serious, right?" asked Taylor, who locked eyes with Mac.

"Surely, they mean Reston," offered Mac. Reston, Virginia, was the headquarters of the USGS, a twenty-mile drive from the White House.

"What is it?" asked Finn.

Taylor sighed and typed a quick response on her phone.

"They're sending us to DC," she replied. "To brief the president at the White House."

CHAPTER TWENTY-TWO

United Airlines Flight 2132
Reno, NV, to Washington Dulles

Taylor was in a pensive mood as she and Mac boarded their nonstop United Airlines flight from Reno to Washington, DC. The late booking provided them the only available seating, which was in first class. After the flight attendant provided them their drinks, she settled in for the flight.

The Western United States had changed considerably following the two catastrophic events in California. After Sacramento succumbed to the flood and was buried as Lake California formed during the ARkStorm, surviving residents and businesses relocated elsewhere. Reno was the primary beneficiary of the exodus in the region.

As a result, the airline flight traveling back and forth to the east coast no longer had to connect in cities like Denver, Chicago and Detroit. Many, like this one, were nonstop. The four-and-a-half-hour flight would give them time to regroup from the hectic few days. Plus, meeting the President of the United States in the White House was an enormous weight on their shoulders. He would be looking for answers and suggestions as to how the activity in the region might impact California and the rest of the country.

Inclement weather forced the United flight on a more northerly track than normal, sending them directly over the Yellowstone National Park and the famed caldera that lay beneath it. The sun was beginning to set, casting a gorgeous glow across the massive supervolcano's caldera.

"Atwood, you have a way of taking me on trips full of gorgeous views and sunsets," said Taylor jokingly as Mac leaned across her lap to see Yellowstone. "But I have to ask. Is there a reason all of these trips seem to include the most dangerous places on the planet?"

"You mean like Washington, DC? The den of the lions? The so-called swamp?"

She began chomping her teeth like an alligator attempting to bite him on the neck. "No. I mean, look at that."

"Yellowstone is an incredible sight. I don't think I've ever seen it from this point of view." The Boeing 737-800 had just reached its cruising altitude of thirty-six thousand feet.

"It's hard to imagine that beneath its beauty simmers a catastrophic threat greater than anything in the country. Look at it. The caldera is the size of an upside-down Mount Everest. The superheated magma rises and falls. Breathing like a massive beast."

"Like Long Valley," added Mac.

"Yeah, except its explosivity potential is far greater. Unless ..." Her voice trailed off as she gathered her thoughts.

"Unless what?"

"What if the magma chambers at Mammoth have merged with the caldera? It would rival the size of Yellowstone and then some."

Mac nodded in agreement. The flight attendant interrupted them to offer another round of drinks, which they generously accepted. They'd been served a meal of salmon over wild rice with steamed vegetables. It was an upgrade, Mac quipped, above their usual buffalo wings and beer. He'd often joked that they ate like they were still in college.

Taylor reached into the hip pocket of her jeans to retrieve her phone. She scrolled through the Photos app to find a folder she'd created to show the president if the opportunity arose. She tapped on the overhead view of the three distinct volcanic systems in the Long Valley region. Mac leaned into her shoulder to study it with her.

"I realize you know this already," she began. "However, it would help me to sort of, you know, rehearse what I'm going to say to the president. I don't wanna come across as a complete moron when I try to give him some insight as to what we're dealing with."

Mac squeezed her hand. "You're gonna do a great job. I'm the one who might freeze. Don't forget, I didn't vote for the guy. I'm tempted to bring up his campaign promises and ask, what the hell have you been doing since you got to DC?"

Taylor buried her face in her hand and shook her head. "They'll lock us up in the basement somewhere, never to be heard from again. Or until the next election, anyway."

"No doubt," added Mac. He pointed toward the map. "We've got to keep it simple. Use the plumbing analogy. That always works for the laymen among us."

"That's a good idea. I'm sure once I get started laying out the situation, filling in the details will be the easy part. It's the big question he'll ask that concerns me."

Mac knew what she was referring to. "Honey, predicting volcanic eruptions is not an exact science. You can talk about precursors and all of that. But you can't provide him a definitive answer."

"He should understand that, right?" she asked.

"Yeah," replied Mac. He sighed and leaned back in the comfortable first-class seat. "Listen, I don't want to throw any more pressure on you."

"Why do I feel you're about to?"

"Here's the thing. Why are we the ones being summoned to the White House? Why not a big shot from Reston? Or even Kemp. Don't get me wrong, I consider you and me to be among the sharpest tools in the USGS shed. But presidential advisors?"

Taylor shrugged. "Okay, we're qualified on a scientist level, but advising the president is way above our pay grade. Let's look at it this way. We could say the eruption of the caldera is not imminent. Or even use the standard USGS line that reads something like —don't worry, the volcano won't blow anytime soon."

Mac let out a hearty laugh, which drew the attention of the other passengers across the aisle. "That bullshit always cracks me up. One side of the USGS mouth tells the world volcanoes are impossible to predict. The other side of the mouth says don't worry, there's no danger of an eruption for a long time. Which is it? Don't know, or don't worry because we do know it won't?"

"Exactly my point. If the caldera blows, who cares? He'll have bigger problems than firing us. If Crater Mountain blows, it's just the volcanic system venting. No harm, no foul."

"What if Mammoth erupts? You know, triggered by what's happening underneath?"

Taylor thought for a moment. "It's potential VEI is two but could approach five if the magma chambers have connected. On a national scale, that's manageable. Locally, it would suck."

"Long Valley's volcanic explosivity index is estimated at seven," began Mac. "If the magma chambers have merged, are we looking at an eight?"

Taylor took a deep breath and rolled her head

around her neck. "Yes, possibly equal in size to Yellowstone."

Mac sat back and mumbled, "I love what we do. I hate having to do this."

"Same," Taylor added as she threw back the last of her drink and waggled the glass at the flight attendant for another.

CHAPTER TWENTY-THREE

The Situation Room
Ground Floor, the West Wing
The White House
Washington, DC

Snow began to fall against the early spring sunrise as the Capitol Police Chevy Suburban delivered Taylor and Mac from their hotel near the Washington Mall to the White House. The formality allowed the couple to avoid multiple layers of scrutiny in order to ensure their timely arrival. The driver wove through the concrete barricades onto West Executive Drive. He slowed, tapping his fingers on the steering wheel impatiently as he waited for the heavy black security gate to open, granting him access to the White House grounds. After crunching through the snow-covered ice from the night before, they pulled to an abrupt stop in front of the ground-floor entrance to the West Wing.

After a security team checked the driver's identification and were satisfied that the bomb-sniffing dogs hadn't detected any explosives, the doors were opened. Taylor and Mac exited the vehicle, their eyes darting about in awe as they looked up at the massive mansion, the most famous in the world.

They gave the snow-filled sky one last look as if their fears of being locked away in some secret cell below the White House might become true. Following the instructions of the armed guards outside, the two entered through the double doors where two uniformed officers were posted. From there, they were escorted down a deserted hallway on the ground floor of the West Wing, which served primarily as offices for support staff as well as the location of the cafeteria.

The Oval Office was located directly above the Situation Room. However, the chief of staff wanted the benefit of the audio-visual equipment contained within the Situation Room to assist the two USGS

scientists in their explanation of the threats the volcanoes posed to the nation.

Taylor fought the urge to reach for Mac's hand.
Her palms were sweaty, and she needed the comfort
of the love of her life. Instead, she settled for the
exchange of a knowing glance and the wink of his
eye. *You've got this.* His message was clear.

They were led down a hallway to the right,
where the watch officer, a lieutenant commander in
the United States Navy, stood by the door to the
Situation Room in a sharply pressed black uniform.
He greeted the couple and their escort as he gestured
toward the door. "Good morning. The president and
chief of staff just arrived."

They were instructed to enter through the secure
door with a camera mounted above it. A black-and-
gold plaque with the words *White House Situation
Room: Restricted Access* reminded visitors of the
room's importance.

The White House Situation Room was a five-
thousand-square-foot complex of rooms commonly
referred to as the *Woodshed.*

It was born out of frustration on the part of President John Kennedy after the Bay of Pigs debacle in
Cuba. President Kennedy felt betrayed by the
conflicting advice and information coming into him

from the various agencies that comprised the nation's defense and intelligence departments. Kennedy ordered the bowling alley that had been built during the Truman presidency removed and replaced with the Situation Room.

Initially, before the age of electronics, President Kennedy required at least one Central Intelligence analyst to remain in the Situation Room at all times. The analyst would work a twenty-hour shift and sleep on a cot during the night.

Other presidents, like Nixon and Ford, never used the Situation Room. In most cases, a visit from the president was a formal undertaking, happening only on rare occasions. President George H. W. Bush, a former CIA head, would frequently call and ask if he could stop by and say hello.

On occasion, there had been a foreign policy failure, such as in 2012 when the American Embassy in Benghazi, Libya, was attacked, resulting in the death of the U.S. ambassador and others. The Situation Room became a forum for a tongue-lashing directed at top-level intelligence and national security personnel.

On many occasions when the president faced a crisis, whether man-made or naturally occurring, requiring all hands on deck, they'd convene in the

Situation Room. Today, President Caldwell viewed the small volcanic eruption at Panum Crater to be a harbinger of future events. He'd learned not to ignore odd coincidences, hence the need for this hastily called meeting. He would be probing Taylor and Mac for guidance.

CHAPTER TWENTY-FOUR

The Situation Room
The White House
Washington, DC

The president's chief of staff immediately put them at ease. "Good morning to you both. We'd like to thank you for hustling to Washington to provide us this briefing. Undoubtedly, you have your hands full following the volcanic eruption."

It was Mac who broke the tension in order to give Taylor an opportunity to get acclimated. She was the expert they needed to hear from, although he'd contribute to the briefing when asked about precursors like seismic activity.

"We're honored to be here. I need to mention something first," he began, turning to the president. "Mr. President, I apologize for not voting for you the first time. However, I'm willing to keep an open mind about the next election."

The president, who was known for his sense of humor, laughed. He looked at Taylor. "What about you, Miss Reed?"

Taylor was still nervous. "What about me?"

"Are you willing to tell me who you voted for?"

"Oh, um. Of course, you, Mr. President. I'm really good at picking winners."

This gave the president a hearty laugh. He turned to his chief of staff. "Put her down as a yes and this one, a maybe."

His chief of staff, who'd known the president for many years, joined the banter. "You know, sir, California is a swing state now. Perhaps we can transfer Dr. Atwood to a state where his vote wouldn't make much of a difference."

The president furrowed his brow. "Hey, isn't Yellowstone in Wyoming? What about it, Dr. Atwood? You wanna live next to the supervolcano that could rain hellfire on top of all of us?"

Mac's eyes grew wide. He knew he should've

lied. He pointed at his head. "Mind. Open. However, it is now a strong lean in your favor."

The room erupted in laughter. The president said, "See. There's no such thing as arm twisting in politics. I prefer to look at it as a suggestive sell process."

Taylor and Mac, who'd been standing the whole time, were directed toward their seats. They were offered pastries, coffee or freshly squeezed orange juice from the president's home state. As they unpacked their briefcases, the president began.

"I'm going to be completely transparent with the two of you. I want you to know it's something presidents do at great political risk. Unfortunately, every decision made in this building must be viewed through the prism of politics. Any wrong move is pounced on by my opponents. Proper decisions are still derided as coming too little or too late. I knew this when I took the job, which is why I'm constantly in front of the cameras making my case to the American people.

"I was elected, in part, on this same principle. I effectively chastised the former president for his inaction during the ARkStorm and its aftermath. I was able to hang the disaster around his neck as if it were his idea to conjure up the hellacious series of storms that nearly destroyed California. Now I'm in a new election season, and my opponent will have the opportunity to do the same to me.

"They tried their political tactics following the earthquakes of last summer, but even the most common-sense American couldn't blame me for the quakes. And our FEMA director, a rock star in his own right, stepped up to help the people of California when they needed it."

As the president took a sip of his orange juice, the chief of staff added, "In fact, if I'm not mistaken, the two of you were beneficiaries of the increased funding for seismic and volcanic monitoring when they expanded the USGS center in the Sierra Nevada."

Mac smiled at the president and took a risk. "Suggestive sell or subtle reminder?"

The president burst out laughing. "You know, I'm beginning to like you. You're a straight shooter. Where are you from, originally? I detect a hint of an accent."

"Dyersburg, sir. In West Tennessee."

"I know exactly where it is. Were you there during the New Madrid earthquake?"

Mac nodded. "Yes, sir. That's what led me to a career as a geophysicist studying seismic zones."

The chief of staff chimed in, "Mr. President, according to the background information provided to me by the USGS director in Santa Rosa, they refer to Dr. Atwood as the earth whisperer and, at times, the seismic detective. It seems he has an innate ability to sense trouble beneath his feet."

The president jutted out his chin and nodded. He lowered his eyebrows and studied Mac. "Do you think you can apply those same talents to reading the political tea leaves? I'll get you an office next to mine."

His chief of staff shot him a glance, so the president added, "Not yours, of course."

Mac laughed. "Sorry, I don't know much about tea, political or otherwise. And as for the whole seismic detective thing, I come up with theories based upon what's plausible, not just what is accepted." He turned to Taylor. "This is why the two of us make such a great team. We think the same way."

"Is that right, Miss Reed?" asked the president.

"Yes, sir, Mr. President. As Mac has learned, sometimes it's not the smart thing to espouse contrary scientific theories when you're surrounded by fellow scientists who are ready to poke holes in your thoughts."

"If you were to substitute the words political and

politicians into that sentence, we'd have a full understanding of one another," said the president. "So I'm
gonna make you both a deal. I want your honest
opinions and suggestions. I assure you, there will be
no repercussions for a wrong recommendation. At
the end of the day, I'm the one who will make the
final determination as to the best course of action.
That's what I signed on for."

Taylor smiled. She and Mac had won them over.
She was confident now and ready to proceed. She
placed her hand on her laptop and a binder full of
materials she'd printed for the president.

"Mr. President, I prepared this for you yesterday
before we left. It has volumes of research documents,
written in plain English, that provide you an over-
view of seismic zones and their relationships to the
volcanic systems they're impacted by. May I ask, do
you have a basic understanding of earthquakes and
volcanoes?"

"I do. The New Madrid quakes intrigued me,
after we all got over the initial shock of the death and
destruction they caused. The whole Mississippi-
River-flowing-backwards aspect was especially
fascinating."

"It happened before, Mr. President," interjected
Mac. "In the early 1800s. What most people don't

want to accept is that if it's happened before, it can happen again. Just because we are the most technologically advanced and educationally enlightened society in the history of the world doesn't mean we can stop the San Andreas fault system from rattling California or the Long Valley Caldera from erupting again."

"That's a great point," said the chief of staff. "Mr. President, when the time comes to make an evacuation decision, we could use this premise to justify the expense and inconvenience."

The president nodded. "Oddly, it's the inconvenience that people will object to far more than the cost of an evacuation's implementation. Dr. Atwood is correct, though. If we implement an order to evacuate, after some period of time, if nothing happens, people can return to their lives."

Taylor and Mac nodded in agreement. When they woke up that morning, they had one last discussion about their approach to briefing the president and his staff. After the ARkStorm and the week of massive earthquakes fractured the Earth, the president wouldn't want to take any chances. They knew they'd have to walk a fine line. If they downplayed the threat too much, they could be responsible for hundreds of thousands of deaths. However, if they overstated the threat, and nothing happened, they'd be vilified for being Chicken Littles.

The president continued by cutting to the chase. "This volcano, the caldera, is turning into a potential nightmare. I need to know whether it's out to get us."

Here we go, thought Mac.

CHAPTER TWENTY-FIVE

The Situation Room
The White House
Washington, DC

Taylor began with a response to the premise that a volcano has designs on destroying everything around it. "Mr. President, nature doesn't love, nor does it hate. It simply builds as it destroys. That's what volcanoes do. They make mountains. True, it's a singularly destructive process that's been ongoing for millions of years. It doesn't stop because we happen to live all around them."

"I get it, Miss Reed. I also understand there's nothing we can do about them. However, surely our technology has advanced to where we can predict the eruption of something as large as Yellowstone or the Long Valley Caldera."

"Mr. President, may I speak freely?"

He leaned back in his chair. "I think we've established a level of trust between us. Please do."

Taylor continued, "The science of forecasting an eruption of a supervolcano has significantly advanced over the past twenty-five years. Most scientists think the buildup preceding a catastrophic eruption would be detectable for weeks and perhaps months to years.

"Precursors to volcanic eruptions include strong earthquake swarms and rapid ground deformation and typically take place days to weeks before an actual eruption. Our scientists at the California Volcano Observatory closely monitor the Long Valley region for such precursors. We operate under the premise that the buildup to larger eruptions would include intense precursory activity at multiple spots within the caldera. As is typical of many immense systems around the world, small earthquakes, ground uplift and subsidence, and gas releases are commonplace events and do not necessarily reflect impending eruptions."

The chief of staff interrupted her. "Of these

precursors, how many have you detected at the Long Valley Caldera?"

"Here's where things get complicated, sir," began Taylor in reply. "Established scientific thought provides that we have three distinct and separate magma chambers in the Long Valley area. One very large chamber is under the caldera, of course. Then there are other chambers in very close proximity to the caldera, under Mammoth Mountain and the Mono-Inyo craters where the recent eruption took place."

The president politely raised his hand, indicating he wanted Taylor to pause for a moment. He smiled as he pointed at Taylor and Mac. "You two are very intelligent, from both a scientific perspective and your use of words. I'm a believer that words have meaning. So, Miss Reed, you began your statement by using the phrase *established scientific thought.*"

Taylor hesitated for a moment and then smiled. She and the president had established a rapport, which encouraged her to be lighthearted in her response. "Busted. Mr. President, years ago, during the COVID pandemic, we were taught to respect and not question established scientific thought. Mac and I believe that the very foundation of scientific discovery is to question the norm. Consider alternative theories and explanations, then set out to either prove them or dispel the notions."

"I take it you have a theory related to the size of the caldera that differs from your colleagues'," said the president.

Taylor nodded and squirmed slightly in her chair. She leaned forward and looked the president in the eyes. "Yes, Mr. President, I do. I believe that it's possible, if not probable, that the various magma chambers in the area have merged into one volcanic system, interconnected."

"Please explain," said the president. He glanced over at his chief of staff, who was furiously making notes on a white legal pad tucked into a leather portfolio.

"Recently, a study undertaken by a team of volcanologists from Caltech found that the Hawaiian volcanoes at Mauna Loa and Kilauea are connected deep underneath the Earth's surface. The enormous amount of seismic activity beneath the island's sister volcanoes in the last few years enabled them to create a three-dimensional map of the magma chambers.

"Here's what triggered the study. A few years ago, the two volcanoes stopped erupting almost simultaneously. The Caltech team thought this was more than a coincidence. Following the pause, there were nearly two hundred thousand small seismic events around the sisters. They became active at the same time.

"While their study is ongoing with a new set of eyes led by Dr. Ashby Donovan, a leading volcanologist, the basis for applying this study to the Long Valley area has merit. Obviously, in my opinion. And his." She pointed her thumb at Mac.

The president leaned back in his chair and took a deep breath before letting the air out of his lungs in a whoosh. "Miss Reed, correct me if I've misunderstood what you're implying. The magma chambers at Long Valley, like Hawaii, have merged. Because of this merger, the Long Valley Caldera is even more powerful than once thought."

"Yes, Mr. President. Its volcanic explosivity index would be on par with Yellowstone's."

"Do you think this smaller eruption is a so-called precursor to the big one?"

Taylor exchanged glances with Mac, something that did not go unnoticed by the chief of staff. "Dr. Atwood, are you on board with this theory?"

Mac took a deep breath before supplementing Taylor's statements. "For example, emissions of volcanic gas, as well as earthquake swarms and

ground swelling, commonly precede volcanic eruptions. When they precede an eruption of a central
vent volcano, such as Mount Saint Helens, they
normally last only a few weeks or months. However,
symptoms of volcanic unrest may persist for decades
or centuries at large calderas, such as Long Valley.
Studies indicate that only about one in six such
episodes of unrest at large calderas worldwide actually culminate in an eruption.

"The seismic activity around Long Valley, thus
far, seems to be insufficient to trigger an eruption.
The swarms have only recently begun, but they're
not that far out of the norm for the region. What's
puzzling, as Taylor can explain, are the precursors
that were seemingly unrelated to the Panum Crater
eruption. Seismic activity, fumaroles, um, hot vents
emitting gas, and ground deformation were taking
place in other parts of the Mono-Inyo chain and at
Mammoth. None of which was occurring at the
caldera itself."

Taylor took it from there. "The point being,
Mr. President, that the crater eruption could be
viewed as a way the caldera is letting off steam.
Releasing the pressure in the magma chamber,
which has now joined into one. At Mauna Loa and
Kilauea, they erupt near continuously. The Long

Valley Caldera hasn't in seven hundred sixty thousand years."

"Are you saying these smaller volcanoes, or craters, as you call them, might be helping the caldera remain stable?"

"Yes, sir."

"And what about Mammoth?" asked the chief of staff.

Taylor sighed. "Sir, I want to reiterate this is conjecture on my part. Proving my theory will take a team of dedicated scientists and years of study. That said, a full eruption at Mammoth Mountain would be akin to Mount Saint Helens. The region would be destroyed. If the magma chambers are connected, it's possible the eruption at Mammoth would be more subdued. Destructive ash, gases, and lava would impact eastern California but not be nearly as widespread as it could've been."

"What about the alert levels?" asked the president.

"My suggestion, sir, is to issue a Volcano Activity Notice with an alert-level change to Advisory. The volcanic system is exhibiting elevated unrest above our baseline data. This will put locals on notice who can make a decision whether to evacuate or not, while not causing a panic. As for the VONA notice—"

The chief of staff interrupted her. "VONA?"

"Yes, um, sorry. VONA is an acronym for Volcano Observatory Notification for Aviation. The activity at Panum Crater is insignificant in the scheme of things. I think remaining at green is appropriate until there's an escalation in eruptive activity."

"Miss Reed, what is the worst-case scenario?" asked the president.

"Mr. President, because we've never experienced the eruption of a supervolcano firsthand, my answer is necessarily speculative. We can make an educated guess from the geologic record. The previous eruption at Long Valley was vast, covering thousands of square miles. It's been studied, and the results show ash beds from the previous eruption stretching from the Pacific Coast near Southern California to El Paso along the Mexican border to Yellowstone and as far east as central Nebraska."

"America's breadbasket," the president muttered.

"The evacuation plan would include tens of millions, Mr. President," added the chief of staff, who'd been thumbing through the binder Taylor had provided to the president.

"Do you have an estimate of how many Americans would be killed by the caldera erupting?" the president asked.

Taylor sighed and looked him in the eyes. "It depends on what you mean by *killed*. Killed right away or starved to death over time? Or die from lung disease or dysentery? As the ash gradually settles out of the atmosphere toward the planet's surface, the ability to grow crops, operate motorized vehicles, and breathe become an issue. Not to mention the noxious gases stay aloft much longer. They will create a cloud in the stratosphere that will encircle the globe within weeks. This newly formed cloud cover will both reflect the sun's rays and absorb the sun's radiation, causing the Earth's upper atmosphere to warm and the lower atmosphere to cool. As the temperatures drop at the planet surface by several degrees, the planet will be plunged into a years-long volcanic winter." She paused and glanced at Mac before summarizing the devastation.

"The effects would be sufficiently severe to threaten the very fabric of our civilization."

Taylor's words hung in the air before the meeting was adjourned.

CHAPTER TWENTY-SIX

CalVO
Bridgeport, CA

Taylor and Mac were exhausted by the time they left the White House. Originally, they had plans to see the sights before they went to Washington Dulles. Instead, they asked the driver to take them directly to the airport, where they found a row of empty seats in a quiet corner to discuss the conversation with the president. Mac was being forthright with his assessment. The president was a straight shooter and not an alarmist. And Taylor had been incredible in her laying out the facts without hyperbole. They were not Team Chicken Little.

They caught a second wind and swung by CalVO on the way home from the Reno airport. The chief of staff had insisted upon having a direct line of communication with them. They exchanged cell phone numbers, something many elected leaders didn't have the privilege of doing. For that reason, the two of them vowed to do whatever it took to provide solid data to the president so he could make an informed decision.

They entered the operations center together and were immediately bombarded with questions.

"What's he like in person?"

"I heard he's funny."

"Was it scary?"

"Is he gonna increase our funding?"

Mac rolled his eyes at that one. Their budget was already bigger than it needed to be. He and Taylor were slow rolling the expenditures so they didn't spook anyone in Santa Rosa or Reston. They got what they needed, including a large shipment of the newly designed seismic monitoring equipment they planned on installing when the snow melted.

This was a large priority for Mac after what had happened the summer before.

Scientists who monitor volcanoes often rely heavily on automatic detections of earthquakes as one of the first warning signs that a volcano is acting up. They set up computer scripts that count up the number of earthquakes twenty-four hours a day. They send his team alerts that wake them up in the middle of the night, at times. Obviously, nobody wanted to be woken up for earthquakes that are happening far away from the volcanoes they monitored, so they created computer-generated alert boxes around the areas having a chance of causing earthquakes impacting a volcanic system.

Before addressing the group, Mac studied the monitor of one of his analysts. The Mono Lake polygon was active, with red dots on the south and southeast sides of the lake. He turned his attention to the analyst sitting to his left. He was focused on Mammoth Mountain. The swarm had continued at the south and southwest sides of the mountain. Sandwiched in between was the Long Valley Caldera, resting peacefully as it ignored the restless ground around it.

"Taylor, have you seen the seismic activity?"

She was standing on the other side of the auditorium setting, discussing data compiled by her team. They walked toward each other and met in the middle.

"No, I was looking at the reporting on Crater

Mountain. We have more deformation, and fumaroles are increasing inside the crater itself. What about quake activity there?"

Mac shrugged. "Yeah, a swarm around the south and southeast sides of Mono Lake. I suppose there is a connection. I haven't seen anything that would indicate an imminent eruption at Crater Mountain."

"Mac, there's some question about the release of gases in Crater Mountain following the rapid deformation. Also, there is evidence of ooze coupled with steam vents. If that is the case, the magma chamber beneath Crater Mountain is low in gas. A chamber low in gas equates to magma that is low in pressure, allowing it to slowly ooze upward, deforming the ground overlaying it."

"That's nature's building process you referenced in the Situation Room," observed Mac.

"That's right. If it's oozing magma, it could potentially erupt like Panum Crater, to eventually cool and rebuild the dome, although at a higher elevation." Taylor put her hands on her hips and looked at the large monitors on the former auditorium's stage.

Mac gently placed his hand on her back. "Whadya thinkin'?"

"Volcanic craters look exactly what they sound like. Craters. They are the nostrils of the beast beneath. If the magma chambers of Mono-Inyo and the caldera have merged, the pressure underneath has grown to a point that eruptions of the craters are necessary. Crater Mountain might just blow off steam, literally. In other words, a phreatic explosion where the magma and groundwater meet. Or lava bombs coupled with some ash, similar to Panum, could occur."

"Do you have an opinion as to which way it will go?"

Taylor rolled her head around her neck. "I need to take the day to see if anything develops and to study the data compiled by our teams. The problem is the lack of monitoring equipment in the crater since the deformation took place. I really need to get eyes on the magma ooze and take some readings on the heat flow. Of course, accurate numbers regarding the change in composition and relative abundance of fumarolic gases is a must."

Mac tilted his head and lowered his eyes to study her face. "How do you propose to do that?"

She shrugged. "I need to go in there to be truly accurate in my assessment."

Mac leaned into her and lowered his voice.

"Inside Crater Mountain? Um, the one that's about to blow? Are you crazy?"

"It's not about to blow," she replied. "You just said there's insufficient seismic activity to trigger any eruption."

"Well, I mean. Um, I'm gonna double-check everything. Maybe going into the mouth of a reemerging volcano is not such a good idea."

She patted him on the chest. "No worries. I can do it by myself."

"Nah. Not gonna happen. You're not gonna make me a widower before we're married. I'm going with you. First, let me make sure my people are correct, and write my will."

Mac walked away, leaving Taylor alone in the center of the spacious room.

CHAPTER TWENTY-SEVEN

Bodie's Roadhouse
Lee Vining, CA

Jimmy Bodey was much like his ancestors who risked everything they owned to move west in search of the wild frontier and, of course, gold. He was a hardened man who believed in self-reliance and perseverance. After the eruption of Panum Crater, both the state and federal governments issued a disaster declaration for homes and businesses damaged by the small volcano. It was a magnanimous, feel-good gesture designed to show constituents that their government was doing something. In practicality, only one individual and his business had been impacted by the eruption—Jimmy.

He didn't have time to jump through the hoops and hurdles to apply for FEMA funding. He needed to get his business up and running. The day after the eruption, his regulars came in to check on him. He'd already started cleaning up and had a couple of notepads sitting on the bar. One was for building repairs. The other was for restocking his restaurant.

That day, word spread throughout the community. Jimmy needed their help. Mothers donated plates, glasses, silverware, and pots and pans, commonly referred to as smallwares in the restaurant industry.

Contractors and their do-it-yourself counterparts found building materials stored in their shops and garages. A steady stream of SUVs and pickup trucks descended upon the restaurant over the next two days. The local glass company apologized to its other customers. An emergency order had just come in, they'd explained. Only, it was their gift to Jimmy for the many years of good food, good drink, and good times.

Then the food suppliers stepped up in a big way. They restocked Jimmy with everything he'd lost due to the power outage caused by the eruption, at no charge. The beer and liquor suppliers couldn't provide him free alcoholic beverages, but they could extend him credit for up to a year from purchase. They gladly did so. Even the Mammoth Lakes Fire Department made a contribution by exchanging their two, nearly new pool tables for the ones in Bodie's that had been damaged by flying glass. The firefighters said they'd convert them to Ping-Pong tables until the cloth could be repaired.

Within seventy-two hours, Bodie's was fully operational. It was a testament to what a small community could do when they rallied around one another during a time of crisis. There was no selfish self-interest. It was all about helping a friend and neighbor.

Jimmy's official reopening occurred just in time for Taylor and Mac to get their fill of beer and wings. They needed time to think. Away from the office. Without the aura of the President of the United States hovering over them.

"It's the darndest thing, Taylor. It's as if we don't know where to start or whether to start at all. I mean, we both agree that the Panum eruption may be a one-off."

Jimmy had called in all of his servers for the evening. The evening crowd began to trickle in as they learned of Bodie's being back in business. Taylor and Mac ordered their usual Eureka Blondes and a couple of trays of wings.

Mac proposed a toast. He raised his beer mug, and Taylor joined him.

"Um, here's to beer and wings. I can't think of better things!"

Taylor began laughing as their unmatched mugs clinked together. One was a traditional mug, and the other was from some bar in Arizona.

"That was so lame, sir," she said before taking a long, much-needed gulp. She closed her eyes and soaked in the moment.

Mac tried to avoid talking about what they faced the next day. He and Taylor both needed a break from analyzing what had happened at Panum, and the thought of what might be on the horizon for Mammoth Lakes. After their wings were delivered, they talked about finishing the lean-to project before the upcoming early-spring snow arrived.

When the ARkStorm had destroyed Sacramento and the repeater towers in between, the only available television stations had come out of Reno. KOLO, Channel 8, the ABC affiliate, had broadened their news coverage to include Mammoth Lakes, the furthest outreach of their coverage area.

The reports of the coming snowy weather were near apocalyptic.

The two of them had danced around the topic that was foremost on their minds. Predicting the next volcanic event, if any. They both agreed that an eruption at nearby Crater Mountain appeared to be most likely. To confirm their opinion, they needed to take a closer look. The conversation surrounding the weather immediately found its way to the challenge they faced the next day.

"What's the timing of the storm?" asked Taylor, breaking the unspoken truce to avoid shop talk.

"Tomorrow afternoon, late. Um, we'll wanna get an early start."

"Yeah, but we'll need the sun's help to make sure we don't get tripped up. This is a very unpredictable climb, Mac. I'm totally fine with doing it alone."

"No way," he responded as he finished off the last of his wings. He opened up a Wet Wipe to clean off his hands after licking any excess buffalo sauce off his fingers. It was a guy thing. "I'll be your wingman. Get it?"

Taylor rolled her eyes but couldn't stop a big smile from spreading across her face. "I hate you. You dope."

Mac nodded toward the other end of the restaurant. "Looks like Finn is here, too. He's watching Sammy and Tyler shoot pool."

Taylor finished off her wings. She, too, licked her fingers clean before using the Wet Wipes. She'd always been a guy's kinda girl.

"Let's go hang out with them," she suggested.

Mac flagged down their server and paid their bill. He noticed that Jimmy had added the forty-six dollars from the other day. Through all the turmoil, the man had a memory like an elephant. Mac didn't mind as he heaped a generous tip on top of the tab. He still had per diem money left over from their trip to Washington. Let the government contribute in their own small way, he thought to himself.

Taylor arrived at the pool tables first while Mac grabbed them another round from the bar. Just as Finn acknowledged her, Sammy finished off Tyler in a game of 8-ball.

"Three in a row, big boy," she said proudly as she twirled the pool cue in her fingers. "Keep it up, and I'll own you."

"You already own me," Tyler mumbled. He was very competitive and didn't like losing. Sammy was just as bad. Their Monopoly games were legendary, knock-down, dragged-out death matches.

"Hi, guys! Mind if we join you?" asked Taylor.

She glanced back at the dining area. "We didn't want to take up a table. Jimmy might charge us double."

"Sure," said Finn. "I've been watching Sammy take her husband to the cleaner's."

Mac showed up with the beers just as Tyler racked the balls for another game. "Hey, Ty. Whadya think? Wanna take on the girls?"

Tyler was still salty from the drubbing he'd just endured. "Are you any good? She's a shark." He pointed at Sammy, who was enjoying every minute of Tyler's brooding. He beat her at nearly every sport and game they played. The Monopoly fiasco had nearly ended their relationship because Tyler seemingly let Sammy win. That had angered her more than losing fairly.

"I'm not too bad. I'm a little rusty. Been kinda busy lately."

"Let's do it," said Tyler.

Taylor approached Sammy and whispered into her ear, "Watch this.

"Boys, let's make it interesting, shall we?"

Mac was ready for the challenge. "Yeah. Let's. Whadya have in mind?" Mac was thinking they'd pay for drinks, or receive a night of back scratching. Something simple like that. He was surprised at the stakes.

"If Sammy and I win, you boys will treat us to an all-expenses-paid day at the Double Eagle spa at the Snowcreek Athletic Club."

"Whoa, that's pricey," groaned Mac. Taylor had spent a day getting a massage, a facial, and a mani-pedi. The bill had run nearly six hundred dollars.

"Yes, sir. It is. This is a high-stakes game. If you can't handle it, step aside, and the girls will play."

"Fine," said Mac. "Our turn." He moseyed over to Tyler, and the two men commiserated. Ty's spirits lifted.

"Sounds good," he said, patting Mac on the back.

Mac allowed the rubber end of the pool cue to bounce off the concrete floor as he made his proposal. "If we win, Tyler and I get a trip to Tahoe to gamble. You guys gotta pick up the tab for the gas, lunch and beer."

Taylor leaned over to whisper again. "Are you okay if I break?"

Sammy shrugged and nodded. "Okay."

Taylor continued to whisper. "Trust me."

"Ladies, do we have a deal or not?" asked Mac.

"Just to make it fair, we'll kick in five hundred dollars each for gambling money."

Mac didn't hesitate. "Done. To prove we're gentlemen, you ladies can break. Right, Ty?"

"Yep." The guys stood to the side and sipped on their beer as Taylor took a couple of cue sticks out of the rack. She slowly rolled them across the new slate pool tables obtained from Fire Station Number 1. Satisfied that the cue wasn't warped, she chalked the tip.

Taylor took the cue ball and strategically placed it slightly off center to halfway between the diamond-shaped inlay. She slowly pulled her stick back and let it rip. The white cue ball hit the 1-ball with a solid smack, sending the other four rows of balls scattering in all directions.

The second row of two balls headed for the side pockets. The corner balls on the back row darted all around the table until they approached the corner pockets nearest where they started. Meanwhile, the 1-ball made an unobstructed roll into the corner pocket next to where Taylor and Sammy were standing. The blue 2-ball found its way into a pocket as well.

Taylor grinned at Sammy and then addressed the guys. "We're gonna call our shots, right? There's no place for luck in competitive pool, especially when wagering is involved."

Mac leaned over to Tyler. "I have a bad feeling about this."

"Sammy is really good, too. I think were screwed."

Mac shrugged and replied to Taylor somewhat dejectedly, "I couldn't agree more. Call 'em."

One by one, Taylor sent the remaining solids into one of the six pockets on the table. She even finished off the 8-ball with a long shot along the rail. The trek down the table into the corner pocket nearest where an astonished Mac and Tyler stood was excruciatingly slow for the guys. As it dropped in, Taylor and Sammy cheered themselves and exchanged high fives.

Mac shook his head in disbelief. After all they'd been through together, this was something he'd never known about Taylor. She was a pool hustler.

After their enthusiasm died down, the ladies offered a rematch. "Boys? Double or nothing? Winner breaks?"

Tyler had had enough. Mac was shell-shocked. "Nah, we'll pass for today. Day after tomorrow, you two enjoy your day at the spa."

"Tomorrow sounds better," said Sammy with a laugh as she playfully poked the rubber end of her pool cue at Tyler's ribs.

"Can't tomorrow," said Taylor. "My boyfriend promised me a hike into an active volcano."

"Seriously?" asked Tyler.

"Yeah," Mac replied. "We have several experiments to run to determine whether Crater Mountain is at risk of an eruption. It would be larger and more widespread than what happened at Panum the other day." He pointed through the windows at the crater that once rested peacefully near Mono Lake.

"We're pretty good at climbing, and we don't have any plans for tomorrow," said Tyler.

"Yeah, can we help you in any way?" asked Sammy.

Mac frowned. "I don't know. We're not sure what we'll be getting into."

Taylor set her pool cue on the table. "We could use a spotter. I can't recommend you guys come into the crater with us. It would be nice to have someone at the top to report that we fell into a fumarole or boiling hot lava."

"Nice. Thanks for the visual," said Mac sarcastically. He and Taylor had discussed the risks ad nauseam. The descent into the collapsed crater was necessary to get an accurate assessment of its threat.

"Count us in!" said Tyler enthusiastically.

"Is anyone going to ask my opinion about this lunacy?" asked Finn.

"Well, um," Taylor began before Sammy rescued her.

"No, Dad," she began. "We knew you'd just say no."

"You're right, lass. I am saying no," said Finn, whose face reflected his concern. "I'm not sure I could rescue you from something like this."

"No worries, Finn. I'm from Colorado. I grew up climbing and hiking. We'll be good."

"You too?" Finn asked Mac.

"Um, yep. Same here." Mac's reply essentially said nothing about his abilities to hike into a volcano. This would be a new addition to his résumé, along with surviving massive whirlpools and tsunamis and earthquakes and his boss's ire.

After they set a time to meet at Bodie's parking lot, Finn gave them some instructions on how to reach out for assistance to both Bridgeport and Mammoth Lakes. Then he reminded them about the weather. He laid on the Irish accent thick and heavy.

"Don't forget. A wicked storm is comin'."

CHAPTER TWENTY-EIGHT

Crater Mountain
Mono County, CA

Crater Mountain was just over a mile from where Panum Crater had erupted. It was about seven miles from the rim of the Long Valley Caldera. The hike up the rocky face of the mountain was complicated by the eruptive material that had found its way from Panum. That, and the potential instability of the mountain due to the deformation of the crater, made their ascent to the crater's rim challenging.

Taylor was immediately glad that Sammy and Tyler came along. They were every bit as experienced as she was. In fact, Tyler had a knack for spotting the easiest, most direct route to the summit. He was especially helpful in pointing out difficult footholds and grips along the way, something that Mac was appreciative of. He'd hiked rocky terrain many times. He rarely climbed up vertical faces of mountains.

"Okay," began Taylor breathlessly as Tyler gave Mac a hand to join the women at the top. "We can set up a base camp here."

"I've got a cell signal," announced Sammy.

"Me too," said Mac. He looked down over the edge of the crater onto the snow-covered rocks inside Crater Mountain. There was scant evidence of volcanic material other than steam rising from a few outcroppings. "I'm thinking close to six hundred feet down."

"Maybe more," said Taylor. "About half the distance of what we just climbed up. Not too bad."

Mac's face contorted somewhat. He begged to disagree.

Sammy, too, was concerned about the descent. "What about the terrain, Taylor? It's gonna be unstable, and we got just enough snow last night to cover up the loose stuff." She assisted Taylor with her backpack.

Tyler, who'd been wandering around the crater's edge as the two scientists got prepared, approached the group. "I have an indirect route you can take. Let's call it the path of least resistance. It'll take a little longer, but you're less likely to run into trouble."

Taylor and Mac followed Tyler to a point forty feet from their base camp. He pointed out the route and identified landmarks for Taylor to focus on. He stood with his hands on his hips for a moment before speaking.

"Listen, I can help you guys get down. Sammy, too. We can find our way back up without a problem."

Taylor nodded and then rested her hand on his shoulder. "I know you can, Ty. However, I could never live with myself if something happened to you guys. We get paid for this but not near enough. I probably shouldn't have brought you this close to a potentially eruptive volcano to begin with."

"Okay. At least let me hover over the edge to spot you. I can give you directions for so long as you can hear my voice."

"Deal," said Mac as he and Tyler bumped fists.

Mac turned to Taylor, who was adjusting the fit of her backpack with Sammy's assistance.

"Thank you, Sammy. I think we're ready."

The two of them took a deep breath of the fresh air atop Crater Mountain and began their descent as snowflakes began to settle in their hair.

CHAPTER TWENTY-NINE

**Crater Mountain
Mono County, CA**

The seven-hundred-foot wall created by the deformation of Crater Mountain was just that. A wall. Nearly straight up and down with the few places to catch your breath. It was the snow-covered footing that gave Taylor pause. There was no margin for error. Mistakes would be unforgivable and could result in death.

The snow was beginning to fall in thicker flakes as the two made their way deeper into the crater. Taylor, following Tyler's direction from above, carefully led Mac along an intact rock outcropping that sloped downwards. Their descent had slowed, but their heart rates slowed as well.

Taylor stopped for a minute on a small ledge sturdy enough to hold them both. She contemplated turning around. Risking their lives like this for the benefit of others was noble, but their efforts would be long forgotten. Mac reached her side and took a deep breath.

"Mac, we can go back. This may not be worth it."

He leaned over the ledge slightly and looked toward the bottom. His view was far better than what they had at the top of the crater. "I'm okay, if you're concerned about me making it to the bottom."

"I'm worried about both of us. Why are we doing this daredevil shit?"

"One word. Dedication. It's kind of like medical professionals taking the Hippocratic Oath. We've made a promise to people who'll never know our names to give them a chance to survive a catastrophe. They didn't listen to us during the quake sequence last summer. If we can uncover a new threat, maybe they'll listen to us this time."

A gust of wind swept across the mountain, causing an updraft of air from the bottom of the crater. The telltale signs of sulfur dioxide reached their nostrils. For Mac, it smelled like lighting a wooden match. Taylor always associated the pungent, irritating odor with rotten eggs.

"Masks?" asked Mac.

Taylor slowly turned him around to gain easy access to his backpack. She'd brought along purified air respirator mask kits for them to wear in the event they encountered the noxious gas. She wasn't going to die from something she couldn't see.

Once they were in place, the two of them continued. The first part of the climb had taken just under an hour. The rest of the climb to the bottom was a little easier, as they had rubble from the crater collapse to use for their path. At the upper part of the crater, a misstep would result in a cracked skull. Down here, a different threat faced the couple.

A large boulder blocked their descent. Taylor, with Mac's help, hoisted herself on top. Mac pushed several rocks together to climb up next to her. They both looked down as a burst of steam rushed upward right in front of them. They both felt the searing heat through their clothing. Any snow around the heated vent melted instantly.

"Welcome to the gates of hell," said Taylor as she pointed toward magma gurgling at the bottom of the crater.

"I see!" shouted Mac as the noise of the heated

vent grew louder. He pointed toward a large void in between several rock formations. "Check it out!"

"Wow! That's a sulfur flow. You expect to see magma gurgling, but this is unusual." Sulfur flows, as the name implies, are a form of molten sulfur, which, like molten lava, can be pushed from the magma chamber of a potentially eruptive volcano. They're less dramatic than the sight of lava bombs spewing into the sky, but they are just as potentially deadly, as people don't understand the deadly nature of the gas the flows emit.

Taylor removed her camera from her utility pack wrapped around her waist. She began taking photographs of everything. As she did, Mac explored ways to get deeper into the crater. He looked into the sky. The altostratus clouds, or snow clouds, were gathering over them. The blue-gray clouds were filled with ice crystals and water droplets that produced snow. He shook his head in dismay because the storm had arrived early. He wondered if there would ever be a weather forecaster who got it right.

"I need to get closer," said Taylor.

Mac pointed to their right. "I can get us to that ledge. But that's it, Taylor. The storm is moving in faster than we thought. We've gotta get out of here, remember?"

Mac led the way, sliding slowly off the boulder until he was on solid ground. Taylor did the same. As they made their way downward, the noise made by the now potentially eruptive volcano grew louder. So did the heat. Snow was nonexistent, which made their task easier. At the same time, it was a reminder of how close they were to the beast below.

They reached a flat, solid rock ledge that seemed to hover over the gurgling lava. The sulfur flow was directly across from them.

"This is close enough!" yelled Taylor, a relief to Mac. He was in awe. Studying earthquakes was child's play compared to nosing around volcanoes.

The two worked deliberately to gather the samples Taylor needed. They pulled out their detection devices one at a time, immediately stowing them into their backpacks when the data collection was complete. Both were keenly aware that they might have to hustle out of Crater Mountain if the situation changed. She didn't want their risky adventure to be a waste.

Working near the heat and steam being discharged from below the planet surface, the two were wholly unaware of the amount of snow that had begun to fall. The skies had opened up as the potentially intense blizzard approached.

"We're good!" proclaimed Taylor as she pointed upward without looking.

Mac immediately searched for the least onerous way to get back onto their trail without having to build a stairwell out of rocks to return to the top of the boulder.

"Follow me!" he yelled.

"Are you sure?"

"Yeah! I'm better at getting out of a pickle that I am at getting into it."

Taylor smirked as she thought to herself, *I could disagree. Mac's always getting into a pickle.*

However, he did have a plan. He'd observed their surroundings during the descent. What good is going to the bottom if you can't find your way back up? They were making decent progress, taking a more circuitous route than their trip to the bottom. It was less taxing and safer as the heavy snow began to accumulate within the crater.

Then a slow, noticeable rumble was felt beneath his feet. This was Mac's biggest fear besides the volcano erupting. Even a slight tremor might bury them under a crush of rock and snow.

"No, no, no! Not now!" he shouted, looking up to

the sky. He wasn't sure if he was screaming at the side of the crater or seeking divine intervention. Regardless, once again, he and Taylor had found themselves in trouble.

Taylor screamed, "Mac! Look!" As the roar around them rose to a crescendo, a snowpack at the top of the crater broke loose and came cascading down the rock wall. The roar was deafening and relentless, exacerbating an already dangerous situation as snowball-sized chunks began to pummel them, breaking along the rocks before sending icy powder onto their heads.

"Curl up in a ball!" yelled Mac, who reached for Taylor to join his side. The tremor continued, over twenty seconds at this point. They dropped to their hands and knees. They pushed their bodies against one another as more of the snowpack fell apart, creating a mini avalanche. Their backpacks protected them from the onslaught of snow that was now mixed with rock.

"Dammit!" shouted Taylor as the tremor stopped. The respite from the earth shaking didn't stop the snow pouring over them until it accumulated at the bottom of the crater, only to melt.

Mac was an expert at measuring the magnitude of an earthquake by using a basic method of counting seconds. However, rather than using one Mississippi, two Mississippi as most kids learned when playing, he liked one potato, two potato. It was far more accurate. However, this time, when the battle was man versus mountain, with a gurgling volcano below them, just for the added adrenaline rush, every instant was a lifetime.

Satisfied the tremor had stopped, he helped Taylor to her feet and shook the snow out of his hair. He gently dusted the snow away from her face and made an effort to untangle her long hair.

Remarkably, Taylor took it all in stride. "Well, Mac, that was fun."

"Yup, another résumé builder for sure." The last of the falling snow and rock skidded past them. Mac stepped back from the rock wall and looked upward. Snow immediately pelted his face and got into his eyes. He pointed upward. "Look at the wind."

Taylor saw the windswept snow rushing across the top of Crater Mountain. The blizzard was close, and luckily, the quickening winds kept the snow from entering the crater. They needed to take advantage of their good fortune.

"Mac, let's get moving. If the winds die down, the heavy snow will make the ascent almost impossible."

They'd lost track of the way they'd come down. After the tremor, the landscape below them had changed, so it was difficult to get their bearings. Here, the side of the crater sloped up at a forty-five-degree angle with ledges jutting out every few feet. Despite the howling wind and blowing snow above the crater, they would be protected until the last fifty feet of their climb.

They were nearing exhaustion as their clothing became soaked by the snow that found its way into the crater. Joints ached. Bruises seemed to create bullseyes for another shot from a falling rock. Muscles screamed in agony as they climbed upward. Slowly. Deliberately. Careful not to backslide to the bottom and a certain death.

Taylor knew they were close although visibility had worsened. Between the color of the sky and the blizzard raging around Crater Mountain, she wasn't sure if they were a hundred feet away or just a few.

As they neared the crater's rim, their adrenaline coursed through their bodies. The howling wind was every bit as loud as the steaming gases they encountered escaping the planet. The heavy snow was whirling furiously around the crater's wall as they made the last, nearly vertical climb to the top.

Taylor and Mac took a brief respite to encourage

one another. They even exchanged a kiss. They'd cheated death together. They could do it again. Rejuvenated and with a renewed sense of purpose, they started the vertical climb.

There were fewer outcroppings now. Taylor knew they were getting closer to the surface. She dug her fingers into an icy crack and pulled herself up to get a footing. She saw another handhold above her head. She struggled but pulled herself up. Muscles were straining, hurting from carrying the additional weight of the backpack filled with scientific gear.

She glanced down to confirm Mac was keeping up. She was so proud of him. He had no business entering the volcano with her. It was not his job. Yet he'd told her the night before that everything she did was his job too. He was her ride or die, he'd promised. She'd never experienced this kind of love before. It was comforting. Invigorating. Inspiring.

Jaws set. Eyes focused. Muscles tensed. Survival instincts at their peak. Taylor looked ahead for the next grip. The swirling snow was thicker now. They were near the top. Almost there.

Don't think, Taylor. Just do it.

She stretched again, feeling the wall for another crack. Another firm rock to grasp. She found one. And then another. And another. So close.

Then, without warning, two strong hands grasped her wrist. It was Tyler, hanging over the ledge. He was tied off and secured by Sammy. Like a couple of trapeze artists in the circus, they were there to pull Taylor onto the crater's rim and do the same for Mac as he reached the edge.

As soon as they emerged from the face of the cliff, they both threw off their backpacks and fell into the gathering snow. Exhausted, they allowed the cold ground to ease the burning pain in their back muscles.

Sammy and Tyler immediately brought water for them to get rehydrated. They also had a dozen Hot Hands, air-activated packets, to provide much-needed heat to warm their hands and feet, if necessary.

"That was hell," said Taylor finally in a voice barely loud enough to be heard over the wind-driven snowstorm.

"Literally!" shouted Mac.

The four returned to their base camp on the other side of the crater. Taylor and Mac had gotten turned around and climbed out of the east side of Crater Mountain. During their ascent, as the snowstorm began, Sammy and Tyler continuously patrolled the crater rim to locate the two scientists.

When Sammy spotted them, Tyler came running with ropes and climbing gear he'd brought with them, just in case. They were able to rig up a way for him to hang over the edge and lend a hand, or two.

Just as they were packing up, Sammy's phone rang. It was Finn. She could barely hear him but got the gist of what he was saying. She reported the conversation to the others.

"That was Finn. The blizzard is brutal."

"No shit," said Mac half-jokingly.

"He said an avalanche has closed the road to Bald Mountain. He wants all of us to get up to his place immediately. He's on his way as well."

Mac turned to Taylor. "If he has internet, can you transfer your data to CalVO?"

"Hey, if he's got internet and beer, I can analyze it myself."

"Stamp it," said Mac. "Let's go."

CHAPTER THIRTY

Finn's Cabin
Lookout Mountain
Mono County, CA

Sammy set up the third bedroom for Taylor and Mac while Tyler gave them a quick tour. Finn's cabin had never been designed to be a full-time residence. It had been built as a vacation rental. The spacious interior resembled a lodge with a massive stone fireplace on one end of the A-frame structure, flanked by floor-to-ceiling windows with a view of Long Valley. There were three bedrooms. Besides Finn's master, the other two rooms were equipped with two sets of bunk beds each. The prior owner was able to

advertise the cabin as capable of sleeping ten
—sardines.

As a bachelor's pad, it was perfect. Finn had
plenty of options to relax, from his large, leather easy
chair to a massive sectional sofa. A wraparound deck
afforded views of the valley to the southeast and
Mammoth Mountain to the southwest. A rarely used
hot tub sat on the westernmost part of the deck next
to a propane-fueled grill.

Despite their exhaustion, the scientists were too
hyped up to sleep. They even rejected Tyler's offer
of a beer, as they were afraid it might make them
drowsy. Before they could relax, they needed to
analyze their findings.

Finn relied upon DirecTV for entertainment
programming and Starlink satellite internet. In a loft
overlooking the living area, Finn had created an
office with a library full of reference materials related
to firefighting, paramedic duties, as well as search
and rescue operations. He'd never lost his hunger for
learning despite his temporary retirement before a
change of careers.

Taylor and Mac set up shop in Finn's loft,
spreading out their monitoring equipment for easy
access as they transferred data to their laptop
computers. For the next hour, they compiled the

information until they agreed they were ready to transmit both the raw data and their report to CalVO.

While they worked, dozens of emails and messages poured in from their teams in Santa Rosa and Bridgeport. In the last twelve hours, the earthquake swarms had increased in both numbers and intensity. The single tremor they'd experienced inside Crater Mountain was gentle compared to the seismic activity south and west of Mammoth Mountain.

"Mac, I wish I could erase everything I know about these volcanic systems," began Taylor. Her voice reflected both her fatigue and her concern. "The assumptions we've always made regarding the caldera, Mono-Inyo, and Mammoth directly conflict with what we're looking at here."

"I agree. The data points to Crater Mountain being in impending danger of an eruption. Yet the seismic activity doesn't support it."

"Right. The seismic data supports activity at Mammoth, but there aren't any of the other precursors."

"Well, there was the one fumarole we investigated."

"One being the operative word. Big whoop.

There are hot vents opening and closing around volcanoes like Mammoth all the time. That doesn't mean an eruption is imminent."

"So what's our next step?" asked Mac.

Taylor thought for a moment. "I think we've been looking in the wrong place. I'd like to return to Mammoth in the morning. Let's start at Horseshoe Lake."

Suddenly, the front door flew open, and a gust of cold air coupled with blustery snow entered the living room. Finn emerged in the doorway and struck a pose emulating Yukon Cornelius of *Rudolph the Red-Nosed Reindeer* fame.

"It's not fit for man nor beast out there!" he shouted, followed by a hearty laugh. Under one arm was tucked a twelve-pack of Harp Lager, an Irish beer, and his other arm held two shopping totes full of groceries.

Tyler rushed to close the door behind him before a snowdrift could gather around their host's feet. "Here, let me help." He grabbed the beer, a gesture Finn found hilarious, as it probably never crossed Tyler's mind to take the groceries. *Priorities*, Finn thought to himself. Clearly, he was in good spirits.

"I hope everyone is hungry. I'm going to whip up a pot of my famous firehouse chili."

Taylor and Mac were leaning over the railing, taking it all in. For a brief moment, they'd abandoned their serious discussion and enjoyed Finn's antics.

Mac whispered to Taylor, "Does it surprise you that his firehouse chili is famous?"

"Nah, not really. Everybody's recipe has its own twist. His is probably adding Irish beer."

"I doubt it," said Mac with a chuckle. "He wouldn't waste it in chili."

Taylor laughed, which helped her relieve some stress. "Whatever it is, I'll take it. I'm starving!"

Mac stood upright. "Come to think about it, we haven't eaten all day. Let's transmit all this stuff and let the analysts take a look. A different set of eyes might be helpful."

"Agreed. My brain hurts. My stomach's empty. And I'm parched."

In unison, the two turned to their laptops, fired off messages to their staff, and bounded down the spiral staircase in search of good friends and good cheer.

CHAPTER THIRTY-ONE

Mammoth Mountain

Some say a volcano eruption and the spewing of lava is like the uncorking of a bottle of champagne. Imagine a race car driver standing victorious atop a podium. Or the baseball players inside their locker room, shaking the bottle of bubbly before releasing the cork. After the bottle blows its top, bubbly liquid gushes out of the opening and creates a helluva mess.

The analogy of celebratory champagne to a volcanic eruption is appropriate in most cases, but not all. To be sure, the addition of carbon dioxide gas forces the wine-like alcohol to become carbonated. The gases build to the point they must escape. The uncorking of the bottle gives the built-up gas an outlet. The more the exuberant celebrant shakes the bottle, the higher the pressure, resulting in more force to spray the champagne around a room to greater distances.

Inside Mammoth Mountain, a similar pressure had been building. Hot liquid in the form of magma and poisonous levels of gas filled the voids beneath the Earth's surface where Mammoth stood. These voids, or chambers, were formed over millions of years of seismic activity.

In some parts of Mammoth's complex geology, the historic amount of water, snow, and ice delivered to the Sierra Nevada Mountains during the ARkStorm hastened changes within the volcanic system. As the water made its way through the many thousands of cracks and crevices toward the center of the planet, they collided with the superheated magma. The water evaporated, creating steam that became trapped inside the volcanic system, and an immense pressure began to build underneath the ground.

At Mammoth, the magma was on the move. It was on a mission to find more space, travelling around the boundary between the Earth's crust and the underlying mantle—the thick, rocky layer that makes up most of the planet's interior.

However, in the last several weeks, the magma found deeper reservoirs than had previously been mapped by volcanologists. The unfathomable heat of the magma and gases worked together to create tubes branching out and away from the magma chamber. Mammoth Mountain was transformed into a complex system of tunnels stretching toward the planet's surface that was capable of delivering magma at an enormous rate of speed.

As the magma quickly filled voids, the earth began to expand and contract, causing numerous earthquakes. They varied in intensity and strength, proving the statement often made by geologists that no two earthquakes were alike.

Mammoth had reached the first stage of its eruption.

As the superheated, ever-expanding gases sensed freedom above the planet surface, fissures and cracks in the rocky surface of Mammoth opened up. These fumaroles began to spew steam, carbon dioxide, sulfur, and other poisonous gases.

The initial venting with the accompanying expulsion of ash and steam caused instability throughout Mammoth's volcanic system. The steam led the way, moving through the tunnels, forcing its way into every available crack in the mountain. The stability of the rocky surface was compromised as the ground began to shake from the violence occurring beneath it.

Mammoth had reached the second stage of its eruption.

Invisible to the naked eye, a lava dome within Mammoth was building. Ordinarily, as a volcano becomes more active, it goes through a series of dome buildups and collapses picked up on modern man's technologically advanced equipment.

Mammoth was anything but ordinary. It was in a hurry. It was not interested in being studied. It cared not for the safety or well-being of humankind nearby. It was bloated and needed to release the pressures built up within it. It was almost time.

Mammoth had reached its final stage before eruption.

CHAPTER THIRTY-TWO

Station 1
Mammoth Lakes Fire Department
Mammoth Lakes, CA

Finn had just completed a briefing with his captains and their lieutenants. As predicted, visitors came from all directions to view the fireworks at Panum Crater. As sensationalist news reports predicted additional volcanic activity near Mono Lake, the visitors decided to stay the week nonetheless. Every available hotel room and vacation rental was filled to capacity and then some. College kids overstayed their reservations, resulting in headaches for the police, whose hands were tied to remove them. Court orders were required to evict an overstaying guest in California. The legal process of filing, service, and hearing required at least thirty days.

The mayor had already emailed the department heads in Mammoth Lakes to apprise them of the situation. To his knowledge, and that of the town's leaders who'd lived in Mammoth Lakes their entire lives, they'd never seen the temporary population swell to such numbers.

And that was before the snowstorm had hit last night. Blizzard-like conditions had existed across Mono County during the evening hours only to give way to a windy, but sunny morning. The westerly winds would be carrying more moisture during the afternoon, resulting in another forecast of heavy snows that night.

To their credit, the road crews did a remarkable job in getting the plows working after the snowfall lessened. Their initial focus was on clearing the major highways leading across the county, like U.S. 395. Next, streets leading to Ski Mammoth and into the Village received priority. Most likely, the mayor's email said, they'd have the most frequented streets cleared just before the next deluge of snow hit that afternoon.

The fire department issued warnings via their

social media outlets to clear snow from roofs and propane equipment. In the past, they'd been inundated with residential structure fires and rescue operations as the heavy snow caused roofing systems to fail. With the roads covered with snow measured in feet in most places, their inability to respond was a concern.

Many properties were heated by aboveground propane tanks. They were at risk for leaks as the heavy weight of the snow compromised fittings, joints, and even the tank's base. A structure fire combined with a damaged propane tank nearby could level a family's home and their neighbors'.

To his credit, the mayor had been receptive to input from Finn and his law enforcement counterparts. Although Finn had gained the bulk of his firefighting experience in sunny LA or the nearby, fire-ravaged mountains, he'd studied the effect of heavy snows on structures. He'd conveyed a lot of this to the mayor, who had incorporated the warnings into an evacuation warning disseminated through several means, from social media to posting notices in local businesses.

From what Finn had observed that morning, nobody heeded the warning.

He'd requested all of his firefighters as well as his search and rescue teams to be on call or actually on duty. He treated the situation as if he were coordinating a wildfire in the Santa Monica Mountains overlooking idyllic Malibu Beach. He had plenty of money available in his budget to pay double-time and a great rapport with the unions representing his people, so there wouldn't be any grumbling.

The contingent at the fire station that morning was so large, they had to clear snow out of the entire parking lot to remove the trucks and ambulances from the garage to conduct the morning meeting. Finn covered every aspect of their emergency protocols and evacuation procedures.

During the briefing, a fairly large tremor was felt in Mammoth Lakes. Earthquakes were commonplace in the areas surrounding Mammoth Mountain and the Long Valley Caldera. Locals took it in stride. Visitors froze in place as their eyes grew wide from anxiety. When the short tremors passed, nervous laughter would fill a room, and life went on. Oddly, for the firefighters present for the briefing that morning, the room broke out with laughter as one of the wildfire crew quipped, "That's one way to get the snow off everybody's roof."

The statement would've been truly funny had it not been for the danger the tremors foreshadowed for them all.

CHAPTER THIRTY-THREE

Mammoth Mountain Ski Resort
Mammoth Lakes, CA

For many snowboarders and skiers, the allure of bounding down a fluffy slope covered in fresh, powdery snow fueled an irresistible desire that bordered on obsession. They loved it. They pined for it. They skipped work for it. They even risked their lives on treacherous roads to get to a mountain, any mountain, where the white stuff awaited them.

If a skiing enthusiast was questioned about this insatiable urge to mess up a pristine snowfall, they might answer that it's fun. Well, so was watching cats herding grizzlies in Alaska. Or they might say it was a once-in-a-lifetime opportunity to feel like you owned the snowy mountain and its singularly natural beauty. Many that week might've said the same thing about flocking to Mammoth Lakes to see the eruption of Panum Crater.

Regardless of why the fresh powder seemed to touch the psyche of skiers or tickle awake the third eye of snowboarders, the slopes of Mammoth Mountain were about to have a historic day. Before the chairlifts and gondolas began running, the resort had to cut off lift ticket sales.

Sammy and Tyler sensed a potential deluge of skiers would descend upon Mammoth. They were awake well before dawn anyway because of the time differential between Pennsylvania in the eastern time zone and California, where it was three hours earlier. By the time they made their way down Lookout Mountain in Finn's Jeep, the snowplows had already cleared a single lane of the highway leading into town. When two cars met, they inched past one another in the spirit of cooperation.

When the former Californians arrived at the parking lot at Eagle Lodge, it was quickly filling up. Their thoughts of being the first down a slope had been dashed. However, it didn't throw cold water on their day of incredible skiing.

They were not disappointed. Despite the large crowds pouring into the parking lots, the two managed to jump ahead of many skiers by choosing Eagle Lodge to begin their day. Most of the skiers were coming into Ski Mammoth from the Village or the many lodging options on the north and east sides of the mountain. While overall, the slopes were more challenging on the south side, the Holiday, Bridges, and Lupin runs were well within the couple's capabilities.

Sammy wasted no time after she and Tyler exited the Eagle Express lift to the top of Holiday. Excited, she activated the GoPro camera attached to the front of her jacket and raised her poles triumphantly in the air.

"Are you ready, Ty?"

He pushed himself alongside her.

"Hell yeah! Let's gooo!"

Sammy shoved off first. She shouted, channeling the Grinch, "C'mon, Ty, the sun is bright, and the powder's bitchin'."

And they were off. The two were enjoying the best day of skiing since they'd taken up the sport years ago. Throughout the day, the powdery snow began to pack down as skiers groomed the slopes. There were still rarely used trail runs available that had a virgin-snow feel about them. The snow that had accumulated on the tall trees flanking the trails would blow over the top of them from time to time when the wind made its way across the mountain, adding to the feeling of being all alone with nature.

At one point, the earth shook. Most of the skiers took this in stride, as it was commonplace for Ski Mammoth. Sammy and Tyler paused their downhill run for a moment in a crosscut trail surrounded by tall pines. The stresses of looking for Taylor and Mac inside an active volcano as the earthquake hit near Mono Lake were still fresh in their mind.

After the shaking, the two took a moment to drink some water and catch their breath. The adrenaline that had fueled them since their first run down the pristine slopes had taken its toll. The couple, who remained in excellent condition, rarely found themselves tired except at the end of the frequent half-marathons they ran.

The stop also gave them the opportunity to take in the incredible beauty of the wooded trails Mammoth Mountain had to offer. While they were enjoying the moment, Tyler announced his intentions to defile the snow.

"I need to take a leak."

"What? Now? Let's ski to the lodge."

"No way. It'll take too long to go through all of that. I'll just walk into the trees a little bit. Maybe over there at the base of that ledge."

Sammy scowled. "I don't know, Ty," she began before lying to her husband. "I need to pee also. Let's just go to the lodge." Tyler didn't buy it.

"That was lame, Sammy. Just hold on. I'll only be a minute."

Tyler removed his skis and began trudging through the deep snow toward a rock formation obscured by a thick stand of trees. Maneuvering his way out of his ski clothing wasn't that easy, but he managed to create the proverbial yellow snow that every skier knew not to eat, as the saying goes. As he struggled to get dressed, he looked around the rock outcropping.

"Hey, Sammy! You should see this!"

"I've already seen it. We're married, remember? Besides, I'm not interested in whatever design you drew in the snow with your pee!" she shouted back.

Tyler wasn't amused, although on any other occasion he'd enjoy the back-and-forth wisecracks.

"No, it's something else. There are a bunch of dead animals at the base of this ledge. And there's steam coming out of the rocks!"

CHAPTER THIRTY-FOUR

Horseshoe Lake
Mammoth Lakes, CA

The road leading to Horseshoe Lake had been plowed up to where the Twin Lakes campground entrance was located. Beyond that point, the marina was closed, and the campground had been declared off-limits after the deaths caused by carbon dioxide inhalation earlier in the week. Taylor and Mac secured his truck, loaded their backpacks, and began the two-and-a-half-mile trek through the heavy snow to the lake's basin.

Because of the thick snow that had accumulated overnight, coupled with that which had blown off of

Mammoth Mountain, every step required extraordinary effort. A walk of this distance on a normal summer day might take them forty to fifty minutes. Today, it took nearly two hours.

"I was a little disappointed that our overnight people didn't dive into the data for us," said Mac as he led the way. His larger feet, coupled with his exaggerated shuffling motion, made it easier for Taylor to follow in his tracks.

"Same here," said Taylor as she hustled to keep up. "Your seismic reports were helpful."

Mac continued to trudge along. "Were they? I mean, it was really more of the same. A few tremors around Mono Lake. Small-to-medium-sized quakes on this side of Mammoth appeared with more frequency. Other than that, all quiet at the *big guy*." Mac was referring to the Long Valley Caldera.

"That at least strengthens my position that Mammoth is worthy of closer scrutiny."

Mac pointed as they crested a hill that gave them a complete view of Horseshoe Lake several thousand feet away. "Okay," he began, stretching out the word. "I get that the snow has been clinging to the pine trees. That's different from what I'm seeing. It's a helluva ghostly graveyard."

"Geez," said Taylor. "There's been an enormous

die-off around the lake since we were last here. We need our masks, and also make sure your skin is covered. This doesn't look good, Mac."

As they got ready, Taylor checked her cell phone for messages from CalVO. She had no signal. She sighed and looked around the sky. It was clear. She'd had perfect reception here in the past. She surmised a cell tower had been damaged by ice and wind.

They checked each other's masks and clothing to make sure they were mostly protected from the poisonous gases they presumed to be hovering around the lake. As they got closer to the lake's edge, they discovered the fresh carcasses of several California mule deer, which were known to inhabit the lower altitudes of the Sierra Nevada mountain range.

Mac examined the dead animals. "Taylor, they weren't attacked. They succumbed to the poisonous gases."

"What's odd to me is that we're not in the forest die-off yet. Has the gas hovered and spread this far away from the lake?"

"If they were poisoned at the water's edge, I can't imagine how they were able to walk this far and stay in their herd," Mac observed.

"Help me unload the equipment. I wanna take

measurements here and then again on the other side of the lake."

They stopped for a moment while Taylor gathered the data. She sent it by both text and email to CalVO, hoping that at some point, her cell phone would catch a tower and her messages would be transmitted.

They continued on. She recorded the level of gases at the lake's edge and then again on the other side about two hundred yards into the existing forest die-off. Like before, she tried to send the data to their Bridgeport office, but they still had no cell service.

It was getting late in the day, and the same grayish clouds they'd encountered at Crater Mountain yesterday began to move across the mountains. Snow was beginning to fall, and the winds were picking up. Another massive snowfall, if not a downright blizzard, was about to sweep across the Sierra Nevada.

Finished gathering data, Taylor turned to return to the truck. "I'm ready," she said as she adjusted her outerwear. The combination of soreness from their climb in and out of the crater plus the suddenly dropping temperatures was taking its toll on her body.

Mac stopped her. "Hey! Do you see that?"

Taylor returned to his side. She sensed appre-
hension in his voice. "Show me."

He stood behind her, hugging her waist with his
left arm while using his right to point toward steam
shooting from the side of Mammoth Mountain.

"Do you see it? At the side of a large rock
outcropping."

Taylor nodded. "That's steam. Water has found
its way into the volcanic system."

"Hang on. Let me look through the binoculars."

Mac removed his backpack and rummaged
toward the bottom of the largest compartment to
retrieve the binoculars. He located the hot vent visu-
ally and then zeroed in on the rock formation.

"Holy shit!" he exclaimed, suddenly pulling the
field glasses away from his face. He handed them to
Taylor, who immediately got her bearings before
looking through the lenses. Her excited voice rose an
octave or two. "That's lava! Mac! That's lava!"

Before he could agree, an earthquake struck
Mammoth Mountain. Mac started counting the
potatoes, determined to identify the magnitude of
the quake in seconds. Even as they were knocked off
their feet and thrown into a snowdrift, he counted.

He lost track at twenty seconds as the rumble of
tumbling rock and large pines toppling took his

breath away. As the southwestern flank of Mammoth Mountain collapsed, it sent rock and trees down the mountainside. The roar of the earthquake coupled with the destruction of the side of the mountain was deafening.

Mac crawled to Taylor, who was lying facedown. He shouted to be heard. "Taylor! Are you okay?"

Just as he arrived by her side, her arm moved in an attempt to push herself onto her side. Mac gently helped her to sit upright. She took a deep breath to regain her composure and then shielded her eyes from the tiny rocks mixed with snow that rained down upon them.

"Do you have the binoculars?" she asked.

Mac turned to look behind him and then up the side of the mountain where they'd stood less than a minute ago. The deluge had dragged them downhill more than a hundred feet.

"No. We have to go," he said as he reached under her armpits to help Taylor to her feet.

"Deformation, Mac. The side of Mammoth has collapsed. The earthquake didn't do that. The volcano is going to erupt."

"All the more reason to get the hell out of here!" he shouted in response as the roar coming from the mountain increased in intensity.

She grasped his hand and stared at the deluge that seemingly headed directly for them. She mumbled barely above a whisper, but loud enough for Mac to discern, "We can't outrun it."

Mac thought she was delirious. He examined her scalp, looking for signs of trauma. Relieved there was no evidence of a blow, he tried to remove her backpack so they could run through the snow faster. She wrestled with him to stop.

"I'm fine, Mac. Please trust me." She tilted her head up, and her nostrils flared.

Mac did the same. The slight smell of sulfur caused him to wince. "I smell it."

"It will get much worse. We need to put our respirators back on."

Both of them had worn the devices once they arrived at Horseshoe Lake. However, they had been ripped off their faces as they tumbled down the hillside. There was now a hundred feet of terrain to search while Mammoth Mountain fell apart.

"Taylor, we'll never find them," he said calmly. He looked back toward the lake. He tried to visualize an overhead view of the lake, the road leading to it, and the location of his truck. "What if we cut through the woods along the base of the mountain. We can avoid the gases around the lake and use the trees for cover from all of this crap falling on top of us."

Taylor had regained her composure although her eyes were transfixed on the unfolding disaster. The earthquake had ended. She was open to the possibility that the seismic event being so close to Mammoth was the reason for the sudden deformation. Maybe, she thought, they could escape the deluge.

They couldn't.

CHAPTER THIRTY-FIVE

Ski Mammoth
Mammoth Mountain, CA

It all happened in an instant. Yet to Sammy and Tyler, every moment lasted an eternity. After Tyler told Sammy about the dead animals at the base of the rock outcropping, her curiosity and his insistence drew her in. She had to see for herself, primarily because she recalled Taylor mentioning that poisonous gases could cause mountain mammals to die off unexpectedly. This might be something the two scientists needed to know.

As the couple studied the dead critters, they took a respite from the approaching blizzard. The winds and the sideways-blowing snow had begun attacking Ski Mammoth from the northwest. With their backs against the twenty-foot-tall rock outcropping towering over them, the wind was practically nonexistent. Tyler quipped they could hold a pile of feathers in their palms, and it wouldn't blow away despite the howling wind above and to the sides of where they stood.

They shared a kiss, marveling at the beauty of the mountain even as the storm was moving in. They both agreed this would be their last run of the day. Nature couldn't agree more.

The ground beneath them began to shake. For a moment, they were frozen in time, unable to will their feet to move, uncertain as to whether the tremor was just one of many that beset the region daily. What began as a low rumble roared to life as a deep, guttural roar spoiling the quiet of the mountain. Rocks began to dislodge themselves from the rock outcropping, pelting them on the head as the earthquake continued.

Tyler reacted first, screaming, "Run!" He grabbed Sammy by the hand in an attempt to tow her away from the falling rocks. However, it wasn't the loosened dacite volcanic rock that had been built up by enormous forces over hundreds of thousands of years that threatened them. It was the avalanche that buried them in snow.

Sammy's hesitation caused her feet to be stuck in place. Tyler had turned to her to urge her to move. He glanced upward and saw the massive avalanche of snow pouring over the edge of the rock outcropping. He quickly turned, tackled his wife, and the two of them rolled together toward the base of the rock wall. Then darkness swept over them.

They'd been buried alive in snow.

Tyler groaned as he tried to move. He'd landed hard against the unforgiving quartz-like rock wall. The jagged edges had bruised his back and caused a gash in the top of his scalp. He felt his warm blood oozing from the wound, although that was the least of his concerns.

"Sammy," he yelled. "Sam, where are you?"

Tyler tried to move his arms, but they were pinned down by the snow. Frantically, he tried to flail about to free himself, but his rapid movements dislodged the packed snow from the avalanche. It covered more of his upper body.

"Ty." Sammy's voice was muffled and weak. Far away, it seemed to Tyler. "I can't move."

"Don't! It'll make it worse." Tyler tried to force himself to remain calm. He closed his eyes to concentrate on slowing his breathing. Panic was not their friend.

"I can't see," Sammy said, her voice somewhat stronger.

Tyler did his own self-assessment as he asked his wife about her condition. Other than his back screaming at him from the beating it took, and the warm blood making its way down his face, which felt oddly comforting in the frigid temperatures, he was fine. It was proof of life, for now.

"Okay. Okay. Are you hurt?"

Tyler was shouting his questions as his hopes lifted. The earthquake had ended. The bleeding had stopped, figuratively speaking. Soon, the ski patrol would see their abandoned skis near the avalanche, and help would be on the way. They just needed to stay alive.

"I don't think so," she replied finally.

"Great! Okay, are you near the rock wall?"

"Yes. I can, um—" The ground shuddered briefly, causing Sammy to stop mid-sentence. Both of them held their breath as they prepared themselves mentally for another earthquake. After a few seconds during which another quake didn't materialize, Sammy yelled, "This sucks!"

"Agreed!" Tyler shouted back. He sensed the

trepidation in her voice. He attempted to ease her stress. "I really like Finn and everything, but California does suck. He can come visit us from now on."

His ploy worked. "He could move down the street from Farmer Joe. They'd argue until they're old and gray."

"No doubt," added Tyler, who felt the need to get down to business. "Are you near the wall?"

"Yeah. I fell on my side and then rolled over before the snow fell on me. My left arm is pinned down, but my right can touch the rocks if I stretch."

"Good! You're doin' better than me. I'm like the dad buried in the sand up to his neck by his bratty kids. I tried to squirm, and more snow fell on my head."

"It's awkward, but I can bring my arm down and dig out a little."

"Go slow, Sammy! Breathing is the most important thing until they dig us out."

Tyler didn't want to frighten her, but he was keenly aware of the long odds they faced. Most likely, he assumed this avalanche wasn't the only one at Ski Mammoth. He'd overheard a conversation between two locals earlier that morning while they waited in line. It was part of the ski patrol's daily routine to inspect the mountain after a heavy, overnight snow to determine if any avalanches warranted closing a trail for the day. If the earthquake had triggered this avalanche, there were probably many more.

They had to find a way to avoid suffocation. Without being able to see in the darkness, he got the sense they were in a small, confined space where oxygen could be quickly depleted. To complicate their survival, the dead animals were an indication that noxious gases had seeped out of the rock outcropping. If high levels of carbon dioxide became present without ventilation, it would be game over for them.

So, as much as he wanted to reunite with his wife to find a way out from under the massive amount of snow heaped upon them, neither one of them needed to bring more snow into the open space they needed to breathe.

"I have my other arm free!" she shouted.

"Yes!" Tyler's exuberance caused powdery snow to fall onto his face. He took another deep breath and calmed down.

"My feet and calves are getting numb," said Sammy.

Tyler had an idea. "Hey! Can you get to your phone?"

"I'll try. It's in the zipper pocket on my leg."

Tyler's extremities were also becoming numb. He tried to slowly wiggle his fingers and toes to keep the blood circulating. At first, he was overly cautious, as he had no means to protect his face if the snow fell on top of it. He had to be patient, or he'd die before Sammy could free herself.

"Got it!" she shouted. "Dammit! I don't have a signal."

"Try the flashlight and tell me what you see," said Tyler.

Seconds later, Sammy let out a bloodcurdling scream.

CHAPTER THIRTY-SIX

Ski Mammoth
Mammoth Lakes, CA

"Sammy! Are you okay? Please talk to me!" Tyler reacted to her screaming and forced his shoulders to move back and forth. He desperately wanted to free one arm so he could dig his way out of the snow.

"No. I mean yes! I'm fine. I turned on the flashlight, and this dead rabbit was staring at me. His paws are huge."

Tyler closed his eyes. His muscle memory wanted to run his fingers through his hair or bury his face in his palm in dismay as he thought about her reaction to finding the snowshoe hare. He'd already seen the dead creature earlier, one of the reasons he'd called her to the rock wall to begin with.

He didn't admonish her for scaring the bejesus out of him. That wouldn't do any good. Besides, she was able to maneuver now, and he knew exactly where she was.

"You're only ten feet away from me," he said.

"I got knocked sideways when the earthquake hit, and then rolled over to avoid the snow." She paused for a moment and then added, "Ty, if I can get free, there's room to crawl around here. The rocks taper outward."

"I see your flashlight! Barely, but I can see you!" Tyler's face beamed in the darkness. He was now certain they'd survive this.

"Stupid animals!" a squeamish Sammy screamed.

Tyler didn't react, as he needed her to remain calm. He waited patiently for her to report her progress. He didn't want to put undue pressure on her, as she might overreact or panic.

"I'm free! I was able to slide out, and now I'm at the base of the wall next to these stupid, dead animals."

Tyler needed to confirm her location while being keenly aware of her battery life. Fortunately, that day, they hadn't taken a lot of pictures or videos, focusing on their day of skiing rather than creating Instagram memories. He chuckled to himself. It would be a new way of doing things in the future, assuming they had one.

"Shine your flashlight away from my voice!"

"Like this?" she asked. His inability to see the light answered his question.

"Okay, can you roll onto your stomach and shine the light in the other direction?"

"Yep!" Seconds later, a bright light found its way along the base of the rock outcropping. She'd have some work to do, but she could dig toward him.

"Okay, Sammy. We can do this. Turn off your flashlight and use the display for illumination. It's so dark down here you can probably turn down the brightness to save battery life."

"Sounds good!" she shouted back. "Done."

"Now see if you can shimmy along the edge of the wall. You'll pack down the loose snow as you move forward. The hard part will be using your arms to create a chute without causing the avalanche to fall on top of you."

"Makes sense. Hold tight!"

Tyler wanted to laugh and respond *no problem,*

but he didn't want to distract her with unnecessary conversation.

Several minutes later, he hadn't heard from her, so he wanted to offer her words of encouragement. *You've got this, babe,* had been the subject of jokes and arguments over the years. Normally, she'd snap back at him. Oftentimes, when they ran half-marathons, he'd try to encourage her to make it to the end. He'd learned when Sammy was exhausted, and her legs were turning to rubber, she didn't need encouragement. She needed focus. Now was one of those times.

Finally, she illuminated the flashlight to check her progress. Tyler didn't complain when it blinded him temporarily.

"Hell yes!" he shouted.

"I see you!"

Sammy continued sweeping the snow behind her with her right arm as she inched closer. Little by little, she dug out the loosely packed snow and moved it to her side, shimmying her body as she eased forward to create a tube adjacent to the rocks. Minutes later, her hand reached out to touch her husband's cheek. His tears of happiness had begun to freeze.

"We're gonna make it, Sammy. I'm so proud of you."

"I've got this, babe," she replied confidently, the flashlight illuminating her grin. Tyler laughed and then began to cough. The weight of the snow on his chest was taking its toll. His breathing had become more difficult, partly because of the confined space but also because of the restricted air flow to his lungs.

"Um, I'm ready to get out of this coffin. How about you?" he asked. The cold was beginning to seep into his bones.

"I prefer to think of it as an igloo. Coffins are so morbid."

"Good point," said Tyler with a chuckle that hurt. He was growing concerned. "My right arm seems to have a little more room than the left. If you can get the right free, then I can clear my chest while you work on the left. It's kinda hard for me to take a breath."

Sammy took this news better than he expected. She understood that freeing Tyler from the snow's grip was only part of the challenge. They still needed to find a way out. Like Tyler, she didn't expect any help from outside.

For ten minutes or more, they worked together to

create an opening large enough for Tyler to wiggle his way out. Just as he freed himself, the two shared a kiss, and the void he left behind immediately collapsed. Their faces were covered with powdery snow. Sammy gently rubbed it off his face and wiped the crusty blood off his forehead. She powered on the flashlight again and took a look at his scalp. The wound was superficial and had already begun to scab over.

Within their snow cave, they huddled together to warm their bodies. They whispered to one another, promising to do all the things they had on their bucket list. Agreeing that life was too short. Then they formulated a plan.

Sammy had created a tube bordered by the rock outcropping on one side and the snow on the other. It was fifteen to twenty feet long, but it was a start. Neither could recall with certainty whether they were closer to one end of the outcropping or the other, so they decided to follow the path Sammy had cleared.

Turning their bodies around in the confined space was no simple task. They moved deliberately. Careful not to disrupt the progress she'd made. Fully aware of what might happen if they caused the snow tube to collapse on top of them.

Tyler led the way, digging through the snow well

beyond where Sammy had started. Not that it mattered, but Sammy kept an eye on the clock. Their ability to breathe was becoming labored. Soon, it would be getting dark. She prayed they'd make it out alive and thanked God for giving them the chance to live on.

Then the enormous pressure of the gases and magma inside Mammoth Mountain blasted out a huge section of its south face. The force of the blast dwarfed the earthquake they'd experienced earlier.

Sammy and Tyler were buried again.

CHAPTER THIRTY-SEVEN

Mammoth Mountain Ski Resort
Mammoth Lakes, CA

Deep in the heart of Mammoth Mountain, miles beneath the Earth's surface, tectonic forces were quietly building up pressure along the fault lines. The Earth's crust had been silently shifting, preparing to unleash its pent-up fury upon the world above. Unbeknownst to the residents and visitors in the vicinity, a cataclysmic event was brewing.

The pristine, snowy mountain was shaken by a deafening rumble. The ground began to tremble violently, causing gondolas full of skiers to sway back and forth until the structural supports holding them aloft broke free of their bases. People were thrown upward, immediately losing their balance before their bodies tumbled and slid down the ski slopes, crashing into trees, rocks, or one another.

From the ski lodges at the base of the mountain to the Village at Mammoth Lakes, and for miles in all directions, the magnitude 7.2 earthquake with its epicenter beneath the volcanic system wreaked havoc. Highways buckled. Power lines were downed. Buildings crumbled. Chaos ensued.

And that was just the beginning.

The massive earthquake also had a profound effect on the mountain's stability. The immense pressure on the fault line triggered a chain reaction that traveled upward, destabilizing the southwest side of Mammoth Mountain. Enormous sections of the mountain began to crumble and collapse, sending a cloud of snow and debris into the air. The winds accompanying the blizzard whipped the cloud into a frenzy before sending it across the shaken landscape near Horseshoe Lake and toward the Village at Mammoth Lakes.

Amidst the mayhem, the unmistakable smell of sulfur permeated the surroundings, signaling the awakening of the volcano's inner fury. Deep within Mammoth, magma surged and bubbled, seeking any available path to release the pressure that had built up over hundreds of thousands of years. Fissures appeared on the mountain's slopes, and from them, fumaroles belched thick, sulfurous gases, poisoning any living being that hadn't already been killed by the quake.

Emergency sirens blared throughout the region, alerting residents of the impending danger, although nothing could be done to stop what came next. As if the mountain could no longer contain its fury, a loud explosion shook the area.

From the southwestern side of Mammoth Mountain, a colossal plume of ash and smoke surged into the sky. The volcano had awakened, and its fiery temperament was on full display. Then part of the northern side of Mammoth exploded as if it had been hit by a nuclear missile. In response, the mountain fought back, shooting lava bombs in all directions. The glowing rocks covered in fiery magma were catapulted high into the air before raining down on the surrounding terrain. It was a terrifying spectacle that painted the horizon a foreboding shade of red against the backdrop of a raging blizzard.

As the eruption progressed, lava streams flowed down the mountain's slopes, carving new paths and devouring anything in their way. The southwest side, weakened by the earthquake's force, succumbed to the onslaught of lava, collapsing farther into the depths of the mountain.

What was once a beautiful snow-covered mountain was now a fiery hell for everyone near it.

CHAPTER THIRTY-EIGHT

Station 1
Mammoth Lakes Fire Department
Mammoth Lakes, CA

Having a sixth sense was an extraordinary experience that went beyond the five traditional senses of sight, hearing, taste, smell, and touch. Some called it a gut feeling. For others, it was referred to as intuition, empathy, or simply an unexplained awareness. Regardless, a sixth sense enabled people, and animals, to perceive things beyond what was immediately visible or evident to others.

Finn's experiences as a firefighter certainly blessed him with a heightened sense of awareness.

His superiors and peers praised his ability to sense the movement of a wildfire, which allowed them to head it off before it destroyed people's lives. Living through the ARkStorm had also expanded the knowledge base of his brain, enhancing his sixth sense, if you will.

The blizzard had descended upon Mammoth Lakes with fury, coating everything in a thick blanket of snow. The town was a winter wonderland, much to the delight of its visitors. However, this beauty was in imminent danger from what lurked beneath the surface. Nothing could prepare them for what was about to unfold.

Finn sat in his office, reviewing the latest weather reports, with Rebel dutifully by his side. His fire and rescue response teams were stretched thin as they responded to calls throughout the area of collapsed roofs, avalanches, and structure fires caused by negligence. A slight tremor had rumbled beneath the Village an hour ago, causing little concern. He'd been convinced that any potential volcanic activity would occur many miles away at Crater Mountain.

If at all. Then everything changed.

The moment the M7.2 earthquake struck at Mammoth Mountain, the shock waves reached the Village in barely a second. Rebel was the first to notice the sudden change beneath the earth. Finn, although a little slower to comprehend what had just happened, had lived in the Sierra Nevada long enough to differentiate between the earthquakes deemed normal for the region and the extraordinary catastrophic event that was unfolding. Perhaps it was the fact California had been beset by catastrophes in recent years only a novelist or moviemaker could conjure up. Or, in the moment, he was experiencing a deeply personal, transformative experience that he'd waited his entire life to confront.

Without hesitation, Finn jumped up from his desk and ran into the center of the fire hall. He screamed instructions, the alarm in his voice every bit as disconcerting to his team as if the electronic notification of a fire had shouted it through the speakers.

"Take cover! Get away from the outer walls. Avoid the windows!"

Rebel ran into the corridors of the fire hall to reach the sleeping quarters, barking incessantly to wake up anyone slumbering while off duty.

Seconds later, the stress placed on the building caused the garage doors enclosing the engine bays to buckle and explode inward. Windows throughout the fire station cracked under the immense pressure and twisting caused by the earthquake. Shards of glass pelted the firefighters, most of whom were relaxing in the open break area, eating a late lunch while discussing the heavy snowfall caused by the blizzard.

The concept of drop, cover and hold on had been engrained in the first responders since the day they were accepted into the fire academy at Mammoth Lakes. However, nothing prepared them for what happened next.

With the force of a seven-megaton nuclear bomb, the southwestern flank of Mammoth Mountain blew apart. The blast's shock wave carried across the mountain directly toward the Village. By the time it roared across the landscape, it picked up debris, from building materials to small automobiles. A red Kia crashed into what used to be Finn's corner office with such force that he would've been immediately killed had he not raced to warn the others.

Now sirens and electronic messages filled the air. Screams of panic could be heard outside on Main Street, where unlucky skiers unable to get lift tickets had been strolling in and out of the shops on the frontage road. Some were, however, lucky enough to not be at Ski Mammoth that day.

"Captain! Lieutenants!" Finn shouted during the chaos. "Account for every firefighter!"

Soon, people's names were being called out, as those who weren't present in the break room at the time were missing. As they searched, Rebel returned to Finn's side. He instructed Rebel to help. He didn't need to explain. His Labrador knew what to do.

Finn crawled through the broken glass, making every effort to avoid getting cut. He didn't realize a shard of the plate-glass window had sliced open his forehead until warm blood began to drip from his eyebrows. He hurriedly wiped it away and continued toward the communications center.

What he found there caused his stomach to retch. The young lady who'd been hired barely four weeks ago was slumped over the communications equipment. The condition of her head told the story. There was no hope to save her.

Finn shook it off and crawled toward the communications equipment. He needed to reach out to his firefighters and rescue teams. He pulled himself up to the counter. After wiping the blood out of his eyes, he located the microphone.

That was when the power grid collapsed.

CHAPTER THIRTY-NINE

Horseshoe Lake
South of Mammoth Mountain, CA

When Taylor and Mac set out to gather data about the potential eruption of the volcano at Mammoth Mountain, little did they know their need to predict the next eruption was about to transform into a perilous dance with nature's fury.

The forest surrounding them, once serene and peaceful, now took on an ominous demeanor as the blizzard began to intensify. The wind howled like an enraged demon, whipping the snow into a frenzy and reducing visibility to a mere few feet. Undeterred by the ferocity of Mammoth Mountain's volcanic eruption and the blinding blizzard, the couple shed their backpacks and began trudging through the snow.

"Follow in my footsteps the best you can!" Mac shouted over the roar of the deluge. They tried to remain focused despite their adrenaline levels threatening to beat their hearts out of their chests.

Several times, the explosion of eruptive material from Mammoth's flanks frightened them into a mistake, causing them to lose their footing. It was human nature to turn and see if the attacker chasing them was closing the gap. With every rumble coming from the collapsing mountain, they'd turn to see the spectacle, only to crash into a tree or trip over a rock hidden under the deep snow.

"Mac!" Taylor struggled to get the words out. "I. Can't. Breathe."

Taylor fell to her knees, her chest heaving. In their panicked state, they'd forgotten the effect of the noxious gases that hovered in the low-lying areas at the base of the mountain. Mac had failed to lead them far enough away from the high carbon dioxide levels they'd recorded around Horseshoe Lake. Now Taylor's chest was heaving as she fought for every breath.

"Oh, God, honey. I'm so sorry. Let me help."

Mac dropped to his knees and comforted her. She was bent over, gasping. Mac forced himself not to yell over the howling winds and the eruption of the volcano, no easy task.

Rubbing her shoulders and neck, he spoke to her in a calm tone of voice. "Relax, Taylor. We're gonna be fine. Breathe through your nose and out through your mouth. Pretend you're trying to blow out a candle, okay."

She took a deep breath as Mac counted aloud, "One. Two. Blow out the candle."

Taylor puckered her lips and let out a long exhale that generated a whistle similar to the sound the wind-blown snow was making as it washed over them.

"Good. Try it again. One. Two. Blow out the candle."

Taylor followed his instructions, and then oddly, a smile came across her face as she pointed her thumb back over her shoulder. Mac was overwhelmed with relief when she began to laugh.

"I visualized blowing out the volcano," she said with a chuckle.

Mac laughed as well as his anxiety was relieved. To add to the lighthearted moment, he pretended to blow out a hundred candles on a three-foot-wide sheet cake.

Taylor stood with Mac's assistance. She shook her head as she took one final exaggerated inhale and exhale. "Well, we've proven a blowhard blizzard is no match for a raging volcano."

Mac smiled and kissed her. "Yeah, there's that. You wanna collaborate on a research paper for the *Journal of Volcanology?*"

Before she could answer, a loud whistling sound could be heard in the distance that increased in pitch and became louder.

"Do you hear that, Mac?"

"Is the storm strengthening?" He looked through the pine trees toward the sky. There visibility was fifty feet, at best.

Without warning, a fiery lava bomb crashed into the center of shallow Horseshoe Lake. The speed of the molten rock increased with the aid of gravity until it reached terminal velocity. As it returned to earth, the whistling became a demonic screech before impact. It struck the water with so much force it created an open space, allowing it to embed in the wet lake bottom, throwing mud and basalt high into the air. The highly concentrated carbon dioxide spewed upwards and joined the snowy winds. It was carried to the south away from Mammoth.

"Shit!" exclaimed Mac. "Come on."

He grabbed Taylor's hand and began dragging her away from the lake. They crawled up the slope at times to get to a high enough elevation to avoid the poisonous gases. With every step to a higher elevation, albeit slight, the snow was piled higher, making their footing more uncertain.

The biting cold gnawed at their exposed skin, but they pushed higher. Mac paused and held up his hand. "Listen."

It was the whistling sound again. They both looked toward the sky but could see nothing. It grew louder. Closer. Screeching now.

BOOM!

With the force of dynamite being detonated nearby, another lava bomb struck the planet, causing the ground to shake. Taylor and Mac were knocked off their feet and were immediately covered in heavy snow falling from the tops of the pine trees.

The ground began to tremble again as another flank of Mammoth exploded outward. Trees swayed to the side as a gust of hot wind momentarily chased the blizzard away. In that instant, the snowy white sky appeared to have an orangish glow.

Their visibility improved for a brief moment, long enough to see what was flying toward them. Lava bombs were sailing out of the collapsed flank of Mammoth; fiery tails of orange and red trailed behind the projectiles. As hellfire began to rain upon them, the blizzard blew hot ash and gases over their heads.

"Run!" shouted Mac, pointing up the mountain in the direction of the ski slopes.

Taylor raced past him, looking for rocks or fallen trees to step on, hoping to propel herself farther up the mountain and away from the poison moving toward them from the lake.

Seconds later, another lava bomb struck nearby, knocking them face-first into the snow. The impact shook the ground and threw rock and frozen dirt into the air. Taylor and Mac huddled together at the back side of the boulder as the tops of the pine trees near the last lava bomb caught fire. The wet needles sizzled under the intense heat of molten lava that hung up in the pines.

While the blizzard had been a formidable adversary for the scientists as they gathered data, it seemed tame in comparison to the volcano's wrath.

"We need to keep moving!" Mac shouted, urging Taylor to get onto her feet.

Together, arm in arm, they bolted up the mountain, slipping to the ground and struggling to remain upright. They'd make a dozen feet of progress only to be knocked backwards by the shaking of the earth or when they ducked for cover from the continuous bombardment of the molten lava rocks flying around them.

They navigated their way through the labyrinth of rock outcroppings and snowdrifts, desperately seeking a way out of the forest. Mac steered them toward the right, ostensibly toward their truck. He still couldn't see more than fifty feet in front of them. He only had the terrain and the trajectory of the lava bombs to go by.

Their legs were exhausted. Their chests were heaving as they gasped for air. Their minds fought for the will to survive. It was their bond and unwavering trust that drove them forward until they reached a clearing.

It was a road.

CHAPTER FORTY

South of Mammoth Mountain, CA

Taylor's and Mac's hearts pounded in unison as they sprinted onto the snow-covered road, their breaths visible in the frigid air. In the open without the protective cover of the thicket of pine trees, the full intensity of the blizzard was felt. Swirling snowflakes, racing across the twenty-foot-wide opening in the forest, continued to obscure their vision. The high-pitched whistling of another lava bomb reminded them they had to keep moving. But which way?

Mac presumed they needed to bear right. However, the road took a steep climb upward to the crest of a hill. The road they'd taken into Horseshoe

Lake was mostly flat except for a gentle rise just before it entered the clearing where the lake was situated. Now, to the left, the road meandered into the woods again, taking a level path until it disappeared in the blizzard.

He spun around and looked skyward. Darkness was setting in, but the sky continued to appear white due to the blizzard. Even the incoming lava bombs didn't provide a definitive clue as to which way they should turn. Their trajectory seemed to be straight up and straight down until impact.

"Taylor, this doesn't make sense. It seems that if we turn right, we'll head back toward the lake. But left doesn't make sense. I feel like that would be back towards the mountain."

Taylor wandered into the clearing and slowly turned, allowing her face to be exposed to the blizzard conditions. She closed her eyes, ignoring the ground, which shuddered with each lava bomb finding its way back to earth. Suddenly, she stopped and pointed.

"That's the wrong way, Mac. I can smell the burnt ash and feel the difference in the heat. Even the winds are swirling in the opening. I'm sure of where the danger is."

"Right we go!" said Mac with confidence and

trust in Taylor's judgment. He shuffled his feet until he reached her side and took her hand. Together, they turned to walk up the steep slope. With each step, the ground beneath their feet seemed to tremble out of fear. The continuous volcanic eruption caused shock waves to be sent throughout the region although it was especially pronounced close to Mammoth.

Taylor quickly became fatigued, so Mac took the lead. His legs, muscular and strong from years of swimming in Lake California, acted like snowplows to clear the heavy snow out of her way. Taylor followed close behind, using his footprints and the trenches created by his legs to keep up before the accumulating snow filled them up.

"Keep going, Taylor! We can't slow down now," Mac shouted in an attempt to encourage Taylor.

The volume of the wind-blown snow had increased, making his voice barely audible over the fury of the storm. He led the way to the top of the hill, pushing through the thick snow. Taylor remained close behind. Their footprints were quickly filled by the accumulating snow that was now blowing into drifts.

The long road continued with no end in sight, at least as far as their visibility allowed. Mac thought of his old truck. The transportation capable of taking them to safety. It was like an oasis in the midst of chaos, offering the hope of survival. Yet he couldn't ignore the peril of the lava bombs raining down around them.

The ground shook again, and they saw fiery projectiles soar into the sky, seemingly carried by the blizzard winds in unpredictable directions. It was an illusion. Seconds later, one flew over their heads with a whooshing sound.

"Watch out!" Taylor yelled, grabbing Mac's arm and pulling him away from the path of the descending lava bomb. The intense heat from the projectile seared their faces as it landed with a thud in the middle of the road just out of their field of vision.

They both jumped to the side, landing face-first in the snow. The icy-cold moisture helped soothe the burning sensation felt on their exposed skin.

"Are you okay?" asked Mac.

Taylor fought back her emotions. She was mentally and physically exhausted. "No, I'm not okay. This freakin' sucks."

She shrieked as another lava bomb landed behind them at the base of the hill they'd just climbed. The snow and gravel from the road were lifted into the air and caught in the brisk winds of the blizzard, eventually pelting them.

Mac took her face in his hands and gently kissed her lips chapped from the cold wind and now the searing heat of the lava bomb. They locked eyes.

"I love you, Taylor. We will get through this. I promise."

She smiled. "You're always full of big promises, Atwood."

"Have I ever let you down?"

Taylor furrowed her brow. For a moment, she was able to put the danger out of her mind. "You promised me a mountaintop wedding."

Mac laughed and helped her to her feet. "Hey, you picked the top of a volcano, remember?"

Her face contorted, and then she snarled at him. "I guess the wedding's off, huh?"

"No, not off. Postponed and relocated. We'll find the perfect spot. Trust me."

She hugged him. "I love you back, Mac Atwood. And yes, I do trust you. Lead the way."

Taylor's vision blurred with every gust of wind, and she felt the cold seeping through her clothes. Her determination, however, was unwavering, driven by the need to survive and escape this catastrophe with Mac.

They pressed on, opting to step into the forest ten to fifteen feet to gain some protective cover from the blizzard's winds. With a renewed sense of purpose, they pushed their bodies to the limit as they moved through the pines. As hoped, the trees provided some protection from the flying debris, but the blizzard raged on, making it challenging to trudge through the dense woods.

They reached another clearing. A fork in the road. A turning point where they had to make another decision. This time, Mac's sense of direction came through again. They exited the forest and made their way into the center of the intersection. They felt vulnerable without the trees hugging them to protect them from the blowing snow and ash.

The snow-covered ground beneath them was no longer pristine white but darkened with volcanic ash. Taylor tried not to think about what could happen if they were caught in a pyroclastic flow, focusing instead on the footfalls of Mac ahead of her.

And the fury of the volcano behind her.

CHAPTER FORTY-ONE

The Village at Mammoth Lakes, CA

In the heart of Mammoth Lakes, the Village provided visitors and locals the opportunity to shop and go to restaurants in an open-air, pedestrian mall setting. Nestled between towering mountains, a storm of chaos had taken hold. Thick, heavy snowflakes fell from the late-afternoon sky, wrapping the small town in a freezing embrace. The wind howled and whistled through the narrow alleys, tossing debris and causing visitors to huddle inside stores and bars. However, amidst this tempest stood a lone figure, a seven-year-old girl named Lily, who was inexplicably drawn to the chaos outside.

Her parents had wandered into McCoy Sports, a

local sporting goods retailer who carried cold-weather clothes befitting the Mammoth Lakes climate. Lily had grown bored with her parents' shopping expedition. She would've preferred staying at their rented cabin to play in the snow and make s'mores by the fire. As her parents avoided the blizzard and tried on clothes, Lily moseyed outside to take in the heavy snowfall.

Lily's curiosity was insatiable, and she had a reputation for her vivid imagination. With her wide, curious eyes and a mop of unruly curls peeking out from beneath her woolen hat, she was the embodiment of innocence in the midst of approaching turmoil.

She walked along the snow-laden sidewalks of the Village, noticing people scurrying about, their faces etched with worry and urgency as the blizzard conditions worsened. But Lily was different. She felt a strange allure to the snow, drawing her towards the center of the Village, where she tried to get a better view of the majestic mountains in the distance.

When the earthquake hit, she was at the base of the gondola station, looking toward Mammoth Mountain. She immediately shrieked, as she'd never experienced an earthquake before at the family's home in Florida. In fact, this was her first time to see snow.

She fell down as the ground relentlessly shook. Twice, she tried to regain her footing only to be knocked over again. Lily didn't know what to do. People rushed out of buildings and ran toward the center of the Village near a stone firepit. Pine trees swayed back and forth, windows broke, and snow flew off the roofs of the buildings in huge chunks.

"Mommy! Daddy!" she shouted although she couldn't be heard over the screams of the panicked visitors. Lily spun around, trying to locate the store they were in. She never imagined being lost in such a small place.

Then, inexplicably, the shaking stopped. The earthquake had ended. Tourists laughed nervously and then joined one another in spontaneous applause not that much different than nervous airline passengers might do following a turbulent landing.

Lily walked away from the group of people who were discussing the earthquake. She needed to find her parents. The blizzard conditions distracted and confused her. She tried to locate the mountain above the ski lift. The storm obscured the sky, making it difficult to see.

She turned to her right. *Yes,* she thought to herself. *That's where my parents are.* She'd come from the clothing store over there. However, as she walked toward McCoy's, the ground shook again, followed by an enormous explosion that filled the air. Nearly everyone fell to the ground and covered their heads.

Not Lily. She turned toward Mammoth Mountain. The blowing snow hurt her eyeballs as it smacked into her fifty-pound body. She covered the front of her face with her arm so she could see what had caused the explosion.

She could make out the faint glow of lava and ash spewing from the side of the Mammoth volcano. It was as if the mountain itself had come to life, casting an eerie orange light that cut through the blizzard's veil.

Her tiny feet carried her closer to the spectacle, and as she approached, the deafening roar of the erupting volcano filled her ears. It was a sound that demanded respect and humility, yet Lily found herself strangely enchanted by the fury unfolding before her. The vivid colors dancing across the horizon caused by the numerous lava bombs held her attention. She stood there, mesmerized, as if she were gazing upon a magical painting.

The blizzard seemingly hushed the relentless assault of lava bombs descending upon parts of Mammoth Lakes, allowing Lily to feel the raw power of the volcano. She reached out her hand, as if trying to touch the fiery orbs as they flew out in the distance. Her fingers trembled with a mix of trepidation and fascination. In her young mind, she imagined that the volcano was speaking to her, telling a tale of ancient times and untold mysteries. It was better than Harry Potter. This was real.

Lost in her fantasy, Lily felt a sudden gust of wind that nearly knocked her off her feet. Startled, she stumbled backward, snapping her out of her trance. Reality crashed back upon her, and she remembered she was standing alone, far away from the safety of her loving parents' arms.

Her heart began to race as her head turned on a swivel, but the blizzard's ferocity had increased. The snowflakes whipped around her like icy needles. Panic clawed at her, and she fought to keep her bearings. Her little footprints were already beginning to disappear under the blanket of snow, and Lily knew she was in trouble when the lava bombs began landing closer to town.

Struggling against the biting cold and the relentless storm, Lily pushed forward toward the clothing store. Tears stung her cheeks, and she was on the verge of panic when suddenly a strong hand grabbed hold of her, pulling her close. It was her father, worry etched deeply on his face.

"Lily! Oh, God, we found you!" he exclaimed, relief evident in his voice. He scooped her up into his arms, wrapping her in his warm coat.

Her mother hugged her as well; her sobbing turned from despair to joy as the family was reunited. Her father spun around, unsure of where to hide from the volcano's wrath. He led them back to the store, hoping the structure would give them some cover.

Lily clung to her father, shivering and still in awe of the volcanic display she'd witnessed. As he carried her back to safety, she couldn't help but steal one last glance at the erupting mountain, its fiery dance still visible through the blur of the blizzard. In that moment, she realized some wonders were best appreciated from a distance, as she learned nature was both beautiful and potentially deadly.

CHAPTER FORTY-TWO

Southeast of Mammoth Mountain, CA

"I know where we are now!" exclaimed Mac. He directed Taylor's attention to the sign that marked the old lodge nearby that had closed due to condemnation proceedings. After the heavy snows associated with the ARkStorm, the roof had caved in. The owners went out of business waiting for the insurance money to fix the property. Once they were paid, they simply abandoned the building.

"You're right. I'm over this crap."

She took a couple of steps and slipped, immediately falling to her knees in the ash-covered snow. It was a reminder that she needed to cover her face to avoid breathing the volcanic ash, which could damage her respiratory system. Mac pulled his undershirt over his nose and mouth. He located the partially filled footsteps from when they'd entered the area earlier that day. The ash mixed with snow was soft and somewhat powdery. It was the wind that aggravated their eyes and skin the most.

The unrelenting blizzard helped obscure the threat of the lava bombs. The inability to track their trajectory added the element of the unknown to Taylor and Mac's escape. Neither the road nor the forest was safe from the blazing balls of partially molten rock. The pyroclastic projectiles of rock varied in size as they fell apart during flight. The blizzard conditions served to expedite the cooling process, which accounted for the lack of forest fires. The farther the couple traveled from Mammoth's eruption, the smaller and more rocklike the lava bombs became. Nonetheless, they were still deadly.

Darkness had set in, but the blizzard didn't let up. Taylor sensed the volcano's explosivity had waned, perhaps because it had begun to ooze rivers of lava. She wished the strong winds would stop so she could get a glimpse of the orange and red molten lava finding its way down the mountain.

They continued toward Mac's truck, periodically seeking shelter from a lava bomb hurled in their direction. As they progressed, the size and number of the molten rocks diminished. However, the race against the erupting volcano and the merciless blizzard was far from over. Taylor was not fully aware of the nature of the eruption. Based on what they'd experienced, she presumed the flank eruption was limited to the south and southwest sides of Mammoth. Thus far, the summit had not collapsed or blown outward. If it had, there would be no doubt in her mind as to the devastation the eruption would bring.

"Almost there!" said Mac; the excitement in his voice encouraged Taylor to focus and not allow her mind to wander.

There would be plenty of time to determine the next course of action once they were safe. Now was not the time to tell Mac what her concerns were. She now had more questions than when they started their day. Was this eruption at Mammoth the culmination of everything that had happened in Mono County recently? Or was it just the beginning of something far worse?

They plowed their way through snow, following the winding road leading to their truck. Their pace was quickened as familiar landmarks came into view. The acrid smell of smoke caused by a fire reached their nostrils. The blizzard coupled with darkness obscured their view of the once serene wonderland turned into a treacherous battleground.

Mac grasped Taylor by the hand. "This way. I know where the truck is. We can save some time."

They cut through a small stand of pines, into the backyard of a one-story house, and onto their driveway. The small neighborhood looked deserted. Tire tracks were evident on the subdivision's street, as residents had fled at the first sign of trouble. There were no signs of life, and oddly, Mac thought, there were no lights left on.

He picked up the pace, dragging Taylor along. He used the packed snow caused by the vehicles to give them the ability to move faster than at any point during their escape from the volcano's wrath.

Without warning, a lava bomb whistled through the air and landed on the roof of a two-story home to their left. Startled, Taylor and Mac jumped into a snowdrift created by a cleanly plowed driveway. They lay there for a moment as the ground level of the house became engulfed in flames.

After a cursory glance toward Mammoth, they ventured back onto the street, carefully watching the flames as they spread through the downstairs of the home. Then Taylor abruptly stopped.

"Mac, that house doesn't have any tire tracks. Look, their car is still in the driveway. Do you think they decided to ride it out?"

He stepped toward the house and studied its windows on the upper levels, searching for any signs of movement. Taylor was correct. It appeared nobody had left the home since the blizzard had hit.

Mac looked back toward Mammoth and then at the house fire, which was now fully involved. He hung his head for a moment to think.

"If they're still inside, there's nothing we can do to help them," he began. "Stay here while I check the back of the house to see if they ran out. If someone makes their way out the front, find me but stay clear of the building."

Taylor slapped him on the back, encouraging him to go. Mac took a wide berth of the house. He took high, exaggerated steps through the snow as he walked through the yard. The entire time, his eyes darted between the windows of the home, the back-yard, and the bomb-throwing volcano.

"Is anybody here?" Mac shouted to be heard over the blizzard conditions. "Hello!"

Mac continued to make his way to the rear of the house. His eyes grew wide when he saw the sliding glass doors leading to the living area off the deck partially opened. He took a deep breath and immediately began to cough violently.

"Bad idea, dumbass," he mumbled to himself. "I have to make sure."

Mac slowly approached the back of the house, observing every window as the fire spread throughout. He held out little hope for any survivors, but the open door told him somebody either tried to get out or were successful. Either way, he couldn't just abandon them.

He found his way to the deck stairs leading several feet up to the sliding glass door. When he reached the top, he saw the body of an older man lying half in, half out of the opening. Mac rushed to his side and grabbed his arms to pull him through.

That was when the house exploded.

CHAPTER FORTY-THREE

Mammoth Lakes, CA

Mac had been thrown from the deck into the deep snow that had accumulated in the man's yard. He was barely coherent as he tried to make sense of what had happened. He forced his eyes open, only to immediately close them as the incessant wind from the blizzard covered his body in blowing snow and ash. His head pounded, and both ears were ringing. Yet his thoughts went immediately to Taylor.

She was impetuous, which was one of her traits he adored. As long as it didn't get her in trouble, anyway. He hoped she'd heeded his admonition to stay away from the house. He forced himself to roll over and sit up. First, he tried to study the back of the house. It was gone. The explosion had caused the entire first floor to give way to the upper level and the roofing system. The house fire had become a raging bonfire with flames leaping a hundred feet or more into the sky until the wind whipped it into a firenado.

He tried to call out to Taylor, but all he managed to do was induce a coughing fit. His lungs burned, and his chest felt like a sumo wrestler was sitting on it. He tried again.

"Taylor! Can you hear me?" He inwardly cursed the raging blizzard.

Mac found his footing and took a few steps toward the house. He wasn't certain, but most likely the man he tried to drag outside had already been dead when he'd arrived. His hands might have been cold from the snow. Mac had sensed otherwise. They'd felt lifeless. Regardless, the body had been consumed by the burning house.

He walked toward the garage, which had been spared from the flames so far. He continued to shout Taylor's name, but there was no response. Now concern washed over him, and he became frightened. Despite his pain and the nonstop ringing in his ears, he shuffled through the snow, finding his tracks around the garage.

"Taylor! Answer me!"

"I'm here!" she shouted in response.

She'd remained by the street as he'd asked. At one point, she'd made her way to the opposite side of the house, where a five-hundred-gallon aboveground propane tank stood perilously close to the flames. In a matter of seconds, she'd watched the snow covering the tank melt from the intense heat. Then the home's chimney had collapsed on top of the propane tank, causing it to rupture. That was when the explosion occurred. She had been knocked backwards onto the snow-packed street but was unharmed.

The two embraced for a long moment before Taylor pulled back to examine her fiancé.

"Are you hurt?"

"I feel like I got run over by a truck. And my damn ears won't stop ringing."

She ran her hands over his face and slowly touched his ears. "Did you find anybody?"

Mac lied. In the moment, he thought it was the right thing to do although he didn't want to make even a white lie a habit between them.

"No. Let's get to the truck and leave before something else happens."

Ten minutes later, they were wiping the snow off the windows and getting comfortable inside. Taylor offered to drive, but Mac assured her he was fine. That was not a lie. It was simply wishful thinking.

Mac clenched the steering wheel, his heart pounding in his chest. He sensed the concussive wave that struck him might've done some damage, but he intended to work through the pain.

"Are you sure you're okay?" Taylor asked.

His face, despite getting burned by the lava bomb that struck near them, was somewhat pale. His hand trembled slightly as he gripped the steering wheel. He took a deep breath and started the truck.

"Yeah. Yeah, I am. I just got a sick feeling in my gut. I can't really explain it."

He put the truck in gear and began heading out of the residential area at the base of Mammoth. He took an easterly route to avoid town, where they could see fires were raging. It took nearly an hour to travel a short distance. They were near U.S. 395, where the highway was packed with vehicles going in both directions. Their truck inched forward with the long line of traffic. At the intersection ahead, the highway traffic allowed a vehicle escaping town to join those escaping the exodus. No cars were headed toward town.

Mac slapped the steering wheel out of anger and pulled his truck out of line onto Sawmill Road. He forcefully jammed on the brakes, and he suddenly stopped the truck and stared straight ahead—at the Long Valley Caldera.

"What is it?" asked Taylor. "What's wrong? Are you thinking we should forget about getting to the cabin? Do you wanna head toward Nevada?"

When he didn't respond, she joined him in staring straight ahead. The longer they sat there, the more she understood. Even without him responding to her questioning, she knew the answer.

"You're right, Mac. Why did we risk our lives to drop into Crater Mountain? Why did we head over to Horseshoe Lake, nearly killing ourselves in the process?"

He was ready to speak now. "For the same reason I took that submersible to the bottom of the Pacific to investigate the seep near San Andreas. For the same reason you and I had to see about a possible fissure in Lake California. It's what we do. We ask questions that the rest of the damn world asks. The difference is we have to know the answer. It's not good enough to sit in a cubicle and theorize. That's no different than guessing. We have to go see for ourselves."

"Exactly," added Taylor. "That's what we've been put on this earth to do. Try to save as many people as possible from volcanoes like Mammoth or even bigger monsters like that one." She pointed at the caldera.

Mac took a deep breath. "Our work's not done here yet. There's still the looming question of the caldera. But before we address that, there are lives we can help save in Mammoth Lakes. We weren't able to warn them about Mammoth. The least we can do is help them survive its wrath."

Taylor turned in her seat and slowly pried his death grip off the steering wheel. She forced him to look away from the caldera and focus on her.

"This is why I love you. You have a passion for life and for helping people. I am one hundred percent with you, Mac Atwood. Ride or die."

Mac raised his chin and smiled. He became teary eyed as he nodded. Then he muttered, "Ride or die."

CHAPTER FORTY-FOUR

Station 1
Mammoth Lakes Fire Department
Mammoth Lakes, CA

Finn had taken a moment to mourn the loss of the
young woman who'd died at the controls of the fire
department's communications center. He cursed out
loud over the lack of power. However, when he was
informed by one of his lieutenants that the communications with his firefighter and rescue teams had
been taken down because of the volcanic eruption
combined with the seismic activity, he became
genuinely concerned for the safety of his entire
squad.

They were no longer operating a cohesive unit capable of contacting central dispatch to get additional assistance or paramedic support. Their emergency response plan, which would already be tested under the most catastrophic of circumstances, could be thrown out the window. They'd never planned for the eruption of the Mammoth Mountain volcano. As his predecessor had put it during a phone conversation, the response plan was simply *kiss our asses goodbye.*

Even without a plan, Finn was not going to turn his back on Mammoth Lakes. Their efforts were not without challenges. Unable to reach out to his firefighters, he sent one of his people on foot to central dispatch, which monitored and communicated with all first responders, including law enforcement and medical facilities. They faced the same problem. Even the two-way radios were ineffective, as most of the towers were perched along the mountains surrounding Mammoth Lakes and Long Valley.

He ordered his personnel to switch to backup power. The large generator was designed to provide power for several days in the event of a sustained outage. However, it had been damaged when the brick wall adjacent to the fire hall's garage bays collapsed on top of it, damaging wires and cables.

With the modern infrastructure they relied upon taken away from them, Finn had to approach his job as if he'd been thrown back to the 1800s. He didn't have to get official word that the town was being pummeled by lava bombs. He could hear them and feel the ground shake from their forceful impacts. Fires had developed throughout the area, especially in the structures closest to the mountain. He vowed to save as many people as he could, while saving structures at the same time.

"Listen up, people!" shouted Finn as he gathered everyone in the garage bays. The blizzard was sending snow in one set of doors and out the other, carrying with it the smell of smoke. "As you know, we have no comms. All of the units already on calls are on their own. I suspect they'll either continue to address fires and rescues in their immediate vicinity or return here.

"In the meantime, we need to get to work. I want to send all companies, the rescue squad, and para-medics to post up near the Village. With the power outage, we won't receive calls to respond to, so we have to be proactive. As long as our hydrants pump water, we'll fight structure fires.

"We can use word of mouth to help people exit the hotels and find their way toward the airport. I think that's the best staging area to care for the displaced refugees. Any injured in need of triage should be taken to Mammoth Hospital."

Finn glanced outside to view the bumper-to-bumper traffic attempting to leave town. "We're gonna need to form up with all of our equipment and create a convoy into the Village. These people are panicked, rightfully so. They're not gonna be cooperative. Be firm, but patient. If they won't move out of your way, then, well, we have a lot of lives to save. We can't worry about hurt feelings right now."

The firefighters began to disperse to gather their gear when Finn asked an additional question. "Can I have a volunteer to head to town hall and get a message to Mayor DiGregory? Let him know our situation, and if he needs me, I'll be establishing an outpost near the Village."

"I can help you with that, Chief," said a sheriff's deputy who entered the fire hall with his partner. His tone of voice foretold the bad news. "Town hall was hit with a lava bomb. He and his staff have died. I came to report the fire to you."

Finn sighed. They were under attack and had no means to fight back. All they could do was react to the carnage inflicted upon Mammoth Lakes by the mountain that prior to today had put food on their tables.

"Okay, the rest of you, get ready to head into the Village," ordered Finn. "Deputies, I could use your help."

"What can we do?" asked the older of the two.

"We're gonna send our units into the Village to evacuate hotels and fight structure fires. I'm sending all of our vehicles against the flow of traffic. Can you help create an opening and deal with crowd control?"

"Sure. We can't reach our dispatch, so we'll just pitch in where needed."

"I will owe you guys," said Finn as he patted them both on the shoulders. He took a deep breath and donned his gear. He grabbed his Halligan, the only tool he'd brought with him from LA. It had saved many people during his career as a firefighter. The old Irishman expected it to save a few more.

CHAPTER FORTY-FIVE

The Village at Mammoth Lakes, CA

Astoundingly, aided by the sheriff's deputies, Finn led the caravan in the captain's SUV with remarkable ease. Main Street, a four-lane road with a center turn lane, was cleverly flanked by frontage streets on either side, ensuring smooth access to businesses without disruptive sudden stops. The highway was packed with vehicles fleeing the volcanic threat, yet the frontage street provided ample room for vehicles to yield and make way for the noisy procession of fire and rescue vehicles.

The howling winds of the blizzard whipped through the streets, causing the snow to swirl in chaotic patterns, limiting visibility to a hundred yards. The city was in the grip of a relentless storm; however, it was the Mammoth volcano that threatened to turn it to dust.

Flaming lava bombs began to drop around the town with increased frequency. The open-air shopping district, normally packed with shoppers and diners, was now the bullseye of the volcano's dartboard. The dead were strewn about, some dying from concussions caused by collapsing buildings; others were burned beyond recognition as fires raged through the hotels, shops, and restaurants.

Finn strategically staged his fire trucks and rescue vehicles where the various teams could lend one another a hand. Where hydrants were blocked, the firefighters didn't hesitate to break out vehicles' windows to feed their hoses through. The gravity-fed public water system didn't fail despite the power outage. They'd need the enormous pressure the hoses provided, as the blizzard did little to douse the flames. Rather, the high winds enabled a fire caused by a single lava bomb to spread rapidly.

He gathered his lieutenants and their top personnel near the entrance to the Village at Mammoth Lakes. He had to shout to be heard over the wind, screaming, and roaring fires around town.

"We're gonna work together to evacuate the buildings first. Don't get overwhelmed. We're looking at a five-alarm fire without the equipment and numbers of firefighters needed to control it. Focus on the hotels first. People may be trapped in elevators, caught when the power was lost. Then check rooms. Cover one another. No heroes, people. I want every one of you to come out of this alive. Am I clear?"

His captain and the two lieutenants divided up their resources and headed for the Village Lodge. The four-story structure overlooked the open-air shopping and retail stores. Those on the west side of the hotel had an unobstructed view of Mammoth Mountain.

With a tense grip on his Halligan, Finn spoke to the sheriff's deputies. "Get these people out of here. I understand they may be searching for lost loved ones. However, they're at risk of the buildings collapsing on them, not to mention they're in the way of us saving others. Send the injured to the hospital and the others to the airport. I know it's a long walk, but convince them they need to get away from these lava bombs."

Everyone jumped or screamed as a lava bomb sailed to their north, landing in a wooded area that contained a trail for skiers to exit the mountain by skiing to the Village.

Finn remained calm as he turned in a full circle to survey the task before him. His heart sank as he realized the situation was far worse than he'd imagined back at the station. The flames had spread rapidly with the aid of the blizzard winds. People seeking refuge from the volcanic eruption and the inclement weather were likely trapped in the lower-level shops or hotel rooms.

"Save one at a time," he mumbled to himself.

He enlisted the assistance of two volunteers who'd stood out among the rest of the locals who went through his training program. Before they left the fire hall, he made certain they were properly suited up to enter a burning structure. They donned their helmets and ventilator masks. The burly man grabbed a sledgehammer. The female, who worked at the high school as a nurse's assistant, shouldered a trauma kit.

The firefighters fanned out, using their training to battle the emerging inferno. The combination of fire and refrozen snow made for a treacherous environment. With each step, they risked slipping on the ice patches or getting hit by a lava bomb. The whistling sound the projectiles made was unnerving.

"Incoming," many people would shout, causing the others to either look up or to crawl under something they perceived might protect them. A desk or table wouldn't make a difference if their number had been called.

Finn and his volunteers started with the hotel lobby. They stayed close to his hip, ready for his instructions. He was keenly aware this was their first foray into a burning building, and they were most likely frightened. Yet they were there to help, and Finn applauded their bravery.

Inside the lobby, panic ensued. Guests poured out of the library, hacking and coughing to eject the smoke that invaded their lungs. Finn turned to his male volunteer.

"We need to vent this lobby. You take the left side of the doors, and I'll take the right side. Break out the glass, but make sure nobody's on the other side. Understand?"

"Yes, Chief. Meet back at this spot?"

"Yeah," said Finn as he patted the man on the back. He turned to the nurse. "Do not move. No matter what, okay? We won't be long."

"Yes, sir." Her voice trembled, and Finn immediately picked up on it.

"Are you sure you're up for this?"

"I will be. Yes, sir. It's just a little overwhelming. All the screaming."

Finn placed his hand on the outside of her shoulder. "They're afraid. I am, too. I'm just not screaming along with them."

The young woman laughed and broke eye contact as she looked around. "You're afraid?" she asked with a smile.

"Okay, maybe not as much as the others. But I've been through this before. Trust me, and we'll save lives today. Okay?"

She nodded and gave him a gloved thumbs-up. Finn took off and quickly broke out the glass with his Halligan. By the time he returned, his two volunteers were gathered in the spot where he'd left them. They were answering questions and directing people out of the building.

The male volunteer hit Finn with the news he expected but didn't want to hear.

"Chief, there are people trapped in the elevator between the third and fourth floors. They told us the fire hasn't reached that high up yet."

Finn adjusted his backpack filled with rescue gear. He'd made sure he had ropes, pullies and harnesses before he left the fire station. He expected he might need it for a rescue like this or to lower themselves out of upper-floor balconies if the exits were blocked by fire. Finn took a deep breath in his mask and looked toward the ceiling of the lobby.

"Let's go!"

CHAPTER FORTY-SIX

Ski Mammoth
Mammoth Lakes, CA

Sammy and Tyler were enveloped in darkness once again, intensifying their fear. They had the presence of mind to slide under the rock outcropping, closer to where the massive ledge met the ground. To where the mountain mammals had gone to die from the poisonous, volcanic gases they'd breathed in. Mammoth Mountain shook with a fury that placed the trapped couple in a near state of shock. The noise was deafening. The consequences of the volcanic eruption were obvious. They were going to die.

Sammy had a death grip on Tyler's ankles. She was not going to let go of her husband at the moment they lost their lives. The deafening roar of the eruption could be heard through the avalanche that consumed them. Its powerful shaking jolted their spines and pounded their backs as they pressed their bodies against the rock wall.

As the volcanic eruption intensified, the snow cave they'd carved for themselves became a temporary sanctuary from the superheated air and the small projectiles peppering the ski slopes. However, the protection was a mere illusion as the seismic activity associated with the eruption threatened to collapse the rock outcropping above them.

Unable to speak, fear gripped their souls as they confronted their vulnerability in the face of nature's ferocity. The darkness heightened their senses, making every dislodged piece of rock or chunk of snow seem like the blow that would end them. Claustrophobia led to panic as Tyler frantically searched for the cell phone he'd dropped. He'd turned it off again to conserve battery power. Now it was buried in the snow that enveloped him.

Incredibly, in the midst of their fear, they found solace in Sammy's grip on Tyler's ankles. He could feel her squeeze, and she felt him wiggle his legs in response. While they couldn't hear one another because of the growling nature of the volcanic eruption, their touch had created an unspoken bond. They were still alive, and therefore, they had a chance to survive.

Tyler found the cell phone. It was underneath him, easily located if he didn't have what seemed like a hundred rocks jabbing him in the belly. He maneuvered his arm out and lit up the display. He illuminated the flashlight and shined it ahead. While the snow had pushed its way farther under the outcropping, there was still enough room for them to inch forward. Digging out would be difficult, but possible.

Now he placed the phone in his right hand and lit up the space behind him. He twisted slightly, bumping his head repeatedly on the jagged rocks until he could get a look at Sammy. The snow had collapsed across her arms. Tyler gasped. Was her head buried? All he knew was that she continued to grip his ankles.

He tried to shout, but the deafening roar muted his attempts to get her attention. He had to signal her. Keeping his left leg perfectly still, he wiggled his right back and forth to create a wider opening as the soft snow became packed down. Sammy picked up on his technique. Still holding on to his left ankle, she began to move the snow around. He sensed her beating the soft snow flat to the ground as well as against the rock. He imagined this was the technique she'd used when she'd created the snow tube earlier.

The volcanic eruption showed no signs of relenting. It would've been easy to give up, succumbing to the agonizing sense of powerlessness. Yet they continued to fight. Just as they'd done when they'd nearly died multiple times during the ARkStorm, Sammy and Tyler never gave up on life. They'd fight to survive until their last breath.

In the suffocating darkness, they worked together now to create an opening for Sammy to inch forward. When the phone's flashlight illuminated her face, she tried to smile at Tyler through her hair, which had been thrown over her face and covered in snow.

"I see you, Ty!"

"Same! Can you believe this shit? Gimme a break!"

"I know!" yelled Sammy. "We have to keep going, Ty. We have less air than before. I'm already starting to smell rotten eggs."

Tyler knew what that meant. He refused to suffer the same fate as the dead carcasses he was forced to crawl over.

"Okay, slowly. Be aware of every movement you make. Stay on my heels."

"If something happens, I'll squeeze them."

They moved in unison, a foot at a time. Tyler didn't bother to check the timing of their progress. He knew they were in a race against time. Mammoth Mountain felt like it was coming apart, ripped open from the inside out. Either it would swallow them in molten lava, or they'd run out of air. Both were very real possibilities at any minute. Minutes that, by the grace of God and a lot of luck, turned into hours.

For a while, Tyler clung to the hope that rescue teams were nearby or scouring the mountain, searching for people in need of rescue. As the volcano continued to erupt, his hopes were dashed. He knew they'd have to save themselves. They had their own families to consider. He didn't begrudge them for it.

He paused to rest. "How're you doin'?" he asked. Mammoth's anger seemed to have taken a respite for the moment.

"Okay. Tired. How about you?"

"Same." Tyler shook his head in disbelief before adding, "Sammy, this is insane."

She'd had enough of this adventure, too. "I swear,

I'm gonna move into a bubble far away from this crap."

Tyler took a deep breath and set his jaw. "Let's keep going. I don't know if you noticed, but we've been crawling upward for the last hour. It's slight, but we're definitely getting closer to the end of this ledge."

"If you say so."

She sounded defeated. Tyler wanted to add one more observation. He wasn't sure if it was positive news or not. The snow was becoming slightly slushy.

Was it melting? How close were they to the eruption, anyway?

CHAPTER FORTY-SEVEN

The Village at Mammoth Lakes, CA

Finn and his volunteers pushed their way past the panicked hotel guests in order to gain access to the fourth floor. They learned the second floor was now fully engulfed in flames. Panic had spread throughout the building as guests were told by hotel staff to remain in their rooms to avoid the lava bombs. Once the fire spread to the hotel, chaos reigned as every occupant rushed for the exits.

The third floor was filling with thick, black smoke. The flames had not yet reached the corridor, but the floor was heating up, as evidenced by the carpet's backing beginning to melt. They rushed into the stairwell again and made their way to the top floor.

There, he heard his firefighters breaching one door after another at the far end of the hallway. Their shouts were in near unison.

"Firefighters! Call out!"

"Firefighters! Call out!"

Finn turned to the young nurse. "Go down the hall and tell them I need another firefighter to get to this elevator. See if there are any victims in need of medical assistance."

"Yes, sir." She rushed down the hallway and disappeared into the darkness. The only illumination came from the battery-powered fire alarms that emitted a nonstop pulsing light to go with the shrieking alarm.

The power outage had added an extra layer of complexity to the firefighters' efforts. It also created a challenging rescue from the elevator cab. Inside were terrified passengers, trapped in darkness with no means of escape.

Finn turned to his volunteer. "I'll pry the doors open. I need you to keep them apart until I can help you. They'll open on their own after we get past the initial tension."

Using the pry bar end of his Halligan tool, Finn

wedged the blade between the doors. He pushed and pulled until a gap appeared. With his tool wedged in place, he joined the volunteer to spread the doors open. He caught the Halligan with his left hand and grunted to create a wider opening with his right. Seconds later, another firefighter joined the struggle, and they successfully opened the door.

He shouted into the dark elevator shaft, "Firefighter, call out!"

"We're in here!" a woman screamed.

"In here," shouted several others.

All were banging on the inside walls of the elevator cab.

"We can't get the emergency hatch open! It's stuck!"

"Okay, stay calm. How many are inside?"

"Nine!" several occupants shouted back.

"Two kids!" added another.

Finn used his flashlight to illuminate the shaft. It was stuck halfway between the two floors. He shined it around the outer walls of the cab to determine if they could pry open the third-floor doors. The smoke seeping through the elevator doors reminded him the second floor was fully engulfed in flames and moving upward. They didn't have much time.

The firefighter sent by the nurse was a shorter,

wiry young man much better suited for being dropped onto the top of the cab. Using Finn's ropes, pullies and the harness, they outfitted the firefighter with the means to drop six feet to the roof of the cab. He didn't want to risk jumping onto the roof in the event the elevator's emergency brake system had been compromised.

Finn and his muscular volunteer slowly lowered the firefighter to the top of the elevator cab. Using his own Halligan bar, he pried open the emergency hatch. A whoosh of smoke-filled air flowed past him. He illuminated the cab with his light. Nine faces of all ages stared up at him, their eyes hopeful and filled with trepidation.

"Okay, let me hoist up the children first. After I take some weight off the cab, I'll bring another fire-fighter down to help me."

A man placed his young daughter on the shoulder of a taller man who positioned himself under the hatch. The firefighter easily pulled her up by the arms until she was freed. Then, in turn, he placed the child on his shoulders and instructed her to raise her hands into the air. As she did, Finn and the volunteer yanked her upward. This process was repeated for a young boy and then an older woman who was having difficulty breathing.

The volunteer turned to Finn. "May I be honest?"

"Sure."

The volunteer pointed to the firefighter. "He's not gonna be strong enough to lift the adults out. Chief, in the gym, I can deadlift and press double what these people probably weigh. It'll be no problem for me to grab 'em out and push 'em up to you."

Finn studied their options. The man was untested but appeared capable. He was cool under pressure. He looked into the shaft, where his firefighter was standing awaiting direction.

"Come on up. I'm gonna swap you two out."

Less than a minute later, the firefighter and the volunteer traded places. It was a smart decision by Finn. Both men excelled in their new positioning, and in less than five minutes, the elevator cab was completely evacuated just as the fire breached the third floor of the hotel. The passengers all suffered from smoke inhalation, but the relief on their faces reflected their appreciation for being rescued. They were immediately led down the stairwell by the volunteer nurse.

Finn and his volunteer joined the other firefighters and made their way to the fourth floor to clear the rooms. Thankfully, between the Village being bombarded by the lava bombs and the hotel beginning to be destroyed by the fire, all the occupants had the presence of mind to leave. Now it was up to Finn, his volunteer, and four firefighters to find a way out.

CHAPTER FORTY-EIGHT

Ski Mammoth
Mammoth Lakes, CA

That day, ski enthusiasts could hardly contain their excitement as they relished the opportunity to hit the fresh powder at Mammoth Mountain. The snow-covered landscape promised an exhilarating day of skiing or snowboarding. They carved their way down the pristine slopes, oblivious to what the mountain would bring them that day.

The blizzard had begun to arrive early, but the threat of bad weather ran off only a few of the thousands filling the slopes. Some groaned as Ski Mammoth closed the lifts to the higher elevations of the mountain due to high winds. Some overstayed their welcome at the summit, sitting in the restaurant and the bar.

The blizzard had taken away the usual breathtaking views. That afternoon, the massive earthquake, immediately followed by the eruption of the Mammoth volcano, took away their breath, literally. The shock wave caused by the eruption knocked skiers off their feet, causing them to career down the slopes. The fragile human body was not made to withstand the pummeling it took at the hands of the catastrophic event.

Normally crisp mountain air was replaced by blizzard conditions coupled with superheated waves of gas and volcanic ash that choked many to death while permanently scarring the lungs of others. In the skies, the lava bombs chased them down the slopes. Those still on skis didn't bother with making carved turns to slow their descent. They tucked and pointed the tips of their skis toward the bottom in an effort to outrun the lava bombs and emerging lava streams. They crashed into fellow skiers, trees, and rocks, mangling their bodies and garnering the immediate attention of first responders.

As the eruption continued, skiers found their way off the mountain. Soon after the lava bombs attacked the volcano's surroundings, streams of lava began to pour from Mammoth's vents. The red-hot streams of molten rock devoured everything in their path. The ten-foot-deep snowpack was no match for the tremendous heat, which melted the snow instantly, turning it into a churning river of water that soon mixed with volcanic ash.

The ash cloud began to spread upward, joining the ferocious blizzard conditions. It rushed down the slopes like the breath of a massive beast, knocking over anyone trying to flee and burying those who couldn't.

The ski patrols worked diligently to save as many lives as they could. However, with the ski lifts no longer functioning when the power grid collapsed, their efforts were limited to those nearest the bottom of the mountain. The rest were on their own.

Buried under the avalanche, Sammy and Tyler were both aware of the next threat in their really bad day. Tyler began to make extraordinary progress as the snow above them began to melt. The slush was more difficult to move through, as it failed to provide them a compact surface to get a footing.

It also meant one thing. Lava must be nearby.

Tyler's arm broke the surface of the rapidly melting snow. Excited, he dug faster, encouraging

Sammy to do the same. The melting snow was collapsing the tunnel they'd made along the rock ledge. He expected it was melting snow on top of the outcropping as well based upon the amount of water dripping on his scalp.

Tyler emerged first, struggling to steady himself on the snowpack, which was rapidly deteriorating. Sammy crawled out next, and her husband's powerful arms hoisted her upright into a much-needed embrace.

Sammy broke free and pointed up the mountain. "Ty! It's coming right at us!"

Nightfall had arrived, and the blizzard had intensified. The snow melted from the heat of the many vents that had opened at the summit, turning the flakes to water only to refreeze again as it made its way down the slopes. Their faces were peppered with ice crystals that stung their exposed skin and made their eyes water.

An eerie sizzling sound accompanied the howl of the wind and the roar of the erupting volcano. The lava stream carved a path through the snowy slopes, instantaneously boiling everything in its path.

Hand in hand, they rushed away from the approaching lava and searched for high ground that hadn't been impacted by eruptive material. That was when they caught their first glimpse of lava bombs.

"Seriously?" asked Tyler.

"Worse than the bears during the ARkStorm, right?"

"Less predictable," added Tyler.

Sammy shook her head in disbelief. They knew how to get off the mountain; however, their escape routes were becoming impassable, as small streams of lava seemed to percolate to the surface out of nowhere.

"Should we try to find our skis?" Sammy asked.

"No time. Let's head to the left. It seems like the worst of it is on the south side of the mountain."

They began to trudge through the melting snow, looking for a path downward that kept them atop a hill. The low-lying areas seemed to be the path of least resistance for the slow-moving lava. The lava bombs landed indiscriminately all around them. It was a crap shoot, so to speak, as they finally realized any attempt to avoid them was fruitless. They focused entirely on getting as far away from Mammoth Mountain as they could.

It took half an hour, but they made their way to the parking lot, where chaos reigned. Panicked drivers attempted to shove cars out of their way to flee the volcano. Fistfights were taking place throughout the parking area. When gunfire was exchanged, drivers and their passengers abandoned their vehicles to run toward town.

To their credit, employees of Ski Mammoth were manning the entrance in an attempt to direct traffic. The problem was that everyone was leaving the area at once. The roads through the town were now clogged. Reports of U.S. 395 being blocked due to the earthquakes discouraged many from evacuating in that direction. Drivers with four-wheel drive tried to avoid the roads, only to get stuck in the melting snow caused by the heat of the volcano.

Sammy and Tyler, relieved to have made it to the parking lot, located Finn's Jeep and sat inside for a moment. Tyler couldn't wait to bring the interior temperature to a level just below sweltering.

"Let me look at your head," said Sammy as she turned on the overhead light. She felt his scalp through his thick, black hair. Smiling, she ran her fingers through it to remove any matted blood. "You'll live." It was a common phrase used to reassure someone who'd been injured that their wound wasn't that dangerous. On that day, the words lent a special meaning.

"Thanks, doc," said Tyler with a laugh. "So do

you wanna sit here and hope we don't get smacked with these giant, blazing meatballs? Or should we head to the fire station to find Finn?"

Sammy looked into the back of the Jeep and stretched to retrieve her duffel bag. "Let me change out of these clothes first."

"Why?" he asked.

"Because I peed myself when the volcano erupted. I didn't get to make yellow snow like you."

Tyler might normally crack a joke at her revelation. This wasn't a good time.

CHAPTER FORTY-NINE

The Village at Mammoth Lakes, CA

Darkness fell across Mammoth Lakes as the combination of volcanic ash and wind-driven snow collaborated to block out the sun while the power outage left them to rely upon their flashlights to find their way around. After ensuring the fourth floor had been cleared, Finn, his two volunteers, and four firefighters found themselves trapped, as the fire escapes had collapsed at each end of the building. Flames had begun to burst through the floors from below, confirming the third floor was now burning out of control.

Finn gathered the group on the back side of the hotel, facing the brunt of the blizzard. Despite the poor visibility, the orange-red glow of oozing lava coupled with the seemingly never-ending supply of lava bombs reminded them Mammoth was not going to relent in its efforts to destroy the town.

With the windows blown out of the west side of the hotel, the flames emerging from the third floor danced and twisted as they consumed flammable materials. The heat from inside fought the cold from the blizzard, with the seven firefighters caught in the middle.

Outside the room where they'd gathered, a loud crash could be heard and a whooshing sound. Finn reluctantly opened the hotel room door to glance down the hallway. Fire rose upward through a hole in the hallway floor before spreading in all directions as it hit the ceiling above his head. The constant heat and pressure would soon spread throughout the fourth floor.

Finn explained the problem they faced. "We have no comms, so we're on our own. Unless we can get the aerial in place at the back of the building, we're trapped."

"The closest it can get is over at the Forest Trail entrance, Chief. North side of the building."

"Chief, how are you gonna get them into position?"

Finn faced two problems. Dropping one of them to the ground with a rope too short to reach and then safely maneuvering the rest to a part of the building inaccessible due to the fire. He walked to the window and leaned over the aluminum sill. He held his helmet in place as the wind tried to blow it off. He studied the back of the hotel in both directions. Six rooms to their right, toward the north end of the building, were several rooms with balconies. They could make their way down one balcony at a time for so long as the fire didn't engulf the lower-floor rooms first.

"Let's move!" he suddenly shouted. "I'll lead us down the hallway. We don't have much time."

"On your shoulder, Chief," said his male volunteer.

The other firefighters hugged the wall to avoid the opening in the floor allowing fire to roar upwards in search of oxygen. Finn kept his wits about him as he counted the doors to reach the one with a balcony. Exhausted, he turned to his firefighters.

"Let me check for flames on the inside of the room, and then we'll breach it," he shouted.

Finn removed a glove and felt the door with his hand. It was cool to the touch, but that could've been due to the cold wind and snow blowing inside the room. He checked for smoke around the frame. Nothing.

He stood back and pointed to the volunteer. "I'm going to pry the door open slightly with the Halligan. I need you to hit the hinges hard with the sledge."

"The hinges?" he asked.

"Yeah, they're the weakest part of a door."

The two worked together, and after two massive blows and a powerful kick, the volunteer once again proved his capabilities by knocking the door completely free of the frame.

The firefighters rushed inside, and Finn directed them to the balcony. He handed his duffel bag to the wiry firefighter.

"Set up the rigging and see how far you can drop yourself. I'm guessing you'll get to the second floor. Once you're there, let us know if it's safe for the rest of us to join you."

"On it, Chief!" the seasoned veteran replied.

He worked with two other firefighters to prepare to rappel down the side of the hotel to the second floor, where the fire had been raging for more than thirty minutes. The hotel was primarily made of wood to give it a rustic, mountain feel. The fire fed on it with gusto.

Finn supervised as the firefighter climbed over

the rail and lowered himself past the third-floor balcony. He paused as his legs dangled near the second floor. He looked up at Finn and shouted his question.

"How much rope do I have?"

"Not enough! Seven feet. You'll have to swing so you're hovering above the rail. Once your feet touch, you can release and jump onto the balcony."

"It's going to be tight, Chief. Here goes!"

He dropped down farther so that he could see inside the second-floor hotel room. Fire had consumed the room. The blaze was so hot the glass from the broken sliding glass door had melted somewhat.

"Chief! I can climb the railing, dangle and drop. I'm not sure everybody else will be able to pull that off!"

Finn studied the ground below. "How far a drop is it?"

"A dozen feet. It's not gonna be easy."

Finn thought for a moment. He turned to his firefighters. "Anybody see a roof access when clearing the floor?"

"I did, Chief. There was a utility room near the elevator. It was a small, confined space, so a quick glance confirmed it was clear. But I saw a steel ladder leading up to an access hatch. Probably for HVAC repairs."

Finn closed his eyes. They were running out of time. He couldn't trust the fire on the lower floors to be patient while they tried to evacuate outside the burning building.

He looked over the railing. "Make your way down. Bring the aerial to the north side of the building. We'll be on the gable end of the roof."

"On it, Chief!" the man replied. With the dexterity and flexibility of a trapeze artist loaded down with firefighter's gear, he scaled the railing. He eased down until he was dangling over the ground and then dropped.

"Are you okay?" Finn yelled his question.

"Yes, sir. See ya on the north face," replied the expert skier.

Finn pointed toward the door. "Back toward the elevator. Quickly!"

One by one, they exited the room. In just the few minutes they had been assisting their fellow firefighter to the ground, the single void in the floor had become two. They were larger, the flames were broader, and the footing was far more treacherous.

Finn, their chief and leader, took the risk of checking their path to the roof access. If anyone was going to fall through the floor, it would be him. He pressed his back against the wall and kept a wary eye on the carpeted floor under his feet. With each exaggerated step, he pressed down to ensure it was stable. The volunteer nurse held his hand while the other volunteer held hers. The group of six formed a human chain that eased past the fire-breathing beast below them. None of them spoke or, most likely, breathed until they reached the elevator and the utility room.

Finn climbed the ladder first, using his Halligan to break off the padlock secured to a latch. He forced the door open, and they were immediately drenched in wet snow and cold air. A welcome relief from the hot, sooty surroundings they'd been battling.

He helped everyone onto the roof and then directed them to the ridge. The hotel's shingle roof was constructed with a very easy four-twelve pitch, the flattest possible. Now everyone was on the roof and moving toward the north end of the hotel amidst the raging blizzard. Finn could barely hear the rumble of the large aerial truck.

On the ground, his firefighters worked frantically to position the truck as close to the roofline as possible. The sheriff's deputies assisted in clearing vehicles out of the way as well as a few hotel guests who'd stood to watch the structure succumb to the flames.

The aerial truck roared to life, its powerful hydraulic system extending the ladder upwards toward the top of the four-story building. On the ground, the operators adjusted to the wind, attempting to maintain steady control.

The aerial ladder swung back and forth, as the wind was unforgiving. Once it landed at the ridge of the roof, two firefighters struggled to secure it to a massive brick chimney without getting themselves knocked off the roof. Finally, they turned to Finn and gave a thumbs-up.

One of the firefighters issued a stark warning. "Chief, this may not hold if the chimney has been compromised on lower levels. We need to roll."

Two experienced firefighters went first, sepa-rated by the volunteer. After they reached the ground, two more members of the squad made their way to the bottom. Finn was resting on his knees, as he was the last to depart the burning building. As the last of the firefighters crawled onto the aerial's plat-form, Finn looked around one last time, taking a bird's-eye view of his adopted hometown. He fought back emotions as he saw large sections of neighbor-hoods burning. The downtown district was somewhat under control except for the hotel, which would soon collapse within itself. The biting cold penetrated his gear, but his adrenaline was pumping with determination. Their day wasn't done yet, much like the days he'd spent fighting fires on the ridges and mountains of Los Angeles County.

"Get to work, Finn," he admonished himself with a chuckle. "Don't get lazy in your old age." Then, to prove to himself he wasn't as old as he thought he was, he turned around on the ladder and grasped the rails with his gloved hands while positioning his feet on the rungs. Slowly, he repositioned his legs on the outside of the rails to allow himself the ability to slide quickly downward. It was a perfectly executed ladder bailout, something he'd done a hundred times. In his younger days.

CHAPTER FIFTY

Station 1
Mammoth Lakes Fire Department
Mammoth Lakes, CA

The weary warriors of the Mammoth Lakes Fire Department began to return to Station 1. It was after midnight as those fighting the residential fires in the community joined their fellow smoke eaters in the Village at Mammoth Lakes. Finn's heroics lifted the spirits of every woman and man within the department. The trained volunteers spawned a groundswell of support for the fire department. Residents who planned on fleeing changed their minds. They might not be able to defeat the wrath of the

Mammoth volcano, but they could certainly do their part to rescue those who couldn't flee the catastrophe.

Among those helping the fire department were Taylor and Mac as well as Sammy and Tyler. The couple who'd survived the avalanche and the fiery lava bombs sailing around their heads stopped in the Village on their way to the fire hall. Finn immediately waved them over and relayed what he knew. He instructed them to follow the highway out of town to the airport after getting the once-over at the hospital. They stubbornly refused.

As for Taylor and Mac, they helped on many levels. Frightened residents tried to drive vehicles in places they weren't meant to go. The blizzard had completely covered the roads with snow. Although most residents drove all-wheel-drive vehicles, many did not. They blocked roads, causing the exodus to come to a halt. Mac used the power of his winch to pull people out of predicaments, opening up the flow of traffic. They also became a means of transportation for the injured to get to the town's only hospital. His ability to take the four-wheel-drive truck over snow-covered ground allowed him to navigate around the traffic jams.

By three in the morning, the roads were cleared,

as most of the town had escaped Mammoth's wrath. The volunteer firefighters were urged to leave as the volcano continued to erupt, although not ·quite as explosively as it had when it began.

Finn drove Sammy and Tyler to retrieve his Jeep from the parking lot. The lodge and the accompanying parking looked like it had been subjected to a bombing raid during a war. The fiery molten rocks had pummeled everything. The lodge had burned to the ground. Cars had been crushed or caught on fire. Massive pockmarks had been created in the asphalt, which was melting due to the extreme heat. The blizzard had abated somewhat, allowing the three of them a clear view of the lava streams descending the mountain. Tendrils of smoke could be seen against the orange-red glow of the lava as trees were burned and charred.

They had just arrived back at the fire hall when Taylor and Mac returned. One might expect the group of five would have a jubilant and joyous reunion. Certainly, their minds felt the kind of relief true friends might have for one another who'd survived a catastrophic event like a volcanic eruption. However, their bodies were too exhausted to even exchange high fives. A long hug would have to suffice.

The fire hall's generator had been repaired, so the facility had lights but no heat. Plywood had been procured from a local building supply to close up the broken windows, although the garage bay doors were broken beyond repair. Finn's office, which had been destroyed by the Kia, was relocated to the conference room. It and the break room were the only parts of the facility that had space heaters. After everyone stopped for a restroom break, they joined Finn in the conference room.

He'd already placed an unopened bottle of fifteen-year-old Redbreast Irish Whiskey on a table together with a stack of clear plastic cups. The iconic brand of fine whiskey was first distilled in the middle of the nineteenth century. As everyone slid chairs around the folding table in a semicircle, he opened the bottle bearing the red-breasted European robin.

"I'd been saving this for the day I officially retired," he began, his voice raspy from inhaling smoke for hours. He poured a shot into everyone's cups. "Tonight, I'll open it so we can toast those who perished and celebrate our friends who survived.

"*Sláinte!*" he said.

Everyone responded with their cups held high. "*Sláinte!*"

Finn leaned on his desk with his elbows. He

closed his eyes and buried his face for a moment before pushing the hair off his sweat-soaked fore-head. The weariness from decades of fighting fires and saving lives was showing on his wrinkled face.

"We all have stories to tell, I'm sure. There will be a time and place for that. For now, there are decisions to be made."

Taylor and Mac exchanged glances. "We agree," said Mac. "We were at the base of the mountain when it began. I guess we witnessed the first part of Mammoth's eruption. Finn, can you tell us anything else?"

Finn refilled their cups and raised his again. All of them drank it down. Of all the times in their lives when a shot of straight whiskey was warranted, it was then.

He nodded and winced as he swallowed hard. He was certain the medical team at Mammoth Hospital wouldn't approve of trying to douse the burning sensation in his throat with Irish whiskey.

"I received reports from my firefighters who were battling structure blazes from the north side of Mammoth to the south. The worst of it was where you folks were. South. Southwest. There was a crack in the face of the mountain on the north side, but no eruption with it. Lava came out, but that was about it. For the town, it was the damned firebombs that caused the most damage. Nearly every one of them triggered a structure fire. Our people fought like hell to put out a fire only to have to come back when it was reignited by another firebomb."

"Those seem to have dropped off," added Tyler. "We just went back to get Finn's Jeep and only saw a few land near the top of the mountain. None made it as far as the parking lot that we could see. You know, after the first part. Um, we missed that part of the fireworks."

Mac studied Tyler and then glanced at Sammy. Her blank stare reflected the near state of shock she was in. She caught him looking at her and spoke for the first time.

"We found dead animals against a rock ledge before it all started. Then, when we were, um, able to see more after the eruption, lava was flowing down the mountain near the Dragon's Back."

Mac continued to study her, so Sammy averted her eyes and pushed her cup towards Finn. Sammy was in need of a strong drink. Several, apparently. He made a mental note to have Taylor pull her aside to assess her state of mind.

"That's about it, Taylor," said Finn. "Sammy is correct. The eruption seems to be calming down. Is it reloading or something?"

Taylor picked up her cup and stood to wander the office. Her eyes surveyed the plywood over the windows. A small crack had appeared on the west side of Finn's office, enabling her to catch a glimpse of Mammoth. With the blizzard now directing its fury on Nevada, the molten lava was more noticeable from a distance.

She took a sip and then leaned against a file cabinet to address Finn's question. "Nah, they don't work like that. Volcanic eruptions are all about pressure buildup and release. There are very rare exceptions depending on the type of volcano and the nature of its plumbing, so to speak. However, it's most likely the worst Mammoth has to offer is over."

"How does that compare to Mount Saint Helens?" asked Finn.

"Similar," she replied. "The most vigorous eruptive activity for the two comparable volcanoes would take place in the first eight to ten hours or so. Once the cryptodome on the southwestern flank of Mammoth became unstable, it was a matter of time until the volcanic structure moved toward failure."

"So we're good?" asked Tyler.

Taylor looked to Mac. "Aftershocks, right?"

"Yeah, from a seismic perspective, more earthquakes are likely. I can only guess, but it appeared the magnitude was in the neighborhood of seven. It was strong enough to create an abrupt pressure release." He nodded at Taylor.

"That's right. When the cracks formed, the extraordinary depth of the snowpack melted, allowing water into the volcanic system. The water quickly heated up and flashed to steam, which expanded explosively, initiating a hydrothermal blast directed laterally through the compromised southern and southwestern flanks of Mammoth."

Mac continued, "Aftershocks are to be expected throughout the area, not just around Mammoth Mountain."

"You can expect forest fires to the south and west of the mountain as the lava flows across the snow and burns the timber," interjected Taylor. "It appears the shock wave was directed away from town, fortunately. Otherwise, we wouldn't be sitting here."

Finn spun in his chair and stood to approach a map of Mammoth Lakes and the immediate surroundings. He drew a circle around the Long Valley Caldera with his index finger and then rapped the wall map with his knuckles.

"What about this booger?" he asked. Then he added, "I received word that the president has ordered the evacuation of the western states from the Pacific to the Dakotas and south to Texas. There's never been anything like it. Obviously, he thinks the caldera is next."

"What do you think?" Sammy asked Taylor. Her wide eyes reflected her concern.

Taylor stuck her cup out to request a refill from Finn. This time, she didn't sip the whiskey. She looked inside her cup to gauge the amount of the shot, then threw it to the back of her throat. She winced and swallowed hard.

"And the giant sleeps, albeit fitfully," she replied in a solemn tone of voice. "I can speak freely within the confines of this room because I consider us to be friends. I want you to understand the theory I have about the magma chambers under Mono County run contrary to accepted science. However, I firmly believe I'm correct."

"Please explain it to us," said Sammy.

"Okay. The generally accepted scientific belief is that there are separate and distinct magma chambers around us. Panum Crater and nearby Crater Mountain are separate from Mammoth. Each of those two chambers is separate from the caldera. If we go by what is presumed to be true, then several likely precursors to an eruption of the Long Valley Caldera have taken place. Earthquakes, new fumaroles, deforestation, and volcanic activity in several forms. Most of the boxes have been checked, which is why the president probably issued his evacuation order."

"You disagree," said Finn.

"I think the geology has changed. To put in the simplest of terms, I believe the magma chambers have joined underneath the three volcanic systems— Mono-Inyo, Mammoth, and the caldera. If I'm right, then the eruption of the Mammoth volcano, while devastating, may have saved America and the Northern Hemisphere around the globe from a natural disaster form of nuclear winter."

"How will you know if you're right?" asked Sammy.

"I have to go into the caldera. I need to study many things, from poisonous gas emissions to deformation of the ground. I need to search for new fumaroles, fissures, or steam vents. That's the only way I can convince anybody to believe my theory."

Sammy stood and set her cup on Finn's desk. "I believe you."

"Me too," said Tyler without hesitation.

Taylor studied their faces. They were battle

hardened. She knew what they'd gone through during the ARkStorm. She also knew they'd experienced something on Mammoth that they wanted to bury deep in the recesses of their minds.

"You know I'll always trust your judgment, honey. I'll follow you into the caldera if that's what needs to be done."

Tyler whispered to Sammy, and she nodded, looking at Finn as she spoke. She announced their position on behalf of the couple.

"There was a time when I thought I was going to die. Several times, in fact. I had faith in God, and my husband, to help me through it. But it was this old Irishman who stepped up and carried us across the finish line. We should've died that day the ARkStorm peaked. It was Finn who helped us survive. We owe him and, by extension, this town. We believe in you, Taylor. We want to help."

She and Sammy hugged one another. They nervously laughed as they broke their embrace.

Taylor beamed. "Well, if it makes any of you feel better. If the eruption of the caldera is imminent, we wouldn't be able to outrun it anyway."

"Ya gotta go out some way, right?" asked Mac.

For the first time since they'd arrived at the fire hall together, the friends were able to relax as a sense of relief washed over them. Even Rebel, who'd lain dutifully nearby, let out a bark to join the change in mood.

Their fate had been set. The next day, they'd find out if they'd live or die.

CHAPTER FIFTY-ONE

CalVO
Bridgeport, CA

With cell tower coverage nonexistent and power lines down around Mammoth Lakes, Taylor and Mac were unable to contact their office in Bridgeport when they woke up the next morning. The data and notes they'd made prior to Mammoth erupting had been left on the mountain, likely buried by the rocks and mud sliding downhill toward Horseshoe Lake. They hoped CalVO in Bridgeport had managed to remain in contact with the Santa Rosa offices during the ordeal.

They arrived at an empty parking lot and a

darkened building. Either the staff had heeded Kemp's order to evacuate, or they had done so after Mammoth erupted. In any event, nobody was working. Mac entered the building first and paused for a moment to take in his surroundings. He remembered the first time the Realtor showed him the mothballed high school auditorium. It needed more work than the USGS budget originally allowed. He didn't hesitate to roll up his sleeves and get to work. While Taylor worked with her team on the volcanology side, Mac built out the perfectly suited space for their combined operations.

"Do you hear that?" asked Mac.

Taylor held her breath and listened. "Um, no. Just the noisy fans on those lousy PCs. I wish they'd switch to—" Taylor cut her sentence short and ran to the wall where a bank of light switches controlled the entire building. She smacked the rocker switches all at once.

"Yes!" exclaimed Mac. "We've got power, baby!" He did a little happy dance and took Taylor by the hand to lead her into the heart of the building.

"Eerie, isn't it?" she asked. "At any given moment during the day, there were always people in here monitoring these volcanoes and fault zones. It's almost as if once the parents left, the hellions ran wild."

"No doubt," mumbled Mac, who made his way to his group's workstations. He eased into a swivel chair and tapped the space bar. The monitor came to life. He quickly entered his user identification and password to access the USGS computer. His personalized portal appeared on the screen. Across the room, Taylor was doing the same.

"Wow, seventy-seven messages," she exclaimed.

"I've got sixty-eight."

As she scrolled through her messages, she needled Mac. "You know, you can tell the importance of someone by the number of messages they get in a single day."

Mac rolled his eyes. "You mean self-importance. I can't stand people walking down the sidewalk or hallway with their nose in their phone. You aren't the president's best buddy. You don't have to answer everyone within seconds of getting a text or email."

Taylor started laughing. "I've got an alert in here warning me a volcano is erupting in my region."

Mac joined her. "No kidding. Thanks for the heads-up."

"Director Kemp's looking for us," said Taylor. "A

bunch of my messages are from her. Let me touch base—"

Mac interrupted her. "Wait, let me ask you something first."

"What?"

"Do you want to go into the caldera to gather data and observations before we speak to her? I know her better than you do. She's like my mother. She'll tell us not to. She'll order us back to Santa Rosa or, hell, on the other side of the Mississippi River somewhere."

Taylor pushed away from the workstation as if the keyboard had given her a jolt of electricity. "Damn. You're right. Even if we tell her the reasons, she'll lecture us both and order us out. That said, what's she gonna do to us? She can't ground us like our mothers might."

"You don't know Kemp like I do. She has a way. I don't know how to describe it. She's scary. Like a freakin', um, I don't know what."

Taylor was quiet for a moment. She was scrolling through the reports generated by the Santa Rosa office. "M7.2. Is that what your people say?"

"Yep. That's about right. Mammoth must've been on the verge, Taylor. That pressure has been building for some time, and it was hidden from us."

"It helps prove my theory. Several factors could've led to the magma chamber heating up, including the stresses caused by the earthquakes in the Mojave Desert and at Garlock. But to create that kind of intensity in a short period of time, it would have to be the chambers merging."

Mac logged out of his portal and shut down the workstation. He walked across the auditorium to join Taylor. "An M7.2 would certainly destabilize the mountain enough to allow a massive influx of water from melted snow."

"Exactly," added Taylor. "That would explain the flank eruption on the south and southwest sides of the mountain. Their slopes were more pronounced and have been known to suffer from rockslides during heavy rains or snowmelt."

"Let me add something," said Mac as he arched his back to relieve some of the pain he'd endured when the propane tank exploded, destroying the house. "There is little or no seismic activity connected to the caldera. Everything is occurring around Mammoth, both pre-eruption and aftershocks."

Taylor pushed against the workstation with the palms of her hands, rapidly tapping her fingers on the desk as she thought. She, too, logged out of her portal.

"You're right, Mac. Any conversation we have with Kemp has to happen when we have a total picture. We knew yesterday that the precursors at the caldera, if any, were the key." She glanced at her watch. "We're meeting the guys at noon, right?"

Mac nodded. "We need to get rolling. It's a hairy ride down the side of Bald Mountain on snow-mobiles."

"I ain't skeered," said Taylor mockingly. "Ain't that the way you guys talk in Tennessee?"

Mac rolled his eyes and smirked. "That's East Tennessee twang. We speak perfect Midwestern English in West Tennessee."

Taylor gave him a shove and then a kiss on the cheek. "Believe what you want, sir. You've got a little twang in ya."

CHAPTER FIFTY-TWO

Arcularius Ranch
Bishop, CA

Taylor and Mac had explored the caldera before the snows started last fall. Roaming the trails around Long Valley was eye-opening for Mac. The caldera, not unlike Yellowstone except on a smaller scale, showed its life through fumaroles, heated vents, and the occasional release of carbon dioxide causing the death of anything living near the crack in the earth.

They had a full understanding of the incredible power that might be unleashed if the Long Valley Caldera were to erupt. Yet they were willing to live atop Bald Mountain with a direct view of the ticking time bomb underneath the Earth's surface.

Years ago, the Arcularius Ranch had been developed on a five-hundred-sixty-acre tract at the entrance to the caldera. A main house plus numerous other homes were located behind the gates guarding the entrance from anyone venturing into the caldera on Owens River Road. The Upper Owens River meandered through the caldera into the ranch. Guests of the ranch enjoyed green pastures amidst the high desert terrain and unparalleled fly-fishing opportunities.

It was a recognizable landmark suggested by Finn for Sammy and Tyler to locate. They'd gotten a good night's sleep at Finn's house while he and Rebel bunked at the fire station. There were snowmobile trails that led from Finn's place at Lookout Mountain toward Owens River. The Arcularius Ranch entrance was a logical meeting point for what Taylor and Mac needed to accomplish.

Very much like four cowboys on horseback might've met up on a mesa overlooking a valley, the four snowmobilers sat atop their steeds, admiring the serene valley. The snow had stopped, and the sun was shining, causing the temperatures to rise. It would've been a glorious day had it not been for the smoldering volcano to their south.

"Thank you both for your help," began Mac. "We've got a lot of ground to cover, and we're gonna do it in teams. Sammy, you're with Taylor. Ty's gonna have my back for when I get into trouble."

Tyler laughed at the way Mac phrased the statement. "You already know that you're gonna get into trouble."

"He always does," added Taylor. "Please don't let my fiancé get himself killed today. We all survived yesterday. Let's not make a silly mistake."

Mac stuck his tongue out at Taylor. "Anyway, Tyler and I will focus on the geologic side, especially cracks in the earth's surface and deformation."

"Sammy and I will search for new breaches in the form of hot springs, fumaroles, and noxious gas releases. We'll need to mask up, Sammy."

"Ugh, I hate that term. Reminds me of the pandemic."

"Well, our masks actually work, and they'll keep you alive. Plus, these have two-way communications so we can talk while we work."

"Sounds good," said Sammy as she settled onto her snowmobile.

Taylor was anxious to speak with Sammy. She'd

sensed she was in a near state of shock when they had been gathered in Finn's office earlier that morning. She seemed to be in good spirits, so maybe she could relay to Taylor what had happened to them yesterday afternoon.

Mac stood on the side of his snowmobile and pointed to Owens River Road. He looked over at Tyler, who nodded, confirming he was ready. Mac shouted as he gunned the throttle on his ride.

"Hi-yo, Silver. Away!" And off they went.

"He's nuts," said Sammy.

Taylor shook her head in disbelief and laughed. "He's an amazing man, Sammy. There was a point last summer when he and I were going to die. There was no doubt about it. Mac never gave up. He never quit looking for a way to save us. And even though he barely knew me at that point, he never gave up on me even though I was no help whatsoever. We were already in love with one another at that point. However, that was the day I removed any doubt from my mind. Even if he is a nerd."

Sammy laughed. "What are you gonna do about your wedding?"

Taylor shrugged. "Our venue at the top of Mammoth is probably scattered all over three counties. We'll have to find another spot."

Sammy adjusted her clothing and prepared to take off as Taylor did the same. "I always wanted to elope. You know, Las Vegas or the islands."

Taylor thought for a moment. This girl might be onto something.

CHAPTER FIFTY-THREE

The Long Valley Caldera

While not as large as the famed Yellowstone Caldera, Long Valley was certainly formidable. The oval-shaped depression stretched nine by eighteen miles. To the casual observer, it appeared to be a pristine stretch of land surrounded by mountains. To Taylor, it was the center of a huge cauldron of boiling rock ready to regurgitate, as it had seven hundred thousand years ago when its ash and eruptive material covered the western United States.

The caldera at Long Valley had been studied and monitored extensively by the USGS and CalVO. However, following the ARkStorm and the subsequent massive earthquakes of the previous summer, both Taylor and Mac firmly believed the geology making up the caldera's volcanic system might have changed. Its next eruption could be far deadlier than previously imagined, equivalent on a global scale to an eruption at Yellowstone. Or if the magma chambers had merged, its equivalency to Yellowstone would be warranted. However, the recent activity to the caldera's northwest, at Panum Crater, and to the southwest, at Mammoth Mountain, might forestall Long Valley's eventual eruption.

Taylor paused at the outer rim of the resurgent dome, contemplating the power these volcanoes wielded. They built mountains. They've been doing so since the beginning of the Earth's formation. They have never stopped and never will until the planet is pushed so far away from the sun that it is starved of oxygen like Mars.

She repeated her thoughts aloud, as if to drive the point home to anyone who could hear her. "They will never stop erupting. Never."

"What was that?" asked Sammy, unsure of whether Taylor was speaking to her. "I'm still getting used to this respirator thing."

Taylor, who'd been deep in thought, snapped back to the present as Sammy spoke. She needed to focus. The time to contemplate the meaning of life could come later, sitting on the deck with Mac, staring at the beast below.

"Um, sorry. My mind wandered for a moment."

"No problem. Just wanted to make sure I could hear you."

Taylor paused for a moment as she got her bearings. To help plan their day, she revealed to Sammy her mental checklist.

"If we were in a chopper, looking down, we'd be at the edge of what's called the resurgent dome. The caldera is much larger, pretty much contained within the mountains surrounding us."

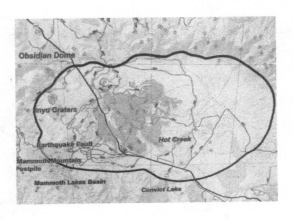

"After the supervolcano erupted, the planet healed itself. It took a couple of hundred thousand years, but during that time, there was an uplift of the caldera floor to form a huge mound. What you see before us is that dome."

"I kinda saw it before we started. It's almost directly in the middle, right?"

"Yes, exactly. It's covered in trees, which sets it apart from the rest of the caldera. Scientists have studied it for longer than you and I have been alive. It's been slowly rising at less than a quarter of an inch per year."

"That's it?" asked Sammy.

Taylor laughed. "Yeah, I know. Most people have the same reaction. We look at volcanoes as one way Earth gives birth to itself. Ask any woman who's had a baby. It's a long painful process."

Sammy laughed. "Yeah, not for me. Thanks. I'm happy with Carly and Fenway, our dogs."

"So this uplift, the caldera's contribution to the birthing process, varies from time to time. In '97 and '98, it rose a whopping seven inches. There were over a hundred and thirty earthquakes greater than magnitude three. The news media picked up on the story, and people freaked out, thinking the caldera was about to blow."

"Obviously, it didn't," interjected Sam. "Is that what we're looking for today? Uplift."

"No, that's the guys' job. When Mac moved in

with me after the earthquakes, the first thing he wanted to do was come into the caldera and look around."

"The first thing?" asked Sammy with a sly grin.

"Okay, maybe the second. But I could tell he was excited about this new direction in his life. He's kinda like me. Science first, personal relationships second."

"I get it."

"As a geophysicist, Mac is focused on the movement of the ground and what's immediately underneath it. He studies cracks in the planet surface. The rising and falling of calderas' resurgent domes. Boring stuff like that.

"Volcanologists are planet plumbers. We want to know what causes changes in the Earth's crust. You know, the cracks, crevices, quakes, and calderas' belching. For me, it's all about the magma. What internal and external pressures are changing the chamber it resides in, or the volume within a volcanic system."

Sammy looked around and then turned to face Taylor. "Last night, when I said I believed you, I meant it. You had a look in your eyes that was very convincing. Now it's just us. I'm gonna ask something. Do you believe yourself?"

Taylor burst out laughing. "I swear we must be soul sisters. You have no idea how many times I doubt myself. Here's what I know, followed by what I think.

"Prior to the ARkStorm, California was in the throes of a decade-long drought. The loss of water reduced the overlying pressure on the magma storage. During that time, hydrothermal fluids accumulated in the layer of rock on top of the magma chamber. This caused the uplift, which in turn relieved the pressure. Low pressure is good. High pressure, not so good. As you learned yesterday.

"Now, along comes the ARkStorm, dropping massive amounts of water on the state. That water had to go somewhere, so it found its way into the rock layers below the surface. A lot of it found its way into the magma chambers underneath all of these volcanoes around us, including the supervolcano beneath our feet.

"This water was turned into superheated steam, which searched for an escape route. It found a couple. At Panum Crater and then at Mammoth.

"Now, if my theory is correct, all of this magma is interconnected into one chamber or connected by geologic formations called tubes. While it makes the supervolcano larger and therefore more dangerous, the eruption at Mammoth served to release all the pressure caused by the ARkStorm's excess water, or melted snow, in the plumbing beneath our feet."

"And that's a good thing?" asked Sammy.

"It is for now. For many, many thousands of years, in fact. The last minor eruption was about one hundred thousand years ago. As the media likes to say, it's overdue for an eruption. I believe Mammoth was that eruption, and therefore, the caldera can rest for another couple of hundred thousand years before it blows off some steam."

"Works for me," said Sammy with a laugh. "Can we go to Bodie's now?"

Taylor reached down and threw a snowball in Sammy's direction, a lame effort that flew wildly behind her.

"You're already turning out to be a lousy volcanologist-in-training."

"I'm a lawyer. I have other ways of blowing shit up."

CHAPTER FIFTY-FOUR

The Long Valley Caldera

Mac stood on the skids of his snowmobile and took in Long Valley. It was a beautiful day to ride. It would've been a better day if they found that nothing had changed as a result of the eruptions at Panum Crater and Mammoth. "Okay, Tyler, we've gotta lot of ground to cover. We're gonna make a half-loop around the base of the mountains before heading into the center to look for any uplift in the caldera. There's a lot of science, if you're interested."

"Hey, I'm along for the ride. Maybe I'll learn something. Also, tell me how I can help."

"All right. First, we're going to ride along the northern side of the caldera's rim," began Mac. He pointed to the north, calling out the names of the rounded hills protruding near the caldera's rim. "Those are called obsidian domes. Technically, they're giant mounds of dense, black volcanic glass. We'll start with Deadman Creek Dome, then work our way along the cliffs at Glass Creek until we hit the third one, known as Obsidian Dome."

"Sounds good. Lead the way!"

Mac, who'd become a seasoned snowmobiler over the winter, took off with Tyler close behind. The fresh snow from the back-to-back storms made their trip across the valley slow going, not that Mac complained. He needed to be out in the fresh air on this crisp, sunny day. He wanted to put the memories of the volcano attacking them and the devastation at Mammoth Lakes out of his mind.

For Tyler, it gave him the opportunity to clear his head as well. He and Sammy had nearly died in the snowy coffin. They'd agreed not to talk about it early that morning when they finally arrived at Finn's cabin. Relieved that it was still standing, they quickly found sleep, and this morning, they vowed to put it behind them.

Yet here they were, in the middle of a supervolcano that rivaled Yellowstone in size. They'd tried to convince themselves they were not adrenaline junkies or crazed daredevils. It was freak circumstances that threw them into these predicaments. Yet when they had the opportunity to head back to the perceived safety of Central Pennsylvania, they chose to stay. *Ya only live once, right?*

Mac slowed as he approached Deadman Creek and the obsidian dome rising above it. Tyler pulled up alongside him.

Mac bent over and rested his arms on the handlebars as he spoke. The pain in his back was not going to give him a break. There wasn't enough Advil at their cabin to give him relief. The snowmobile's rough ride aggravated the injury.

"This thing is like a toddler, geologically speaking," began Mac. "Most were created around six hundred years ago."

"What are we looking for?" asked Tyler.

"Something similar to what we explored at Crater Mountain the other day. When a dome collapses, it could be a sign of an impending volcanic eruption. The caldera's dome is the last thing we'll explore. These smaller obsidian domes can give us an idea if the volcanic system has become unstable. We'll ride to the top, look for changes in the earth's surface, and then move on to the next one."

Tyler gave Mac a thumbs-up, so they started the

ascent to the top of the first dome. Domes can grow on steep slopes or even overspill summit craters, resulting in unstable rock and soil. Mac was careful not to ride too fast so they could react to anything unforeseen hidden beneath the snow.

At the summit of the Deadman Creek dome, they got out and walked around. Tyler took a moment to take pictures for Sammy to post to her Instagram account. The guys even snapped a few goofy selfies.

Once Mac was satisfied the dome was intact and none of the telltale signs of it being fractured existed, they moved on. As they rode along Deadman Creek, Mac introduced the Glass Creek dome.

"I wish you could see this in the summer months. They call it *marble cake* because there are two different magmas combined into a single dome. Since they were from two different sources, Taylor believes Glass Creek Dome is an example of her theory that the magma chambers are capable of merging."

He began up the trail carved out of the steep cliffs of the dome many years ago. He had to slow as a boulder the size of a sofa ottoman appeared in the center of the trail. It was surrounded by a dozen smaller rocks.

"Damn!" he exclaimed in frustration. "I really

didn't want to walk to the top. We don't have time for this."

"It doesn't look that bad," said Tyler. "We can move the big one together, and the smaller ones will be a piece of cake."

Mac turned and studied Tyler. He lowered his eyes. "Did you say that on purpose?"

"Um, yeah. Piece of cake. Marble cake. Right?"

"Yes, and I wish I'd thought of it. I'll have to use it on Taylor sometime."

The guys shared a laugh and talked about their gals as they tossed the smaller rocks over the edge of the lava dome. They dropped to their hands and knees to dig the snow away from the larger boulder.

Then the ground began to shake.

CHAPTER FIFTY-FIVE

The Long Valley Caldera

Taylor and Sammy were making great progress on the checklist the volcanologist had created for them. While at CalVO, Taylor had noticed their monitoring equipment at several key locations within the caldera had gone offline following the eruption at Mammoth. She started with these first, following a logical order that enabled her to observe the rest of the caldera for new fumaroles, boiling springs, and hot groundwater. New activity coupled with higher carbon dioxide and sulfur readings were telltale signs of instability in the volcanic system.

They made great progress, as Taylor was able to

take readings and samples while Sammy recorded the data for her. Next, Taylor led the way to several strategic locations she'd always preferred to observe in person near Hot Creek and around Crowley Lake in the eastern half of the caldera.

She searched for unusual hydrothermal water discharge at the creek bed as well as near rock outcroppings. The snow was deep in areas, making their traveling via snowmobile difficult. On the other hand, it enabled her to quickly identify the hot vents emitting steam and gas from thermal features under the snow.

Their final stop was at the Casa Diablo geothermal power plant on the flanks of the resurgent dome. The plant used hot water from the caldera's hydrothermal system for power production. It was a concept planned for Yellowstone albeit on a much larger scale. A group had proposed to drill deep into the Yellowstone Caldera, inject large amounts of water to create steam, and harvest geothermal energy similar to Casa Diablo.

There was one huge difference, Taylor and other volcanologists argued. Casa Diablo relied upon natural water sources already situated within the volcanic system. The developers of the Yellowstone geothermal project proposed artificially pumping millions of gallons of water underneath the caldera. A reckless notion that could result in a catastrophic event not seen since the last time Yellowstone erupted around the same time as the Long Valley Caldera.

She and Sammy had just cleared the snow away to expose the ground so Taylor could take a soil-temperature measurement at Casa Diablo. The earth's surface began to shake slowly at first. The low rumble spreading throughout the valley warned Taylor that a shallow earthquake was taking place. She rushed to her backpack and retrieved her high-powered binoculars. As she did, she followed Mac's suggested method of counting seconds to guestimate the magnitude of the quake.

She scanned the caldera, rhythmically counting to herself. One potato. Two potatoes. Three pota-toes. She stopped at twenty. It was a minor quake, perhaps an aftershock from the activity from Mammoth. Or it was an indication of trouble at Long Valley.

After the shaking stopped, she scanned the area where the obsidian domes were located. She and Mac had compared notes of how they planned to spend their day. Since they didn't have cell phone service or two-way radio capability, there was no way to communicate with one another. They'd planned on calling it quits around four that afternoon, meeting back at the Arcularius Ranch entrance.

"Oh, shit!" shouted Taylor as she pulled the binoculars away from her eyes. She immediately took another look.

"What is it?" Sammy's concerned voice seemed to wash away the feelings of relief she'd felt while hanging out with Taylor.

"There's snow kicked into the air next to Glass Creek. Dirt, too. That dome may have collapsed."

Sammy looked around, as she was unaware of their planned itinerary. "Where are the guys?"

Taylor quickly stowed away her binoculars. "Over there somewhere. Let's go!"

Mac spun around, searching for the mythical freight train that approached, a description so often attributed to the onset of an earthquake. Internally, he began to count potatoes although at this point, the magnitude of the coming quake was the least of his concerns. Rubble began cascading down the Glass Creek Dome directly toward them.

"Run!" he shouted at Tyler and immediately began to rush up the hill. Tyler presumed he meant back down the access road to the top of the obsidian mountain. He began his descent when a large boulder, bigger than Finn's snowmobile he'd been riding, landed on top of the fiberglass body and crushed it beyond recognition.

The ominous sound grew louder as Mac reached the teens in his potato count. Even as he arrived at twenty-one, the ground continued to shake, and the rocks continued to crash all around them. He noticed Tyler was not by his side.

The avalanche had picked up steam, carrying with it a blinding cloud of powdery snow. It pummeled the trail between Mac and Tyler.

"Tyler! Where are you?"

"Arrrggghhh!" he groaned in response.

Mac turned downhill, dancing and dodging the boulders, which seemed to be growing in size and speed. His visibility was obscured by the snow and debris in the air, but he pressed forward.

"Tyler!" he shouted again as the roar of the avalanche began to subside.

"Over here. I'm hit, but okay."

That didn't stop Mac's adrenaline-fueled body. The earthquake had dislodged enough rock to cause the avalanche to continue toward them. He wanted to believe the M2 or greater quake was an isolated occurrence. That it was one of many that was recorded around the caldera in a given week. That had nothing to do with the eruption of the supervolcano or even the collapse of the Glass Creek Dome.

Inexplicably, time slowed down as he made his way through the boulders tumbling past him. He caught a glimpse of Tyler's white and blue, Penn State University sweatshirt. Tyler was dancing around the rocks as well, looking down the trail for an escape route.

Mac glanced upward to follow the path of the avalanche. As he'd suspected, at the moment the quake began, the bulk of the falling rock came across the access trail downhill from their position. The face of the dome was rockier the higher it stretched from the caldera floor.

"I see you! Can you come this way?" The avalanche had subsided farther up the dome.

"Yeah!" Tyler responded as he darted and hurdled the bounding rocks. He looked like he was running an agility drill during a Steelers football practice.

As he reached Mac, he pointed to his backside. "One of them busted me in the ass. That's gonna make a hella big bruise." Mac was relieved that he wasn't hurt more seriously and that the avalanche was beginning to come to an end.

"Just tell everyone that your wife kicked your ass for bringing her on vacation to an active volcano or two."

"It was her idea!" Tyler protested. "Well, I never really thought about it. But you can bet your ass I'll research every place we go on vacation in the future. I think I'm gonna stick to Florida. What could go wrong there?"

Mega tsunamis, for one, Mac thought to himself, but why burst the guy's bubble? "Can you walk?"

Tyler rotated his hips and grimaced. Painful, but manageable. Mac's back felt the same way. Tyler added to the bad news.

"We'll have to 'cause both snowmobiles are, um ..." Tyler's voice trailed off before he explained. "One got crushed, and the other, um, is down there somewhere."

Mac gauged the distance to the top of the obsidian dome. Maybe a quarter of a mile. It would be easy to call it a day, but they needed to finish the job.

"If you can make it to the top, we can check this off our list, and I can view the next dome through binoculars. Plus, from up there, we can look for Taylor and Sammy. Hopefully, they stuck to the plan and didn't get caught up in the quake."

CHAPTER FIFTY-SIX

The Long Valley Caldera

With a lot of pissin' and moanin', the guys made their way to the top of the Glass Creek Dome. Much to Mac's relief, the dome had not collapsed. The earthquake, not unlike many others that struck from time to time, happened to impact them via the avalanche. He surveilled the entire caldera for several minutes in search of deformation or any other significant change in the planet's surface. It was exactly as he'd hoped it to be—undisturbed.

He also caught a glimpse of Taylor and Sammy racing across the valley toward the three domes. He was glad she remembered his itinerary for the day.

Now he had to signal her to let them know they were safe.

Without communications, they had several means to let the others know they might need help. One was a flare gun stored in the seat of the snowmobile. That option had met the same demise as the machine itself. The other was a signaling mirror they kept in their backpacks as part of their safety protocols. Today's bright sunny day allowed Mac to easily reflect the sun off the mirror.

Tyler took the binoculars to follow the women's progress. "They changed course straight for us. They had to have seen the reflection."

"Great! Now we have to find a way to meet them. Our road is blocked, but the back side of the dome joins the mountains. I'm pretty sure they can find their way around the dome."

Mac began walking toward the far side of the dome, keeping the sun on the mirror where Taylor could see it.

"They changed course again," announced Tyler. "They have to be tracking us, Mac. Keep going."

They slowly and carefully traversed the top of the dome, making sure the reflected light was visible to the oncoming snowmobilers. Several minutes later, Taylor led the charge up the slope through a stand of pine trees. They emerged into a clearing and slowed to a stop.

Taylor removed her ventilator mask and shouted to them, "Are you hurt?"

"I'm good. Tyler's got a boo-boo," said Mac as he burst out laughing. "Show 'em, Tyler."

Tyler turned and mooned the women, much to their delight. Sammy, always quick with the camera, took a snap. This bruised backside would live on in infamy.

The four of them traded notes and observations. While Sammy and Tyler chatted, the scientists made their way to the top of the dome and studied the caldera together.

Taylor took a deep breath, as she had many times that day. Her lungs begged to be cleaned, she thought to herself.

"You haven't been into the resurgent dome yet, have you?"

"Nope. We kinda got derailed. Our rides are crushed."

Taylor shook her head in disbelief. "Kemp will be pissed at you."

"She always is," Mac said with a shrug.

"Sammy and I can double if you guys can."

"Sure. I just have a couple of sites to check for

geophysical signals to check against my baseline conditions. If that's good, I can call it a day. What about you?"

Taylor thought for a moment. She didn't see anything through her binoculars that warranted her attention. "I have some sensor pipes in the resurgent dome I could measure. When we get back to CalVO, I'd like to compare it against the seismic wave data to get a feel of what percent of the upper chamber is melted rock. The quantities of melt have increased over the years. A significantly higher percentage could be a real problem."

Mac leaned in to kiss Taylor on the cheek. "Thanks for rescuing us."

"You owe me," she said with an elbow to the ribs.

"I already owe you. But, my darling rescuer, what can I pay you for today's services?"

Taylor turned toward Mac. She wrapped her arms around his waist and pulled his chest against hers.

"Will you please marry me before we get ourselves killed?"

Mac kissed her again. "You know what? It's time for us to think about us. Let's deal with Kemp this afternoon. Let the chips fall where they may. Tomorrow, come hell or high water, let's get hitched."

She slugged him on the chest. "I am not a horse. I am your bride-to-be. And don't you think we're gonna do this thing on the cheap. I still want my cut of your insurance money. Remember? You promised."

Mac remembered her negotiating for a cut of what the insurance company paid him for his losses caused by the earthquake storm. It was pennies on the dollar, but he gladly would give it all to the love of his life.

"Deal. Tomorrow, we set all of this aside and find the perfect place to get married. I don't care if it's on our deck. We just need to make it legal."

"Not on the deck, you dope. Don't worry about the details. I've got plans."

She began to walk away from him.

"What plans?"

"Big plans!"

"You're a bridezilla!" he shouted after her.

"You have no idea, Atwood. Now catch up before I leave you up here and find a rich doctor to marry."

CHAPTER FIFTY-SEVEN

CalVO
Bridgeport, CA

"What's this?" asked Taylor as she and Mac approached the front door of the CalVO offices in Bridgeport. A notice bearing the Mono County Sheriff's Department logo at the top had been taped to the glass door. While Mac unlocked the door, Taylor used her flashlight to read the notice aloud.

"The President of the United States has declared a national state of emergency. The text of this declaration can be found posted at local federal buildings and military facilities. In conjunction with this Federal Declaration, the Governor of the

State of California issued his Declaration of Martial Law.

"Effective immediately, until ended by a superseding decree, the Governor has declared the following to be in effect. A mandatory evacuation of all residents except for state and local officials who perform first responder duties, and essential medical personnel.

"Local law enforcement and the National Guard, in conjunction with the Federal Emergency Management Agency, will be establishing holding facilities for those displaced from their homes or who are in need of special assistance. Transportation will be provided to remove you from Mono County and the areas surrounding Mammoth Mountain. Your destination will be San Diego.

"In furtherance of these directives, the Governor has instructed the National Guard and local law enforcement to break up any unlawful assemblies and confiscate weapons, magazines, and ammunition, such actions determined to be in the best interests of the state and the safety, health, and general welfare of its citizens.

"Willful violations of the provisions of the Governor's declaration shall be punishable by imprisonment and asset forfeiture. All persons falling under the Federal Disaster Declaration will now fall under the jurisdiction of military tribunals established by this declaration."

Mac leaned against the open door as Taylor finished reading the notice. "This can't be real."

Taylor carefully peeled it off the glass. "It's a photocopy, but that's not surprising. It's a little heavy-handed."

"Do you think?" asked Mac sarcastically. "Okay, I get that you might be concerned about the people who live here. Yes, the noxious gases are a real health issue. But what about busing people to San Diego? And what do our guns have to do with anything?"

"I guess he's concerned about looting and lawlessness," Taylor surmised.

"Exactly why lawful gun owners should be able to protect themselves and their property."

"I don't want to go to San Diego, do you?" asked Taylor.

"Honey, we could hide on Bald Mountain for eternity. That road barely thaws in the summer."

"If they shut everything down, we won't be able to eat."

"We can live off the land," said Mac with a laugh. "I can hunt. You can harvest brine shrimp out of Mono Lake."

"Yuck. I'm serious. What should we do?"

"First, let's deal with Kemp. You talk about the science. I'll negotiate."

Taylor rolled her eyes. *Here he goes again.* "Negotiate for what?"

"Trust me."

She shook her head. They were gonna be on a bus to San Diego. She just knew it.

While they were anxious to call Director Kemp in Santa Rosa to get it over with, they took the time to compile their notes and prepare it in a bullet-point format. It was likely Kemp would need the supporting documents and data. She was just the next person in the chain of command that ultimately led to the president.

They were ready to place the call. Kemp had already been notified by an underling that the two scientists had logged in to their portals at CalVO. She'd messaged them several times, giving them instructions on how to connect with her via the USGS intranet since both cell service and landlines were inoperable in Bridgeport.

Mac suggested they send her the message containing their conclusions with the bullet points. "Let her digest what we have. That way, we can cut to the chase and get the hell out of here before the governor's people grab us up and throw us on a bus."

"I don't think it'll be like that, Mac." She sensed Mac was still salty. She needed to calm him down, or his frustration over the martial law declaration would impact their conversation with Director Kemp. "Let's deal with that later. Whadya think about stopping by Bodie's after our call? You know he's open."

A smile came across Mac's face. The thought about visiting their local hangout in the throes of a catastrophe was so like him—rebellious.

"Great idea. We'll fill up on wings and beer before I start hunting in the morning."

Taylor rolled her eyes and was about to throw cold water on his notion of living off the land when a notification sounded on her computer, indicating Director Kemp was online. After a moment during which the two scientists attempted to figure out the computer technology, they were ready to go.

Director Kemp led the conversation. "Of course, I'm glad both of you appear to have survived the eruption. I trust you stayed away as it took place, avoiding the urge to view it up close and personal."

Mac squeezed Taylor's hand. "Oh, yes, ma'am. Safety first!"

Kemp lowered her eyes as she tried to study

Mac's face. He pretended to cough to avoid her probing his brain.

Kemp continued, "I have already shared your findings with our team so there can be a second set of eyes taking a look. That's just protocol, as you both know, before I send anything to Reston. It's especially important since I'm sure this will land on the president's desk.

"Taylor, let me get to the bottom line. You both look exhausted, as am I, so there's no need to rehash every step of your investigation. I know that *you* are thorough."

Now it was Taylor's turn to squeeze Mac's hand. She was certain he'd picked up on Kemp's insinuation that Mac had a tendency to reach a theory without completely analyzing his hypothesis. Her squeeze was the functional equivalent of instructing a dog to heel.

"Director Kemp, as you know, I've relayed to you as well as the president that there is a strong possibility the magma chambers have merged. I believe the events of the last week plus our investigation today bolster that theory. I firmly believe the eruptions at Panum Crater and Mammoth relieved the pressure in the new, conjoined magma chambers. Therefore, I do not believe the Long Valley Caldera is in danger of eruption for many hundreds if not thousands of years."

Kemp nodded and furrowed her brow as she thumbed through a printed version of Taylor and Mac's report. She was making notes as they spoke. She removed her glasses and returned to Taylor.

"As you're aware, we've analyzed the seismic wave data and found the upper chamber to exceed thirty percent melt. That surpasses Yellowstone around this time last year."

The calderas at Yellowstone and Long Valley contained massive reservoirs of magma beneath them. Volcanologists and scientists from around the world had studied these supervolcanoes. At Long Valley, the deeper reservoir was mostly solid material mixed with approximately two percent melted rock.

A year ago, the upper chamber had risen to at least thirty percent melt. A generally accepted scientific principle was that any level above twenty-eight percent meant that an eruption was likely in the near future.

Kemp asked a follow-up question. "I know you two were very close to Mammoth at the time of eruption. This camera may not be high definition, but I can see the sunburned look on Mac. Now, you can confess your sins at a later date. What I need to know is whether the magma released from Mammoth was commensurate with the satellite images I provided to you in one of my many messages?"

Taylor anticipated this question. "More, in my opinion. Satellite imagery is very one-dimensional. And it couldn't account for the lava flows obscured by the snowpack and the blizzard. I believe the volume of magma released from the volcano on the southern and southwestern flanks of Mammoth was greater than the imagery portrayed."

Kemp studied her notes. "So if you're correct and the magma chambers have merged, then the eruption at Mammoth would necessarily release the pressure under the caldera."

"Yes, ma'am."

Kemp sighed. "Did you relay your theory to the president?"

Taylor hesitated. She'd overstepped her bounds when she relayed her merged-chamber theory to President Caldwell. Mac was right, Kemp had a way of reading them. It was uncanny. She didn't dare lie.

"We did, although, of course, that was before Mammoth's eruption. I understand he's ordered a mass evacuation of the western states. Frankly, I think that decision was premature."

Kemp shrugged. "It is an election year. He's

damned if he doesn't and will be judged harshly if nothing happens. There is no completely right answer at this point until the passage of time."

"We agree," added Taylor.

"Mac, you've been awfully quiet. That's rare for you."

"Taylor has this part of the conversation covered," he said.

"This part? What's the next part other than you two need to evacuate per the governor's orders."

"Yeah, about that," began Mac. "They want us to load onto a bus and travel to San Diego. We'd rather not. In fact, we feel like we could help out by staying here."

"Nope. You gotta go. I've already fought this battle."

Mac squeezed Taylor's hand. "Okay, I respect that. Unfortunately, we can't access our money at the bank because it was, um, destroyed by a lava bomb. May we use our USGS credit cards to cover our expenses while we find a hotel room? You know, room, food, incidentals."

Kemp thought for a moment. "Well, you may not have to go far. That ex-sheriff governor of Nevada didn't obey the president's emergency declaration and mandatory evacuation orders. He made a big speech about how Vegas never sleeps or some such. Anyway, the answer is yes. Hopefully, you can find lodging in Reno or Las Vegas or some of the outlying communities. I'll notify accounting and increase your limits."

"Thank you," said Mac, trying to contain his excitement.

"Nothing crazy, you two," admonished Kemp.

Mac gave her a thumbs-up. "You know me, Director Kemp. I live frugally."

"Yeah, okay," she said, her voice full of sarcasm. "Both of you. Leave first thing in the morning, or you'll be on a bus. The National Guard is due to arrive late morning tomorrow."

They disconnected the intranet feed. The two of them scrambled to log out of their portals so what they said next wouldn't be heard by anyone.

"Are you logged out?" asked Mac.

"Yup! You know what this means, right?"

"Vegas, baby!" Mac exclaimed as he scooped her up in his arms and twirled her around.

"But first, how 'bout Bodie's? I'll buy."

"On the company card?" asked Mac with a sly grin.

"You betcha!"

And they were off.

CHAPTER FIFTY-EIGHT

Bodie's Roadhouse
Lee Vining, CA

Bodie's Roadhouse was living up to its name. It had become a place for the travelers to gather to share stories and the displaced to share a cabin. Word of the governor's martial law declaration had spread throughout the community. Many feared Bodie's would be closed, and they'd be forced out of their homes despite the fact they lived many miles away from Mammoth Mountain.

Once again, even without power, Jimmy managed to keep the doors open and the beer cold, which wasn't much of a problem since he stashed it in snowdrifts behind the bar. The generator enabled him to offer a limited menu, but most of his customers that late afternoon were there for the alcohol.

And so it flowed. The raucous crowd was almost celebratory. Surviving a volcano eruption can do that for one's psyche. Others were angered about the governor's actions. They threatened to move to Nevada, where the governor had kept the state open. Many questioned the president's decision to evacuate. They doubted the Long Valley Caldera was going to blow. They'd always been assured it wouldn't during their lifetimes. However, others pointed out the so-called experts had said the same thing about Mammoth Mountain, and look what had happened.

When Taylor and Mac arrived at the parking lot and realized they'd have to park across the highway, they considered returning to their cabin to relax. Yet they felt compelled to be around their neighbors. Even though they knew very few people outside of work, it was the camaraderie of their fellow survivors they looked forward to.

They entered Bodie's and marveled at the packed crowd. Jimmy had hired a couple of local women to help him serve his customers. He paid them in food and drink. Mac scanned the restaurant, looking for a place to sit or a friendly face to join.

"Mac! Over here!" Tyler slid out of the bench seat he shared with Sammy and waved them over. There were half a dozen beer bottles stacked on the table. "We've been holding a table, figuring you guys or Finn might show up."

He and Tyler exchanged a bro hug while Sammy spoke to Taylor. "How did it go at work? I sensed you were a little nervous about talking with your director."

"Yeah, mainly because I knew that our report would be sitting on the president's desk by the end of the day."

"Did you tell them what you really thought?" Sammy asked.

"Well, let's say I sugarcoated it a little. Here's the thing. He's ordered the evacuation already. It's too late for me to dissuade him. Plus, have you heard about the National Guard coming to evacuate everybody?"

"Yeah, Ty and I talked about it. We figured Finn would be spending his nights at the fire hall, and I've got to get back to the office in a few days. We've got this rental car, so we decided to drive back to Pennsylvania tomorrow, or as far as we can before we run out of gas."

One of Jimmy's temporary servers approached the table. "We have beer and shots. That's about it."

"Eureka?" asked Mac.

"Yep."

"Four of those. And we'll start a tab."

"Mac, right?" the server asked.

Mac scowled. How did she know his name? He glanced past her and saw Jimmy standing with his arms folded, staring between two burly guys to make eye contact with Mac.

"Yeah. So?"

"He said cash—"

Taylor cut her off. She handed the woman her USGS credit card. "I know the power is off, and he has no internet. Just ask him to write the number down and charge it when he can. I'll cover theirs, too."

"Sure thing."

Mac brooded. "I'm so over him hating on me. One of these days, we're gonna have it out."

Taylor laughed. "Big baby. He's just messing with you. I've known Jimmy for a long time. That means he likes you."

Mac was about to belabor the point when Tyler

noticed Finn and Rebel arrive. "I can't believe it. I thought for sure he'd have to stay in town. Hey, Finn!"

Rebel responded with a bark and rushed over to the table. Licks and hugs were exchanged with everyone at the table. They rearranged their seating to make room for Finn on one side and Rebel to sit directly across from him, looking like a big dog. Finn dropped his keys and a handheld radio unit on the table in front of him.

He flagged down the server and asked for a shot of whiskey as he relayed what he'd learned throughout the day. Taylor picked up on his dour mood.

"The sun helped a lot today. The roads are clearing up, which has eliminated a lot of the congestion and accidents to respond to. The winds died down, so we were able to extinguish the structure fires. The woods are still burning around the south side of the mountain near Horseshoe Lake. The CO_2 and sulfur dioxide levels were so bad, we couldn't even consider going in there. The forest fires will burn themselves out eventually."

"What about lava flow?" asked Taylor.

"Slowing down considerably. Again, on the south and west sides of the mountain. I would say the effect of the eruption on the rest of the mountain has stabilized."

The server returned and set a bottle of Jameson's on the table with five shot glasses.

"Where did this come from?" asked Finn.

A voice behind him responded, "From me, you lousy Irishman. I keep it behind the bar for my good customers, not the likes of you." Jimmy let out a hearty laugh.

Finn dropped his chin to his chest. The others thought he'd enjoy the playful back-and-forth he was known for when interacting with Jimmy.

He leaned back against the booth and looked Jimmy in the eye. "You're a good man. I needed this. Thank you." Finn appeared genuinely touched by the gesture.

Jimmy was taken aback by Finn's demeanor. He squeezed Finn on the shoulder and nodded. "So are you, my friend. Thank you for saving the lives of so many friends and neighbors."

"Just doin' my job," he said as he fiddled with the shot glasses.

Jimmy frowned and studied the faces of the two couples. "Well, it needed to be said." He patted Finn on the back and then handed Taylor her credit card. "No need for this, pretty lady. Drinks are on me."

The group thanked Jimmy and then turned their attention to Finn, who poured shots for everyone. However, rather than his customary toast, he slugged it down and poured another.

It was Sammy who tried to get to the bottom of Finn's melancholy state of mind.

"Rough day, huh?"

"Yes, 'twas," he replied. He let out a sigh and was in deep thought for a moment. He reached into his pocket and laid a crumpled copy of the martial law declaration on the table. "Do you all know about this?"

"We do," replied Taylor. "We were just talking about what was next for all of us."

Finn drank another shot. "I've already been visited by their colonel and his captain. I was informed they were bringing in experts to take over the fire and rescue operations. I was then informed my duties would be supervising the engine companies."

Sammy leaned forward. "Wait, what? Were you, um, demoted?"

Finn nodded in response.

Sammy was incredulous. "But why? Look what you did to save the town. You saved lives."

"They have no right," added Tyler.

Finn shrugged. "Yes, they do, Ty. Martial law allows them to do whatever they damn well please. But you know what? I don't have to go along with it."

"What can you do?" asked Tyler.

"I quit. Yes, sir. That's what I did. I quit."

"Whoa!" exclaimed Tyler. "Are you sure? I mean, they'll be gone eventually, and you'll be in charge again."

Finn shook his head. "Maybe. I dunno. Our fair town will never be the same. The ski resort will be closed, maybe forever. That means the tourism will dry up. The businesses will close one by one. Residents will leave to find jobs. Mammoth Lakes will become a ghost town."

"What are you gonna do?" asked Mac.

He poured another shot. "For now, I'm gonna drown my sorrows in the Scotsman's Irish whiskey." He chuckled at his lighthearted response.

Taylor pointed at his radio. "What's that?"

Finn laughed as he slid it over to her. "Yeah, a parting gift or two they forgot about. Before I quit, they'd issued me this satellite telephone so I could direct the engine companies on calls. It works just like a cell phone except uses Starlink. The keys are to the gas and supply depot. I forgot they were in my pocket when I left."

Taylor fiddled with the phone to study how it worked. It was no different than a portable house phone.

"May I make a call?" she asked.

"By all means. It's the government's dime."

Taylor eased out of the booth and exited Bodie's. She was gone for several minutes, during which time they made small talk about the effectiveness of the martial law declaration. Sammy weighed in on its legality. All thought it was overbearing in many respects.

Taylor returned from placing her call with a huge smile on her face.

"Spill," said Mac.

"How would you guys like to drive to Vegas?" Before anyone replied, she laid out the plan. "Tyler, you guys were headed back to Pennsylvania, right? Can you go through Las Vegas?"

"Sure. I don't see why not."

Taylor turned to Finn. "And you have some free time, right?"

"Of course, lass. However, I also have Rebel to tend to, and I have to tell you, hotel rooms will be impossible to find."

"Leave that to me," she said. "Are you in?"

Finn looked at Rebel. "What do you think?"
Rebel barked.

"He's in!" exclaimed Sammy.

Finn shook his head. "Vegas hotels won't allow pets. I just don't think this—"

Taylor politely raised her hand to cut him off. "Everybody, leave the details to me. Are we a green light for Vegas, or what?"

"Hell yeah!" exclaimed Tyler. "Are we leaving now?"

Mac, who'd said nothing since Taylor returned, replied, "What about first thing in the morning? We're gonna need to find gas."

Finn picked up the keys and gave them a jiggle. "The fuel depot is a block behind Station 1. Meet us there at eight in the morning. We'll top off our tanks and head out."

Everyone exchanged high fives and took another shot of Jameson's.

While the others talked, Mac leaned over to whisper to Taylor, "Okay, how did you pull all of this off?"

"Oh, my sweet fiancé, I called your future father-in-law, the ambassador."

CHAPTER FIFTY-NINE

The Golden Nugget
Downtown Las Vegas, Nevada

The three-hundred-mile trek from Mammoth Lakes
to Las Vegas was remarkably uneventful. The only
traffic along the deserted stretch of highway came
from Mammoth Lakes refugees, most of whom had
left the day before or awaited transportation to the
San Diego FEMA holding facilities. Their drive took
them through barren landscape into a valley full of
thousands of homes as they entered North Las
Vegas.

Twice while they were on the road, Finn stopped
to allow Taylor to place phone calls. Her father, who

had substantial contacts throughout the business world, had arranged for them to stay at the famed Golden Nugget casino and hotel in downtown Las Vegas. When she told everyone that a suite large enough to accommodate all of them, plus Rebel, was awaiting them, their excitement was overwhelming. They couldn't get there fast enough.

Upon arrival, they were greeted at valet parking by a concierge who escorted them directly to the elevators. There was no need to check in, she'd said, as everything from food to drinks to the room were compliments of the hotel.

The anticipation and excitement continued as they passed through the elegant lobby. The Golden Nugget exuded a classic charm with chandeliers hanging from the high ceiling and marble floors gleaming under the soft glow of the ornate light fixtures.

"Everything is golden," whispered Sammy to Taylor as they walked through. Their attention was suddenly drawn toward the casino, where a man whooped and hollered over a win at the craps table.

"Yeah, it's paid for by those people," she said, nodding toward the casino gamblers.

The young woman waited by the elevator until it opened. "I'm going to turn you over to William, who will be your valet during your stay. Thank you and enjoy." She made eye contact with everyone and slowly backed away from the group.

"Welcome to the Golden Nugget, ladies and gentlemen," William said with genuine enthusiasm. "We are delighted to have you as our guests in our luxurious Spa Suite in the Spa Tower. You're in for a treat!"

Taylor couldn't help but glance at Mac with a wide grin as their eyes met. He winked at her and turned to William.

"Thank you so much," Mac replied, appreciating the warm hospitality.

"It will be our pleasure. Please, follow me to the Spa Tower."

William led the group through the casino floor, a vibrant atmosphere buzzing with excitement as people tried their luck on the slot machines and gaming tables. The dazzling lights and ringing slot machines created a magical ambiance, typical of Las Vegas. William pointed out the amenities of the hotel as they walked.

"Here at the Golden Nugget, we pride ourselves on providing a first-class experience for all our guests," William explained as they made their way to the dedicated elevators for the Spa Tower. "Our casino offers a wide range of table games and slot machines, all complemented by a variety of restaurants, bars, and entertainment options. You'll never run out of things to do here!"

"Are the shops open?" Taylor asked. "We have limited clothes with us. We, um, had to leave Mammoth Lakes."

"Oh dear. I am so sorry. But the answer is yes. Everything is open in the city that never sleeps."

Taylor leaned over to Sammy. "Are you up for some shopping? I'm pretty sure the boys will wanna gamble."

"Absolutely. At least we'll have something to show for the money we contribute to all of this."

The women continued to conspire as they entered the elevator. The ride up the Spa Tower was swift, and the doors opened to reveal a sumptuous corridor leading to their suite. As they entered, gasps of astonishment and awe escaped from the lips of Taylor, Mac, and their friends.

The Spa Suite was nothing short of spectacular, boasting an expansive living area with plush sofas, a dining table, and a wet bar adorned with crystal glasses. The floor-to-ceiling windows offered an unparalleled view of the glittering Las Vegas Strip, casting a spell on everyone in the room. The master bedroom was equally impressive, adorned with opulent decor and a bed fit for royalty, or honeymooners. But the highlight was the extravagant bathroom, featuring a marble-clad spa tub and a steam shower that promised pure relaxation.

"Wow, this is incredible!" Finn exclaimed, hardly believing their luck. "You have to tell your father thank you."

"I can't believe we get to stay here!" Tyler added, equally amazed.

As if the suite itself wasn't enough, a table in the corner was adorned with champagne bottles chilling in an ice bucket and an assortment of delectable appetizers waiting to be devoured.

"Compliments of the Golden Nugget," William said with a smile. "Please enjoy these treats as you settle in. And if there's anything else you need, don't hesitate to call our concierge service."

"Thank you so much," Taylor said gratefully, her heart filled with happiness and gratitude. She slipped William a twenty-dollar bill.

Once the valet departed, the friends took a moment to soak in the sheer luxury surrounding them. They raised their glasses in a toast to the opportunity to enjoy this opulence, even if it was just for a couple of nights.

"I have another toast," began Mac as he raised his glass. "To my fiancée. The love of my life. The woman who rescued me in more ways than one. I cannot wait to marry you."

The group toasted the happy couple's engagement, their laughter and clinking glasses filling the suite with joy.

"What's the holdup?" asked Sammy. "Vegas is the wedding capital of the world."

Mac thought for a moment. "I don't know. Taylor had something far different in mind before Mammoth had other plans."

Taylor wrapped her arm around Mac's waist. "I'll marry you anywhere, any time. When I said yes, I didn't have conditions."

Mac lowered his eyes and whispered to her, "I seem to remember a couple."

She kissed him. "Consider them waived. Let's get hitched in Vegas. Wanna?"

"What about our families?" he asked.

"We'll take pictures and video. They'll be fine."

Mac reached for the bottle of champagne and topped off their glasses. "Well, there you have it. We're getting married in Vegas!"

"When?" asked Finn.

Taylor and Mac looked at each other and

shrugged. Taylor responded, "They have places that perform wedding ceremonies twenty-four seven. But with a day of planning, we could do something memorable. Sammy, will you help?"

"Sounds good. Tomorrow?"

"Tomorrow it is!" exclaimed Taylor to clinking glasses.

CHAPTER SIXTY

Little White Wedding Chapel
Las Vegas, NV

Since they met, Taylor and Mac knew they were
meant to be together. They embraced adventure and
spontaneity, whether they liked it or not. So when
the time came for them to tie the knot, they decided
to do it in a way that was as unique and
extraordinary as their love. Las Vegas, with its glitzy
lights and a promise of surprises around every
corner, seemed like the perfect destination for their
wedding. It's funny how things work out.

Las Vegas was truly the wedding capital of the
world, and the competition wasn't even close. The

city's most iconic venue, the Little White Wedding Chapel on the Las Vegas Strip, had performed weddings for A-list stars such as Bruce Willis, Demi Moore, Britney Spears, Ben Affleck, and Jennifer Lopez.

For the rest of those who chose the venue, some were in a hurry and wanted a simple, legal wedding. Others took advantage of their many packages, which ranged from Elvis acting as the officiant to getting married in a helicopter. The owner, Charolette Richards, had encouraged her couples to be creative. Make memories, she'd said.

After meeting with the staff at the chapel, Taylor came up with an idea that would be unforgettable and apropos considering what they'd just been through. She and Sammy explored shops around the Strip as well as near downtown to gather everything they needed to pull off the elaborate ceremony.

They were in high spirits when they returned to the Golden Nugget. And so were the guys. Each of them had won money, a remarkable feat in Las Vegas. Eventually, gamblers give back their winnings and then some. The three vowed to quit while they were ahead even though it meant wandering around the casino watching others play.

Finn marveled at the diversity of the players.

They were from all over the world. He struck up conversations with fellow Irishmen as well as a couple of firefighters from Texas. Tyler saw some Steelers fans wearing sweatshirts bearing the colors and logo of the team. Naturally, he stopped to speak with them. Asians seemed to dominate the contingent from foreign countries.

For Mac, he was soaking it all in, wondering what Taylor had in store for them. He'd been contemplating their future together. Just because Mammoth Mountain had erupted didn't mean their work at the deadly Long Valley supervolcano ended. It would require a lifetime of monitoring until a new group of geophysicists and volcanologists stepped in to take over that responsibility.

He and Taylor could take some time off to honeymoon, although it would likely be limited to traveling the country. There was family to visit and sights to see. Flights were grounded because of the threat of the caldera erupting, but that would likely change soon. The wheels of commerce couldn't be stopped for long. Ask the governor of Nevada.

Finally, Taylor and Sammy returned. With the help of the bellman, they brought costumes and props up to the suite and revealed them to the group. After the hilarity died down, she urged everyone to get ready as the hour of the nuptials approached.

The five of them were quite a sight as they made their way to the limousine provided by the Golden Nugget. The short ride down Las Vegas Boulevard past the intersection with Charleston Boulevard was full of picture taking and laughter. And the celebratory champagne was already flowing.

They made a quick stop at the Clark County Marriage License Bureau to obtain their license. The license clerks manned their offices every minute of every day throughout the year. Weddings were a cash cow for Clark County.

Finally, they arrived at the Little White Wedding Chapel and bailed out of the back of the limo. Sammy and Tyler rushed inside with the wedding officiant's costume and props for where the wedding would be performed.

After a lot of scampering around, everyone was ready. The wedding officiant was a great sport. The vast majority of the weddings he performed required him to assume the Elvis persona. The man, a local dentist named Vincent Grosso, was an exceptional Elvis impersonator. His singing voice was indistinguishable from the King himself.

Today, however, he was none other than Bigfoot.

Yes, the big, hairy humanlike creature believed to inhabit the forests of North America, including those around Mammoth Mountain. Sometimes called Sasquatch, visitors to Mammoth enjoyed looking for tracks of the humanoid creature. Some fell for hoaxes. Others swore on their lives that they had been within a few feet of the smelly beast.

Meanwhile, the loving couple to be married stood across from each other, dressed like space aliens. Unidentified flying objects have been associated with volcanoes for decades. Also known as *vufos*, some people believed extraterrestrial spacecraft were attracted to the heat and energy emitted by volcanoes. Naturally, these beliefs were debunked as absolute nonsense until 2023 when a congressional commission successfully pried the truth out of the Pentagon. Both videos and firsthand testimony showed the world that we were not alone.

So space aliens Taylor and Mac prepared to join one another in holy matrimony amidst décor and costumes appropriate for two scientists dedicated to the study of Mammoth Mountain and the ticking time bomb beneath the Long Valley Caldera.

Bigfoot began the ceremony with a heartfelt speech about love, companionship, and the wonders of the world. His deep, resonant voice echoed through the chapel, captivating everyone present, including the next wedding party in line. He spoke about how love could be found in the most unexpected places, ironic considering Taylor and Mac had almost died in the process of falling in love.

The couple exchanged vows, promising to love and support each other through all of life's adventures, whether they were exploring active volcanoes or simply sitting on their deck together staring at the caldera on a lazy afternoon. Finn, Sammy, and Tyler couldn't help but smile and shed a few tears of joy as they witnessed the heartfelt words being spoken.

Just as the two extraterrestrial beings, looking like friendly space aliens from a sci-fi movie, were about to exchange rings they'd purchased at the Golden Nugget, the chapel seemed to glow with an otherworldly light. The cosmic witnesses beamed, showcasing their approval with nods and applause. For a time, reality was vanquished during the moment of unity where different worlds came together to celebrate the love of two extraordinary individuals.

After the final pronouncement of their marriage, Taylor and Mac sealed their commitment with a simple kiss through the holes of their space alien masks. The crowd erupted into cheers and applause once again as the newlyweds beamed at each other, feeling an overwhelming sense of happiness and love.

Taylor and Mac left the chapel hand in hand, knowing they had just experienced a wedding like no other. It was a celebration of love, friendship, and the magic of life itself. And with Finn, Tyler, and Sammy by their side, friends who'd come together with a remarkable story of their own, the five had a common bond that they'd carry for the rest of their lives.

THANK YOU FOR READING MAMMOTH!

If you enjoyed it, I'd be grateful if you'd take a moment to write a short review (just a few words are needed) and post it on Amazon. Amazon uses complicated algorithms to determine what books are recommended to readers. Sales are, of course, a factor, but so are the quantities of reviews my books get. By taking a few seconds to leave a review, you help me out and also help new readers learn about my work.

Sign up to my email list to learn about upcoming titles, deals, contests, appearances, and more!

Sign up at BobbyAkart.com

READ ON to see what's coming next and to learn the backstory behind the writing of this novel. Also, I have some news media excerpts related to the story that might be of interest. They're the types of stories you don't ordinarily see. If you did, you might be stocking up on the basics because you never know when the day before, is the day before. Prepare for tomorrow.

**MADE IN CHINA, a Gunner Fox
standalone novel.**

*A daring rescue leads to a startling
discovery.*
*Two geopolitical titans battle over the
sovereignty of a tiny nation.*
*America is under attack as a deadly game
of predator and prey unfolds in
a pulse-pounding race to prevent the
heartbeat of America from being stopped.*

A standalone thriller from international bestselling
author, Bobby Akart, one of America's favorite story-

tellers, who delivers up-all-night thrillers to readers in 245 countries and territories worldwide.

Gunner Fox returns as the world teeters on the brink of chaos. The decades-old political battle between the United States and China over Taiwan takes a menacing new turn. As diplomats exchange heated words on the global stage, a far more dangerous battle unfolds in the shadows—a battle where the combatants are elusive, and the stakes are nothing less than the destruction of the American way of life.

"... if you like Sigma Force, Mitch Rapp or Scot Horvath, you will love Gunner Fox!"

As the war of words escalate, a clandestine group of Chinese operatives forge an unholy alliance with a Mexican drug cartel to enter the United States with a singular goal - destroy the American way of life and methodically bring the nation to its knees.

As Washington escalates economic and geopolitical sanctions, Beijing attacks the very fabric of America by targeting our critical infrastructure from banking to medical to the power grid. Only, this battle wasn't fought with bullets or bombs. They simply used the parts they've been selling to America for years to bring us to our knees.

*"With a **Gunner Fox** novel, your emotions are on a roller coaster, and it's a ride that will leave you breathless."*

As tensions escalate, Gunner Fox and the Gray Fox unit must outwit, outmaneuver, and outfight an enemy that knows no boundaries. With the fate of a nation hanging in the balance, can Gunner Fox hunt team the elusive operatives behind the chaos before the ultimate act of terrorism plunges the United States into darkness forever?

"Author Bobby Akart again does a masterful job of blending reality with fiction by providing another well-researched store line with incredibly compelling characters."

437

This modern-day, fact-based thriller will have you whispering just one more chapter until the end.

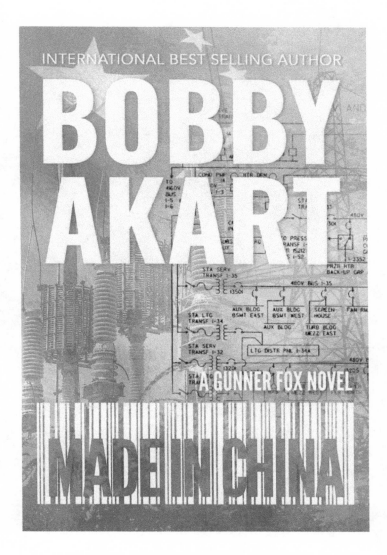

Available on Amazon by clicking here.

AUTHOR'S NOTES

August, 2023

The Volcanoes are, in fact, tailor-made to kill human beings. Scientists believe a supervolcano was responsible for the Permian extinction event that wiped out the dinosaurs while nearly exterminating the budding human race. You can't find a catastrophe much deadlier than that.

However, California's next Big One may not be an earthquake. According to a new study from the USGS, a future volcanic eruption at Mammoth Mountain and the Long Valley Caldera is not only inevitable, it's likely.

The Long Valley Caldera, like her big sister Yellowstone in Wyoming, is getting ready to super-erupt again, possibly covering half of North America in ash. As the magma beneath the caldera gets hot and bothered after 700,000 years, scientists are concerned that the intense focus on Yellowstone is misguided.

Geophysicists warn that the Long Valley Caldera began growing around 1978 and has been doing so ever since. This gradual expansion likely represents the influx of molten rock into the magma chamber below the supervolcano, essentially filling the tank in preparation for the next eruption.

I've included the history and the science I relied on when writing this novel. I've also shared some insider tidbits about the story that I hope you'll enjoy.

WHAT IF FICTION BECOMES REALITY

If a moderately-sized volcano such as Mount Saint Helens and Mount Pinatubo can kill hundreds, what might happen if the Long Valley Caldera let loose with another blast?

It's hard to imagine the destructive force caused by the volumes of magma, ash, and gases unleashed in an explosion of that magnitude. The pyroclastic flows, lava floods, and poisonous gases would destroy the region around Mammoth Falls. The kill zone would stretch from the California coast to Nebraska. Half the United States would be covered in a blanket of utter devastation.

This would be just the beginning. The impact on America would be unfathomable. Forget about mundane things like loss of the power grid, internet, and all forms of transportation. Natural disasters are often measured in terms of economic losses. When the Long Valley Caldera erupts, the impact will be measured by the small percentage of Americans who survive.

You see, the death toll will be determined two ways: One, by the number of people who are killed immediately. Two, by the number of people who will die of respiratory disease, starvation, and dysentery.

Looking for a bright side? Calderas around the world huff and puff for decades without producing a cataclysmic eruption. Until they do.

Now, for some interesting tidbits that went into the writing of this novel.

At the ripe old age of 63, there are times when I find myself having difficulty relating to high school and college kids. When the opportunity arose to introduce the group of four friends in the Prologue who met with a boiling, gassy demise, I had to dig deep in the memory banks to create them. As I explained to you in the novel, dear reader, their nicknames were based on the Bullwinkle and Rocky cartoon series. I had to ask myself, "Self, do younger readers have any idea of who these character names were based upon?" The irony that the cartoon series began during the month of my birth was not lost upon me. That was a long time ago. Honestly, I don't know if kids watch cartoons anymore. One of these days, I'll gather the courage to ask one. My longtime editor, Pauline Nolet, lives in Canada. I'll ask her if she watched Bullwinkle and Rocky.

Oh, yeah. Back in the day, as they say, I was a pretty good skier. I could tackle most advanced slopes during my trips to the Rockies. The black diamond slopes were for the crazies. I valued my life too much.

With Mammoth, my tradition continued by purchasing apparel that was appropriate for the novel I was writing. In Chapter 2, there was reference to a sweatshirt bearing the Ski Mammoth resort's logo. I have a long sleeve tee shirt that has the same logo. Also, as I write these Author's Notes, I'm wearing the red tee shirt referenced in Chapter 2 portraying an erupting volcano graphic and the words, *Volcanoes Kick Ash. Sorry, my Fault*, appeared in Fractured.

In Chapter 3, readers are introduced to Finn's dog, Rebel, named after my wife Dani's Labrador, when she was growing up. Rebel was highly intelligent and loyal to her. We're convinced a little part of Rebel found her way into one of our English Bull-dogs, Woolie Bullie.

For the story, I had to create a local bar and grill that was away from the tourist areas in Mammoth Lakes. While Bodie's Roadhouse was a figment of my imagination, it's the kind of place I would frequent if it existed.

Bodies needed to be a local hangout with a pool table. The backstory of Taylor's pool shark capability was actually based on my own experience. Every year, at Spring Break, I'd travel to Colorado with Pop and two of his friends. We'd drive from Knoxville, twenty-two hours without stopping through blizzard conditions across Kansas and into Eastern Colorado. We stayed in Georgetown, Colorado, an old mining town due west of Denver. We skied A-Basin and Loveland on the eastern side of the Continental Divide and then spent several days in a row at Breckenridge and Keystone. In Georgetown, there was a bar with a couple of pool tables where we'd hang out at night. I was very good at shooting pool and took on all challengers. There were some fussy truckers from time to time. Lol.

In Bodie's, Finn enjoys a shot of rye made by Devils Creek Distillery located in Mammoth Lakes.

In Chapter 8, I elected to transform the mythical jackalope to a real critter just for grins and giggles. I know. I know. I write fact-based science fiction. But I wanted to have a little fun with the jackalope because many people aren't sure whether it exists or not. And, for readers of my Geostorm series, you may have noticed the reference to Dr. Kristi Boone, the zoologist who worked at the Brookfield Zoo during the story. She made a cameo appearance, of sorts, in Mammoth. I like to do that from time to time as a nod of thanks to my long-time readers.

In Chapter 18, I took a moment to relay the story of the ski patrollers who perished marking a fumarole on Mammoth Mountain. The incident occurred on April 6, 2006, on the Christmas Bowl Run on the other side of the mountain. Although I took the creative license to place the horrible tragedy near the location of a new fumarole Taylor and Mac were inspecting on the south side of the mountain, I wanted to honor those who died to help others. These brave men who devoted their lives to protecting skiers from danger and rescuing those who'd been injured, lost their lives in the line of duty. They, and their families, deserve a word in our prayers.

Later in the chapter, I shifted from reverent to

irreverent, simply because the story gave me the opportunity. Taylor and Mac had a playful exchange about this guy Pete. When Taylor asked Mac, *Why do you think this up this shit?*, I couldn't help but feel she was asking your humble author that question, rather than her fictional fiancé. So, as I often do, I turned to Google.

In the early 1900s, the name, Pete, was substituted for Christ to avoid using the Lord's name inappropriately. From there, I fell down the proverbial rabbit hole. Did you know there is an annual *For Pete's Sake Day* in Lebanon, Pennsylvania? What do they do on *For Pete's Sake Day?* Nothing. [Insert eye roll here]. As the rabbit hole got deeper, I learned the town also celebrates, *Hoodie-Hoo Day*. To commemorate the occasion, they go outdoors and yell, Hoodie-Hoo, to chase away winter and make ready for spring. I guess they only have groundhogs in Punxsutawney, P - A.

And there you have it. You learned something new today.

Speaking of learning something new, in Chapter 19, I couldn't help myself. I inserted myself into the story as an unnamed author hosting a book signing for a future thriller series—*Behind the Gates*. I did something similar in Perfect Storm. Now, I've told no one about *Behind the Gates* that will be released in late fall after I publish *Made In China*, a Gunner Fox novel. Those of you loyal readers who've enjoyed these Author's Notes are the first to know the breaking news.

In Chapter 22, I wrote one of the best passages in my sixty-six novels to date. Remember when Taylor and Mac were on the flight to Washington to meet with the president? They discuss the most likely question they'd face—*When will the volcano blow?* Here's what I wrote. You can insert any "expert" or government agency in exchange with USGS and it fits. Think about this the next time the experts feed you a line of bullshit about the threats of solar flares, earthquakes, volcanoes, and tsunamis. Here it is again:

Taylor: "Or even use the standard USGS line that reads something like—don't worry, the volcano won't blow anytime soon."

Mac: Mac let out a hearty laugh which drew the attention of the other passengers across the aisle. "That bullshit always cracks me up. One side of the USGS mouth tells the world volcanoes are impossible to predict. The other side of the mouth says, don't worry, there's no danger of an eruption for a long time. Which is it? Don't know or don't worry because we do know it won't?"

This bears repeating. *Which is it? Don't know or don't worry because we do know it won't.* It's this lack of transparency, among other reasons, that Dani and I always prepare for the worst-case scenario.

As a kid, I enjoyed watching shows like The Lone Ranger and Bonanza. In Chapter 52. when I used the Lone Ranger's famous saying, Hi-yo, Silver. Away!, I didn't make a mistake. That was the correct saying, not Hi-Ho. Those were Snow White's guys.

Taylor and Mac had to get married and what better place than Las Vegas. We used to live in the Soho Lofts overlooking the famed Las Vegas strip. Our loft was eye level to the Stratosphere. Also, you could see the Little White Wedding Chapel from our balcony. Let me say, that place was as busy as a Waffle House on a Friday night.

Finally, the wedding itself needed to be memorable while appropriate to the story. It's custom to get married by Elvis. My first thought was to introduce my friend and dentist, Dr. Vincent Grosso who is a great guy and an incredibly talented Elvis impersonator. I bet you can't say that about your dentist.

Anyway, it's a thing to get married by Elvis if you

choose Vegas. Although, I think it's soooo expected. I had a better idea.

The folklore surrounding Mammoth Mountain is extensive. There are stories of alien aircraft shooting out of the top of the mountain when earthquakes rattle the region. Odd creatures have been sighted in Mono Lake. And, being located in the Sierra Nevada Mountains, Sasquatch, the formidable ape-like creature with the incredibly big feet and stinky armpits, is known to roam the forests. Naturally, Dani found me a tee shirt representing all of this. She's a really good wife like that.

Back to the nuptials. Taylor and Mac, after all they'd been through in my stories, along with their new friends, Finn, Sammy and Tyler, deserved a wedding to be remembered. The happy couple who had more than nine lives between them, certainly could be looked at as space aliens. And, Dr. Grosso (with apologies, my friend), could step out of his usual Elvis role and don the Sasquatch suit. It was a wedding event for the ages.

Thanks y'all for reading another one of my stories. I've got a couple hundred more to come.

GUESS WHAT, CALIFORNIA?
YOU NEED TO PREPARE FOR
ERUPTING VOLCANOES

~ PBS, March 8, 2023

Earthquakes, wildfires, floods. If you live in California, you're likely aware of these natural hazards and the dangers associated with them.

Based on records of volcanic history, geologists calculate the chance of an eruption in California over the next 30 years at 19 percent. For comparison, scientists have pegged the 30-year probability of a major earthquake in the Bay Area along the San Andreas Fault at about 22 percent.

Jessica Ball, a geologist with the California Volcano Observatory (CalVO)says many Californians aren't aware of the possibilities of a volcanic eruption in the state. Volcanoes operate over longer timescales, she said.

"In California, earthquakes tend to take front and center. We have had more of them in the 20th century and 21st century than we have had volcanic activity. So it's sort of out of people's memories that we've got active volcanoes in the state."

CALIFORNIA'S 'BIG ONE' COULD BE A VOLCANIC ERUPTION

~ *CBSNews.com, February 25, 2021*

California's next 'big one' may not be an earthquake. According to a new study from the U.S. Geological Survey, a future volcanic eruption is inevitable.

"Of the eight volcanic areas that exist in California, molten rock resides beneath at least seven of these — Medicine Lake volcano, Mount Shasta, Lassen Volcanic Center, Clear Lake volcanic field, the Long Valley volcanic region including Mammoth Mountain, Coso volcanic field, and Salton Buttes—and are therefore considered "active" volcanoes producing volcanic earthquakes, toxic gas emissions, hot springs, geothermal systems, and (or) ground movement," says a new USGS report.

While Mount Shasta has the largest number of people in harm's way, with a daily population of more than 100,000, it's the Long Valley Caldera that is capable of having a worldwide effect. The threat-impact level there is very high, according to the report.

CALIFORNIA'S SUPERVOLCANO HAS A SPLIT PERSONALILTY

~ NBCNews.com, March 2, 2020

There's some good news and bad news

regarding a sleeping supervolcano in California.

A new study that uses argon isotopes in the lava rocks to refine the timing of different eruptions over the last 160,000 years reveals that when Long Valley has spewed forth in the past, it's been in two very different styles at nearly the same time, which makes it a bit of a volcanic oddity.

One eruption style is a gloppy, not very explosive lava called basalt that poses little blast danger unless it contacts groundwater or snow.

The other sort of eruption involves more glass-rich or "silicic" magma that appears at Long Valley to hitch a ride with the basalt to the surface. When it gets there, it tends to come out of the ground in the more explosive, ashy style of Mount St. Helens.

That official prognosis puts the odds of an eruption in any given year at about the same odds for the San Andreas Fault letting loose another magnitude 8 earthquake like the one that destroyed San Francisco in 1906 on any given day.

"It's a low probability that the caldera erupts," says geologist Gail Mahood. She adds the worst-case scenario is that the eruption would be at Mammoth Mountain.

SCIENTISTS WARN MAMMOTH LAKES DESTINED FOR VOLCANIC ERUPTION

~ Los Angeles Times, July 11, 2019

The bad news is that a volcanic eruption near this Eastern Sierra town is "certain to occur," according to scientists who have reported on the results of 17 years of monitoring possible precursors.

Mammoth Lakes is located within the Long Valley volcanic caldera, the site of hundreds of thousands of years of repeated eruptions. The last--a little outside the caldera--occurred about 250 years ago.

"The pattern of volcanic activity over the past

5,000 years suggests that the next eruption . . . will most likely happen somewhere along the Mono-Inyo volcanic chain" west of Mammoth Lakes and extending northward 25 miles to Mono Lake, said a U.S. Geological Survey statement.

The next eruption may begin with a series of steam-blast explosions as rising molten rock vaporizes underground water near the Earth's surface, the scientists say. Those blasts would throw large blocks of rock and smaller fragments hundreds of feet into the air, and leave deep circular pits such as the Inyo Craters.

The scientists add that past eruptions also generated pyroclastic flows up to five miles long, in which superheated ash, rock, air and gases moved at speeds of 100 mph or greater.

ACKNOWLEDGMENTS

Creating a novel that is both informative and entertaining requires a tremendous team effort. Writing is the easy part.

For their efforts in making this novel a reality, I would like to thank Hristo Argirov Kovatliev for his incredible artistic talents in creating my cover art. He and my loving wife, Dani, collaborate (and conspire) to create the most incredible cover art in the publishing business. A huge hug of appreciation goes out to Pauline Nolet, the *Professor*, for her editorial prowess and patience in correcting this writer's same tics after sixty-plus novels. Thank you, Drew Avera, a United States Navy veteran, who has brought his talented formatting skills from a writer's perspective to create multiple formats for reading my novels.

ACKNOWLEDGMENTS

Thank you, Andrew Wehrlen, an incredible talent and all-star dad who performs the audio narration of my stories.

A few years ago, we met a couple who have become close friends. Their names? You guessed it. Sammy and Tyler, together with their fur babies, Carly and Fenway. There have been many friends and acquaintances who've found their way into my novels as named characters or inspiration for those in the story. I have to say, this has been incredible fun including Sammy and Ty in ARkStorm and now, Mammoth. Dani and I truly admire these two. It was my honor to create characters in this novel who have some of the real personality traits of our friends. When the shit hits the fan, we know we can trust them as we hope they know we'll have their back. Thank you both for being such good sports and providing me lots of material to bring the fictional Sammy and Ty to life!

Once again, as I immersed myself in the science and history, source material and research flooded my inbox from around the globe. Without the assistance of many individuals and organizations, this story could not be told. Please allow me a moment to acknowledge a few of those individuals whom, without their tireless efforts and patience, Mammoth and all the novels in this trilogy could not have been written.

Many thanks to the preeminent researchers and engineers at the United States Geological Survey and the UCLA Center for Climate Science for their research and climate models.

This story couldn't have been written without the research done by Dr. Lucy Jones and Dr. Daniel Swain.

Dr. Lucille Jones is one of the foremost and trusted public authorities on earthquakes, Jones is referred to by many in Southern California as the *seismologist-next-door* who is frequently called up on to provide information on recent earthquakes.

She is currently a research associate at the Seismological Laboratory at Caltech and chief scientist and founder of the Dr. Lucy Jones Center for Science and Society. She was previously at the USGS from 1985 to 2016, where she conducted research in the areas of foreshocks, seismotectonics, and the application of hazards science to improve societal resilience after natural disasters.

At the USGS, she was also part of the team of scientists that developed the Great Shakeout Earthquake Drills, during which millions around the world participate in annual earthquake safety drills.

ACKNOWLEDGMENTS

Dr. Daniel Swain is a climate scientist in the Institute of the Environment and Sustainability at the University of California, Los Angeles, and holds concurrent appointments as a Research Fellow in the Capacity Center for Climate and Weather Extremes at the National Center for Atmospheric Research and as the California Climate Fellow at The Nature Conservancy of California. Dr. Swain studies the changing character, causes, and impacts of extreme weather and climate events on a warming planet—with a particular focus on the physical processes leading to droughts, floods, and wildfires. He holds a PhD in Earth System Science from Stanford University and a B.S. in Atmospheric Science from the University of California, Davis.

Dr. Brian H. Wilcox, an aerospace engineer at the Jet Propulsion Laboratory in Pasadena, California, co-authored a research paper titled Defending Human Civilization Supervolcanic Eruptions. Wilcox boldly raised the proposition that the greatest threat to humankind may not come from above, in the form of a Near-Earth Object, but rather, from below, as an eruption of a supervolcano.

Dr. Michael R. Rampino, Professor of Biology at NYU, conducts research in the area of earth sciences and in the causes of mass extinctions, in particular.

He has focused ongoing research on large supervolcanic explosive events which results in catastrophic climate change. The episodes of volcanic winters in our history may have caused the near extinction of humans. Dr. Rampino believes a reoccurrence would most likely threaten our civilization and existence. I believe he is right. For more on Dr. Rampino's work, purchase Cataclysms, A New Geology for the Twenty-First Century.

Finally, to my new friends at GeoScienceWorld in McLean, Virginia who helped guide me during my initial research into the subjects of earthquakes, volcanoes, and anything else going on under our feet. You folks are way smarter than I am!

Finally, as always, a special thank you to my team of loyal friends and readers who've always supported my work and provided me valuable insight over the years.

Thanks, y'all, and Choose Freedom!

ABOUT THE AUTHOR, BOBBY AKART

Author Bobby Akart has been ranked by Amazon as #25 on the Amazon Charts list of most popular, best-selling authors. He has achieved recognition as the #1 bestselling Horror Author, #1 bestselling Science Fiction Author, #5 bestselling Action & Adventure Author, #7 bestselling Historical Fiction Author and #10 on Amazon's bestselling Thriller Author list.

Mr. Akart has delivered up-all-night thrillers to readers in 245 countries and territories worldwide. He has sold over one million books in all formats, which includes over forty international bestsellers, in nearly fifty fiction and nonfiction genres. He has produced more #1 bestselling novels in Science Fiction's post-apocalyptic genre than any author in Amazon's history.

His novel *Yellowstone: Hellfire* reached the Top 25 on the Amazon bestsellers list and earned him multiple Kindle All-Star awards for most pages read in a month and most pages read as an author. The Yellowstone series vaulted him to the #25 bestselling author on Amazon Charts, and the #1 bestselling science fiction author.

Since its release in December 2020, his stand-alone novel, *New Madrid Earthquake*, has been ranked #1 on Amazon Charts in multiple countries as a natural disaster thriller.

Mr. Akart is a graduate of the University of Tennessee after pursuing a dual major in economics and political science. He went on to obtain his master's degree in business administration and his doctorate degree in law at Tennessee.

With over a million copies of his novels in print, Bobby Akart has provided his readers a diverse range of topics that are both informative and entertaining. His attention to detail and impeccable research has allowed him to capture the imagination of his readers through his fictional works and bring them valuable knowledge through his nonfiction books.

SIGN UP for Bobby Akart's mailing list to learn of special offers, view bonus content, and be the first to receive news about new releases.

Visit www.BobbyAkart.com for details.

The Nuclear Winter Series
First Strike
Armageddon
Whiteout
Devil Storm
Desolation

New Madrid (a standalone, disaster thriller)

Odessa (a Gunner Fox trilogy)
Odessa Reborn
Odessa Rising
Odessa Strikes

The Virus Hunters
Virus Hunters I
Virus Hunters II
Virus Hunters III

The Geostorm Series
The Shift
The Pulse
The Collapse
The Flood
The Tempest
The Pioneers

The Asteroid Series (A Gunner Fox trilogy)

Discovery

Diversion

Destruction

The Doomsday Series

Apocalypse

Haven

Anarchy

Minutemen

Civil War

The Yellowstone Series

Hellfire

Inferno

Fallout

Survival

The Lone Star Series

Axis of Evil

Beyond Borders

Lines in the Sand

Texas Strong

Fifth Column

Suicide Six

The Pandemic Series
Beginnings
The Innocents
Level 6
Quietus

The Blackout Series
36 Hours
Zero Hour
Turning Point
Shiloh Ranch
Hornet's Nest
Devil's Homecoming

The Boston Brahmin Series
The Loyal Nine
Cyber Attack
Martial Law
False Flag
The Mechanics
Choose Freedom

Patriot's Farewell (standalone novel)

Black Friday (standalone novel)

Seeds of Liberty (Companion Guide)

The Prepping for Tomorrow Series (non-fiction)
Cyber Warfare
EMP: Electromagnetic Pulse
Economic Collapse

Printed in the USA
CPSIA information can be obtained
at www.ICGtesting.com
LVHW050755280823
756436LV00031B/898/J